R.L. STINE

Goosebumps

W9-AXS-705

CREEPY CREATURES

graphix

AN IMPRINT OF

SCHOLASTIC

NEW YORK TORONTO LONDON AUCKLAND SYDNEY MEXICO CITY NEW DELHI HONG KONG BUENOS AIRES

The Goosebumps book series created by Parachute Press, Inc.

Library of Congress Cataloging-in-Publication Data is available.
ISBN 0-439-84124-0 (hardcover) / ISBN 0-439-84125-9 (paperback)

12 11 10 9 8 7 6 5 4 3 2 1 06 07 08 09 10
First edition, September 2006
Edited by Sheila Keenan
Book design by Richard Amari
Creative Director: David Saylor
Printed in the United States of America 23

THE WEREWOLF OF FEVER SWAMP

ADAPTED AND ILLUSTRATED BY

Gabriel Hernandez

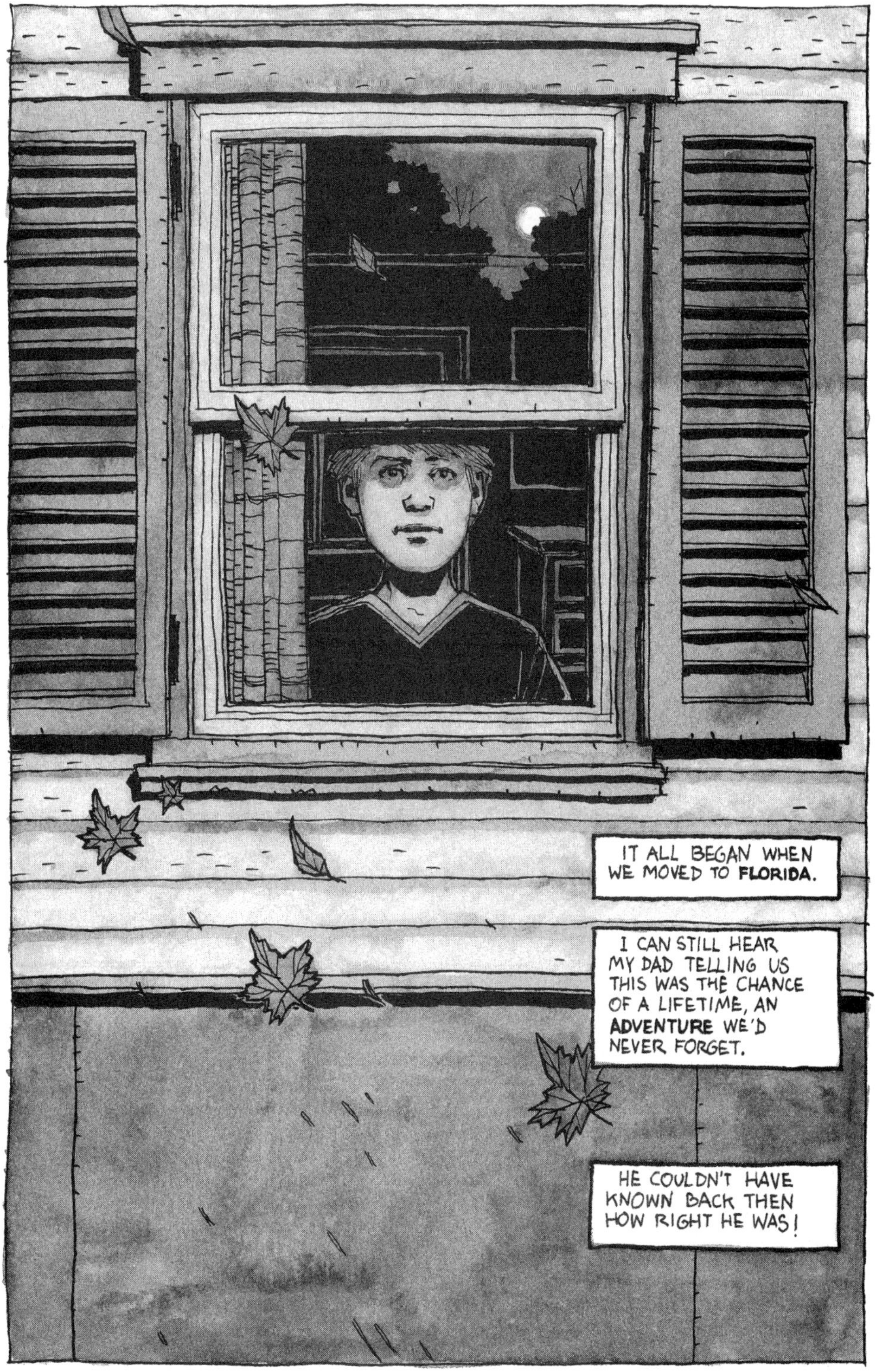
IT ALL BEGAN WHEN WE MOVED TO FLORIDA.
I CAN STILL HEAR MY DAD TELLING US THIS WAS THE CHANCE OF A LIFETIME, AN ADVENTURE WE'D NEVER FORGET.
HE COULDN'T HAVE KNOWN BACK THEN HOW RIGHT HE WAS!

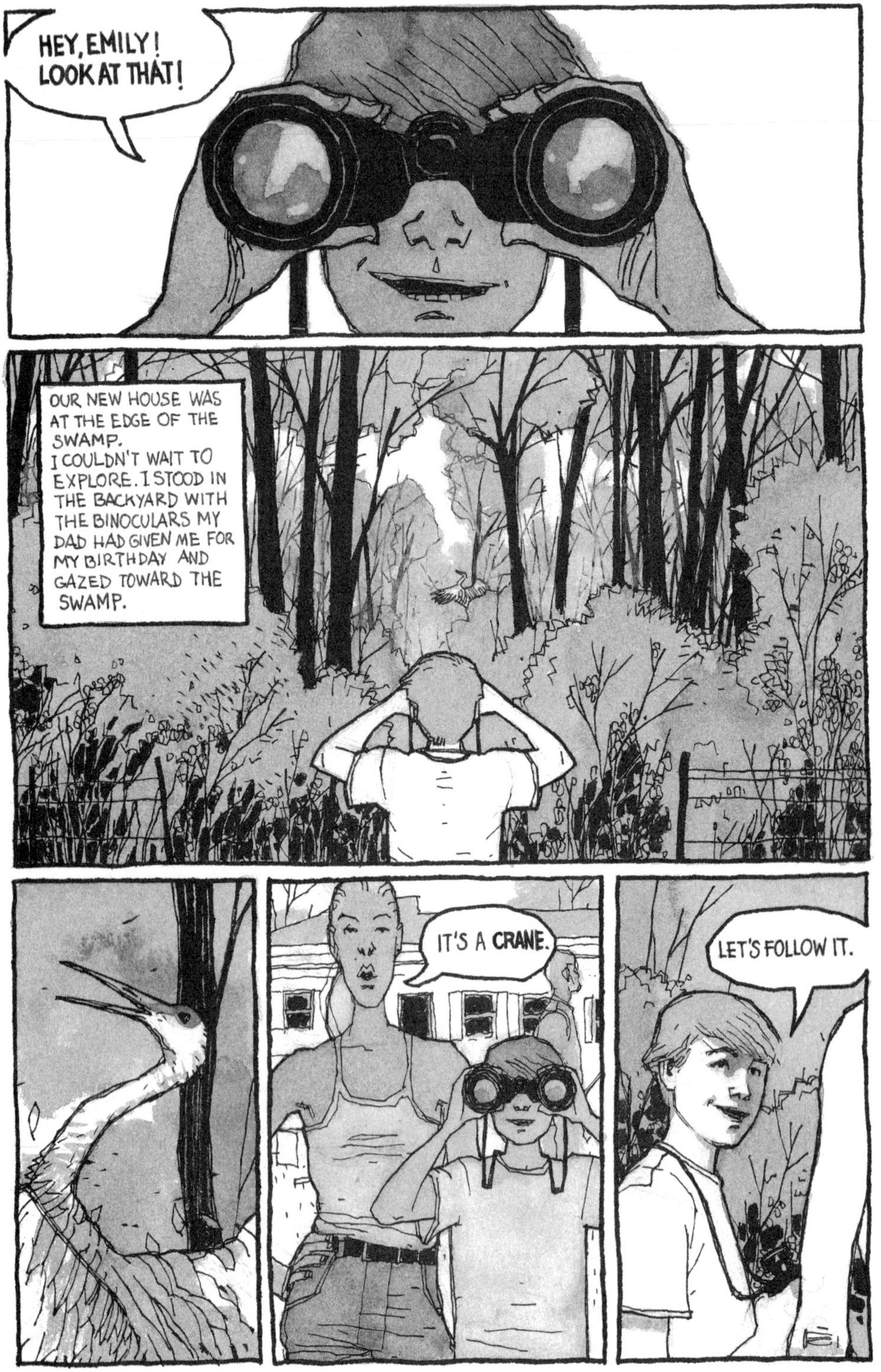
HEY, EMILY! LOOK AT THAT!
OUR NEW HOUSE WAS AT THE EDGE OF THE SWAMP. I COULDN'T WAIT TO EXPLORE. I STOOD IN THE BACKYARD WITH THE BINOCULARS MY DAD HAD GIVEN ME FOR MY BIRTHDAY AND GAZED TOWARD THE SWAMP.
IT'S A **CRANE**.
LET'S FOLLOW IT.

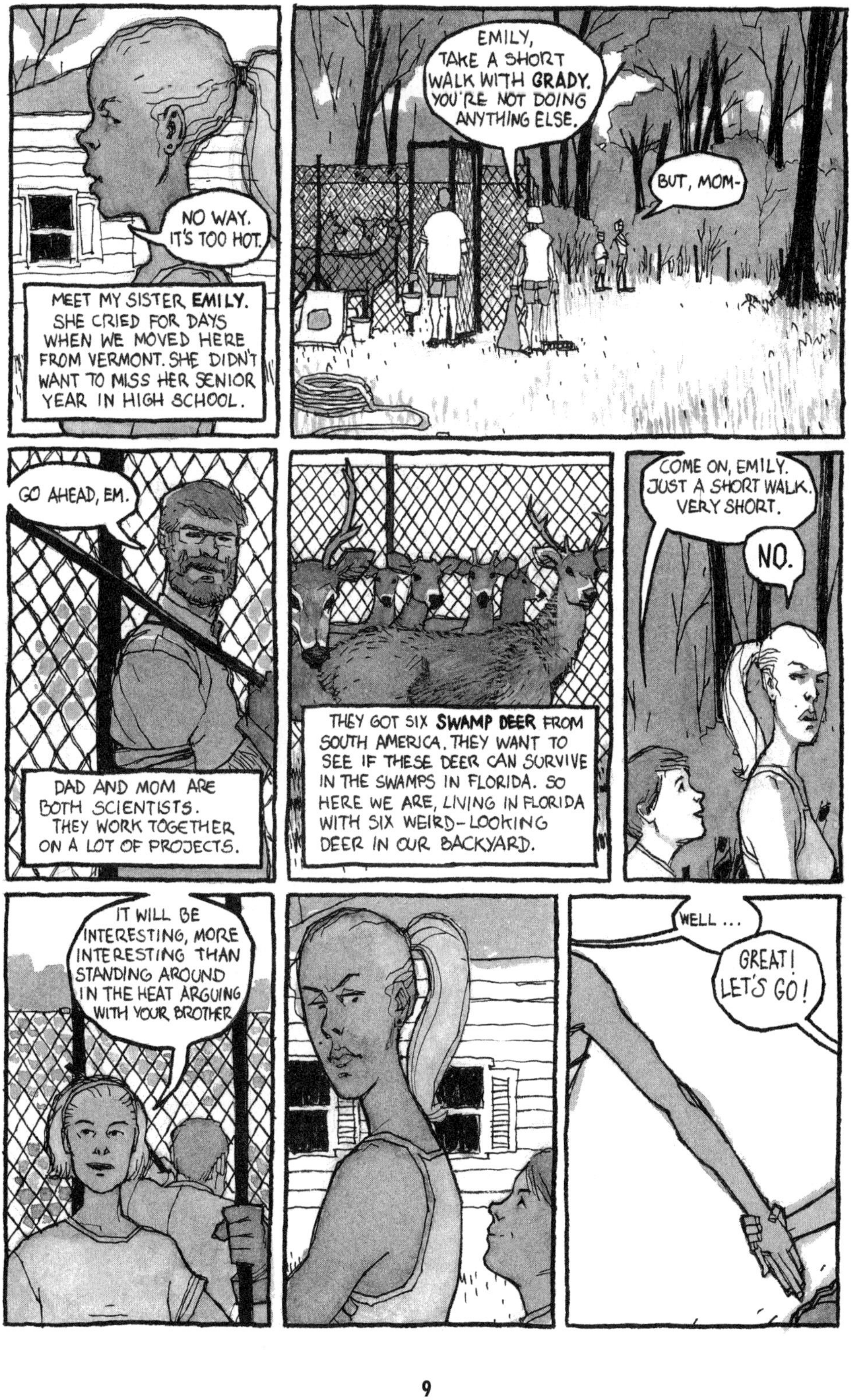
NO WAY. IT'S TOO HOT.
MEET MY SISTER EMILY. SHE CRIED FOR DAYS WHEN WE MOVED HERE FROM VERMONT. SHE DIDN'T WANT TO MISS HER SENIOR YEAR IN HIGH SCHOOL.
EMILY, TAKE A SHORT WALK WITH GRADY. YOU'RE NOT DOING ANYTHING ELSE.
BUT, MOM-
GO AHEAD, EM.
DAD AND MOM ARE BOTH SCIENTISTS. THEY WORK TOGETHER ON A LOT OF PROJECTS.
THEY GOT SIX SWAMP DEER FROM SOUTH AMERICA. THEY WANT TO SEE IF THESE DEER CAN SURVIVE IN THE SWAMPS IN FLORIDA. SO HERE WE ARE, LIVING IN FLORIDA WITH SIX WEIRD-LOOKING DEER IN OUR BACKYARD.
COME ON, EMILY. JUST A SHORT WALK. VERY SHORT.
NO.
IT WILL BE INTERESTING, MORE INTERESTING THAN STANDING AROUND IN THE HEAT ARGUING WITH YOUR BROTHER
WELL ...
GREAT! LET'S GO!

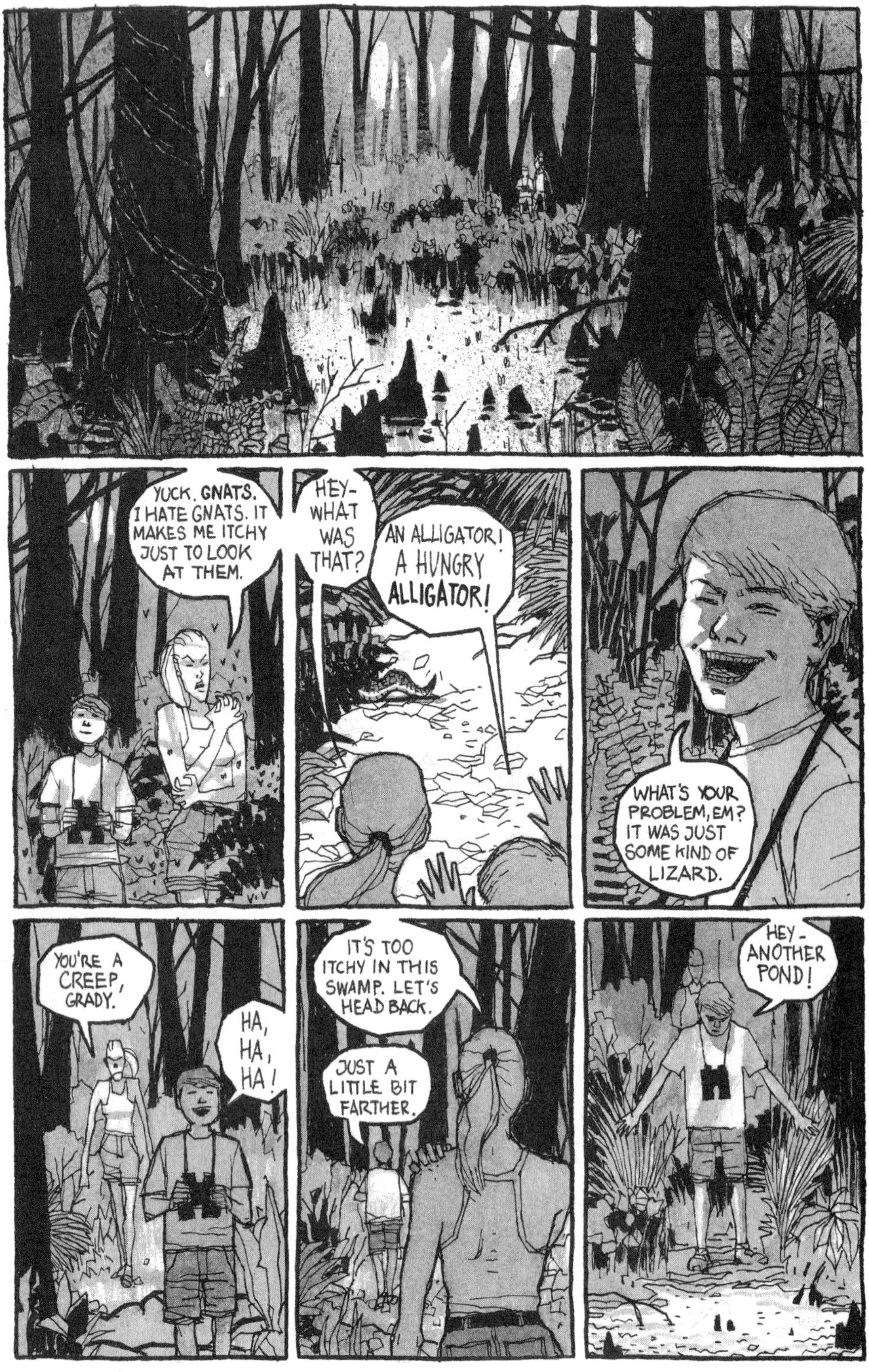
YUCK. GNATS. I HATE GNATS. IT MAKES ME ITCHY JUST TO LOOK AT THEM.
HEY- WHAT WAS THAT?
AN ALLIGATOR! A HUNGRY ALLIGATOR!
WHAT'S YOUR PROBLEM, EM? IT WAS JUST SOME KIND OF LIZARD.
YOU'RE A CREEP, GRADY.
HA, HA, HA!
IT'S TOO ITCHY IN THIS SWAMP. LET'S HEAD BACK.
JUST A LITTLE BIT FARTHER.
HEY- ANOTHER POND!

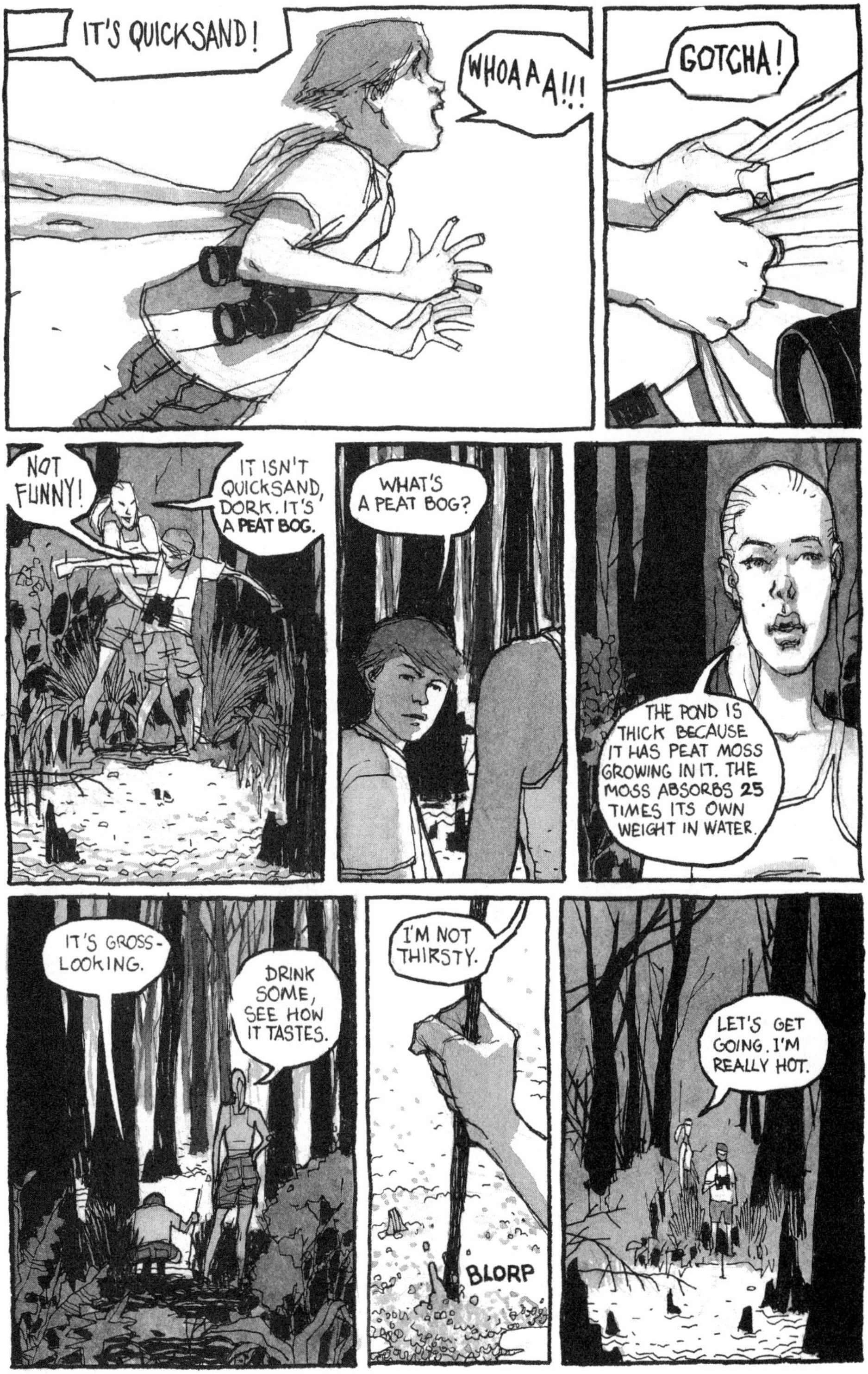
IT'S QUICKSAND!
WHOAAAA!!!
GOTCHA!
NOT FUNNY!
IT ISN'T QUICKSAND, DORK. IT'S A PEAT BOG.
WHAT'S A PEAT BOG?
THE POND IS THICK BECAUSE IT HAS PEAT MOSS GROWING IN IT. THE MOSS ABSORBS 25 TIMES ITS OWN WEIGHT IN WATER.
IT'S GROSS-LOOKING.
DRINK SOME, SEE HOW IT TASTES.
I'M NOT THIRSTY.
BLORP
LET'S GET GOING. I'M REALLY HOT.

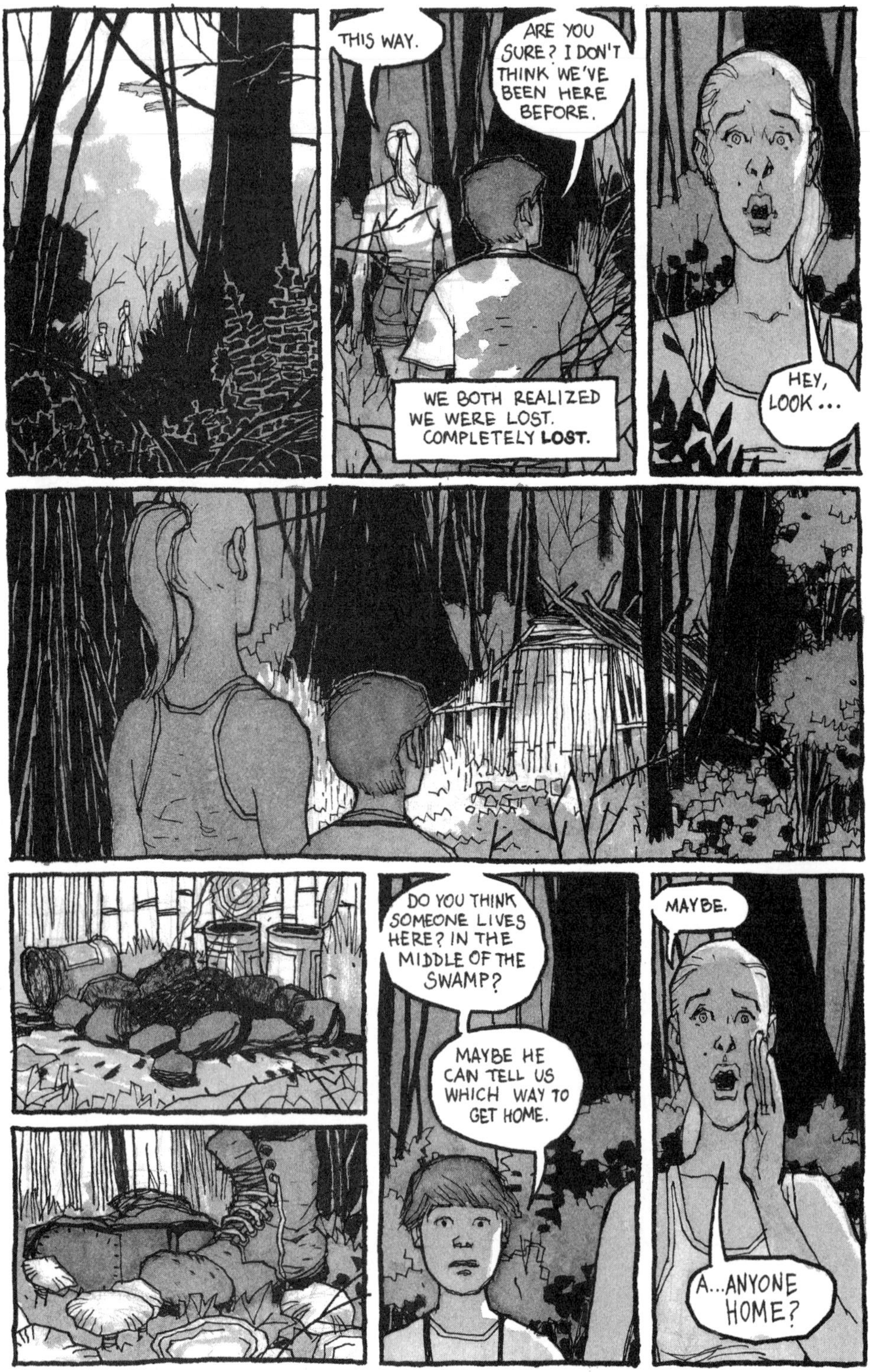
THIS WAY.
ARE YOU SURE? I DON'T THINK WE'VE BEEN HERE BEFORE.
WE BOTH REALIZED WE WERE LOST. COMPLETELY **LOST.**
HEY, LOOK...
DO YOU THINK SOMEONE LIVES HERE? IN THE MIDDLE OF THE SWAMP?
MAYBE HE CAN TELL US WHICH WAY TO GET HOME.
MAYBE.
A...ANYONE HOME?

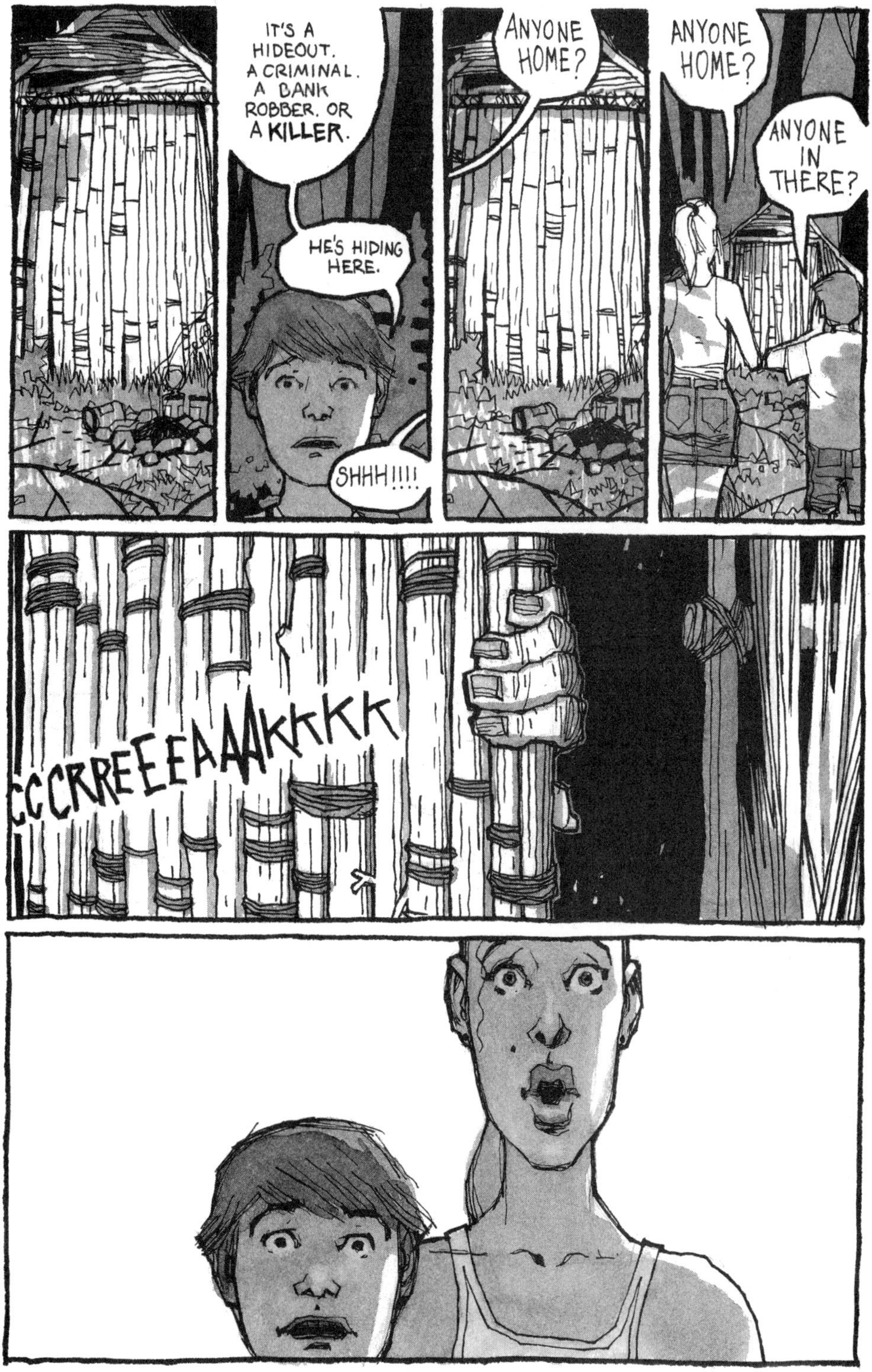
IT'S A HIDEOUT. A CRIMINAL. A BANK ROBBER. OR A KILLER.
HE'S HIDING HERE.
SHHH!!!!
ANYONE HOME?
ANYONE HOME?
ANYONE IN THERE?
CCCRREEEAAAKKKK

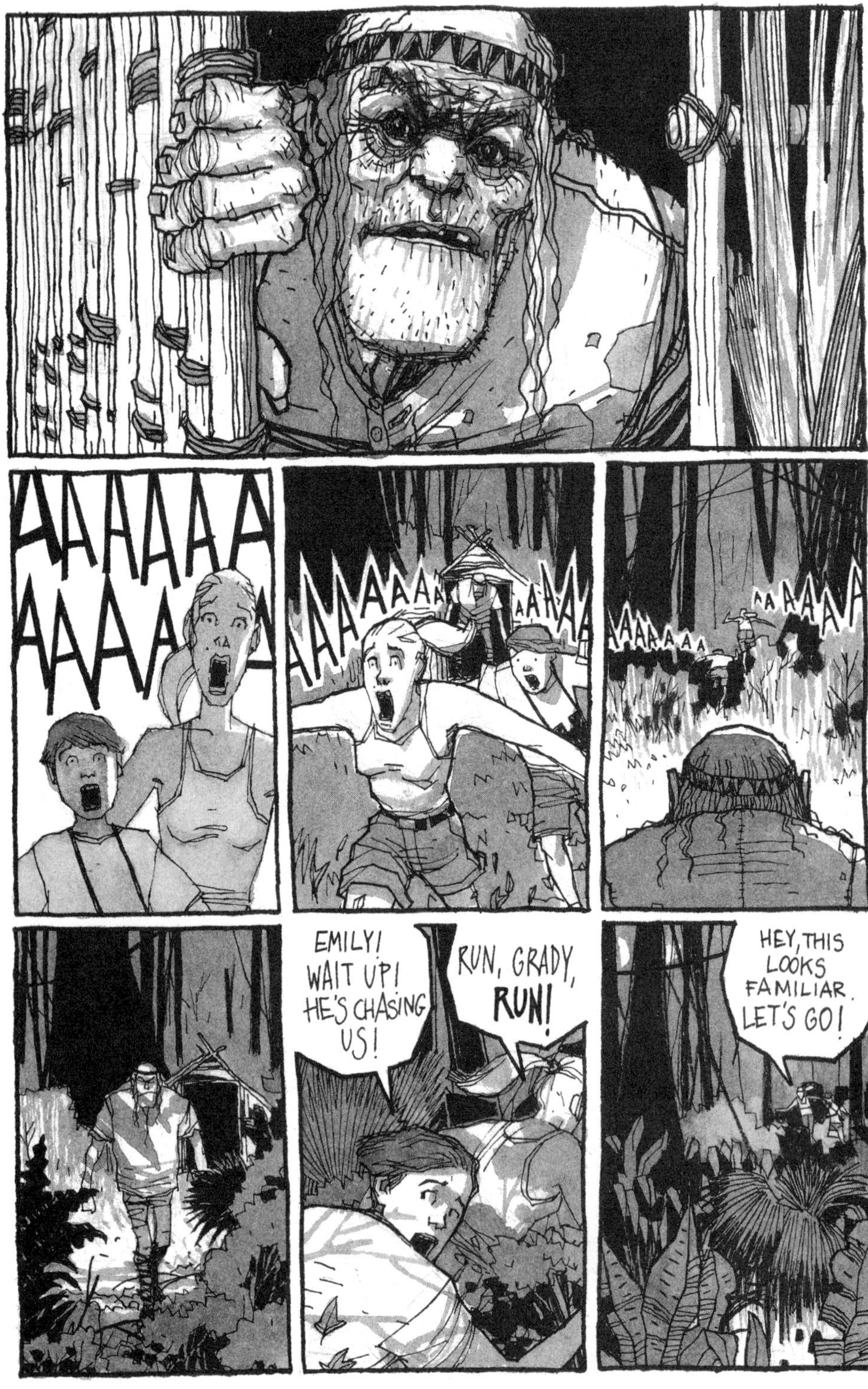
AAAAA AAAAA
AAAAAAAAAA
AAAAAAA AAAA
EMILY! WAIT UP! HE'S CHASING US!
RUN, GRADY, RUN!
HEY, THIS LOOKS FAMILIAR. LET'S GO!

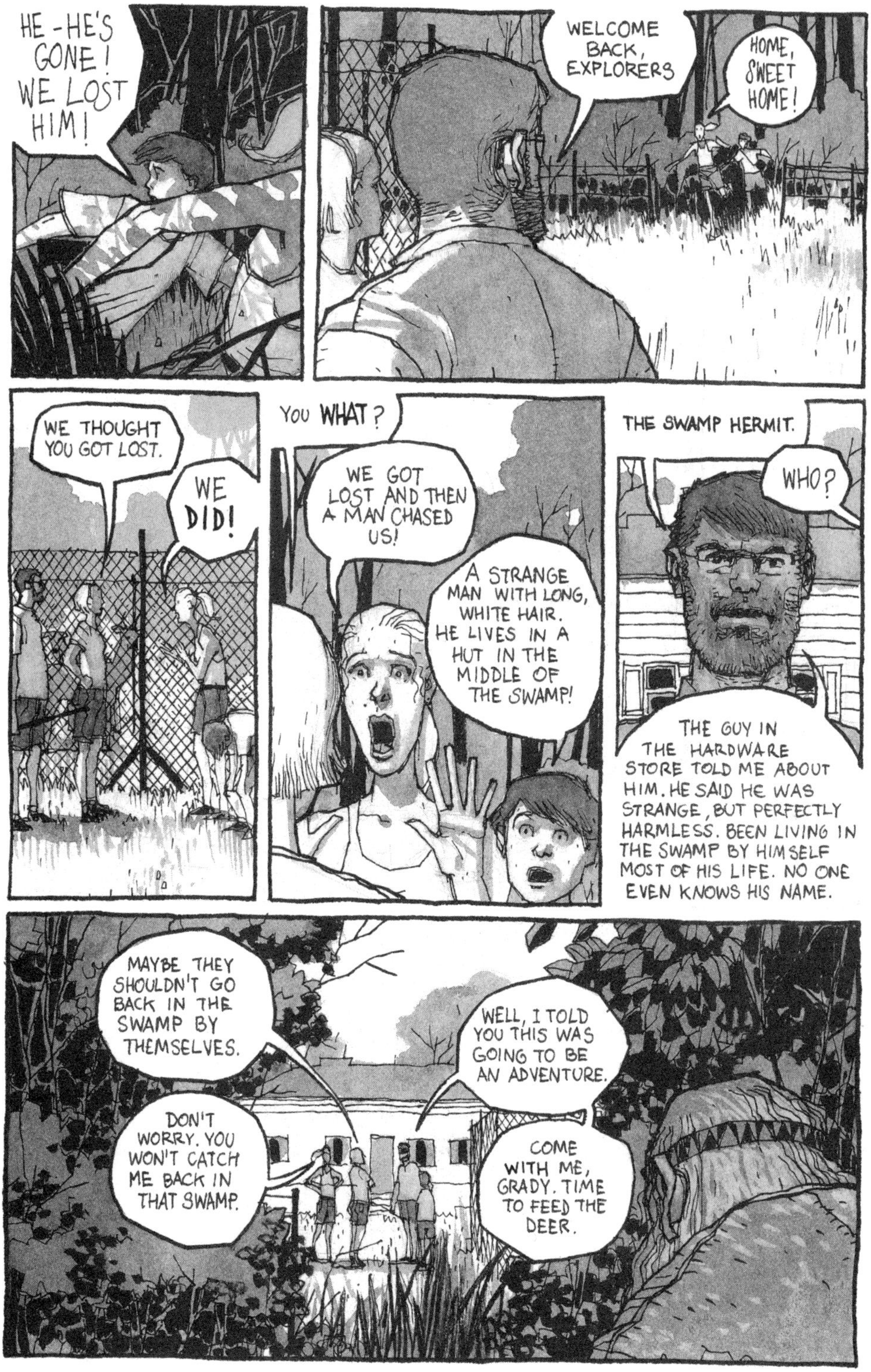
HE-HE'S GONE! WE LOST HIM!
WELCOME BACK, EXPLORERS
HOME, SWEET HOME!
WE THOUGHT YOU GOT LOST.
WE DID!
YOU WHAT?
WE GOT LOST AND THEN A MAN CHASED US!
A STRANGE MAN WITH LONG, WHITE HAIR. HE LIVES IN A HUT IN THE MIDDLE OF THE SWAMP!
THE SWAMP HERMIT.
WHO?
THE GUY IN THE HARDWARE STORE TOLD ME ABOUT HIM. HE SAID HE WAS STRANGE, BUT PERFECTLY HARMLESS. BEEN LIVING IN THE SWAMP BY HIMSELF MOST OF HIS LIFE. NO ONE EVEN KNOWS HIS NAME.
MAYBE THEY SHOULDN'T GO BACK IN THE SWAMP BY THEMSELVES.
WELL, I TOLD YOU THIS WAS GOING TO BE AN ADVENTURE.
DON'T WORRY. YOU WON'T CATCH ME BACK IN THAT SWAMP.
COME WITH ME, GRADY. TIME TO FEED THE DEER.

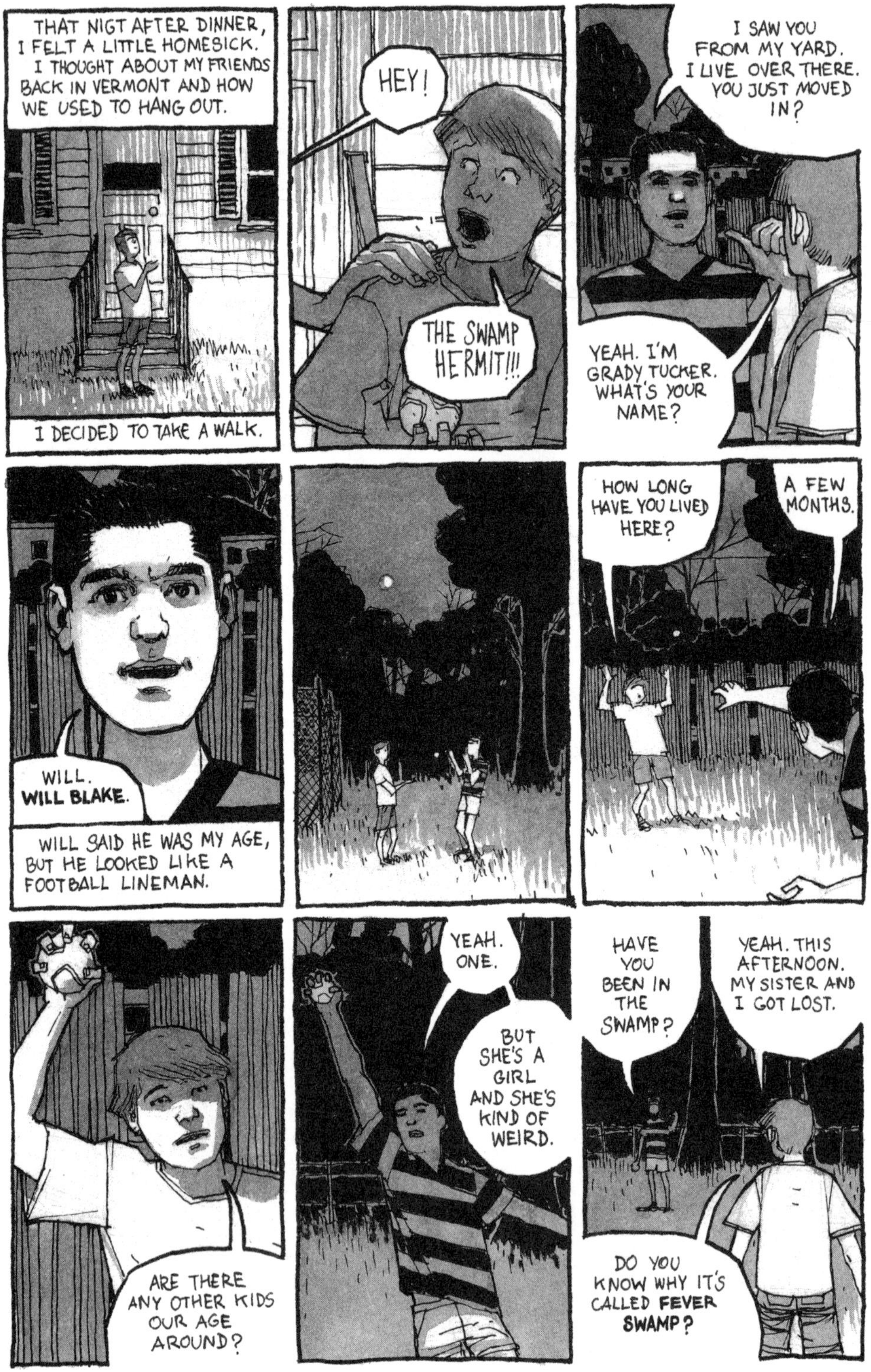
THAT NIGT AFTER DINNER, I FELT A LITTLE HOMESICK. I THOUGHT ABOUT MY FRIENDS BACK IN VERMONT AND HOW WE USED TO HANG OUT.
I DECIDED TO TAKE A WALK.
HEY!
THE SWAMP HERMIT!!!
I SAW YOU FROM MY YARD. I LIVE OVER THERE. YOU JUST MOVED IN?
YEAH. I'M GRADY TUCKER. WHAT'S YOUR NAME?
WILL. **WILL BLAKE.**
WILL SAID HE WAS MY AGE, BUT HE LOOKED LIKE A FOOTBALL LINEMAN.
HOW LONG HAVE YOU LIVED HERE?
A FEW MONTHS.
ARE THERE ANY OTHER KIDS OUR AGE AROUND?
YEAH. ONE.
BUT SHE'S A GIRL AND SHE'S KIND OF WEIRD.
HAVE YOU BEEN IN THE SWAMP?
YEAH. THIS AFTERNOON. MY SISTER AND I GOT LOST.
DO YOU KNOW WHY IT'S CALLED **FEVER SWAMP?**

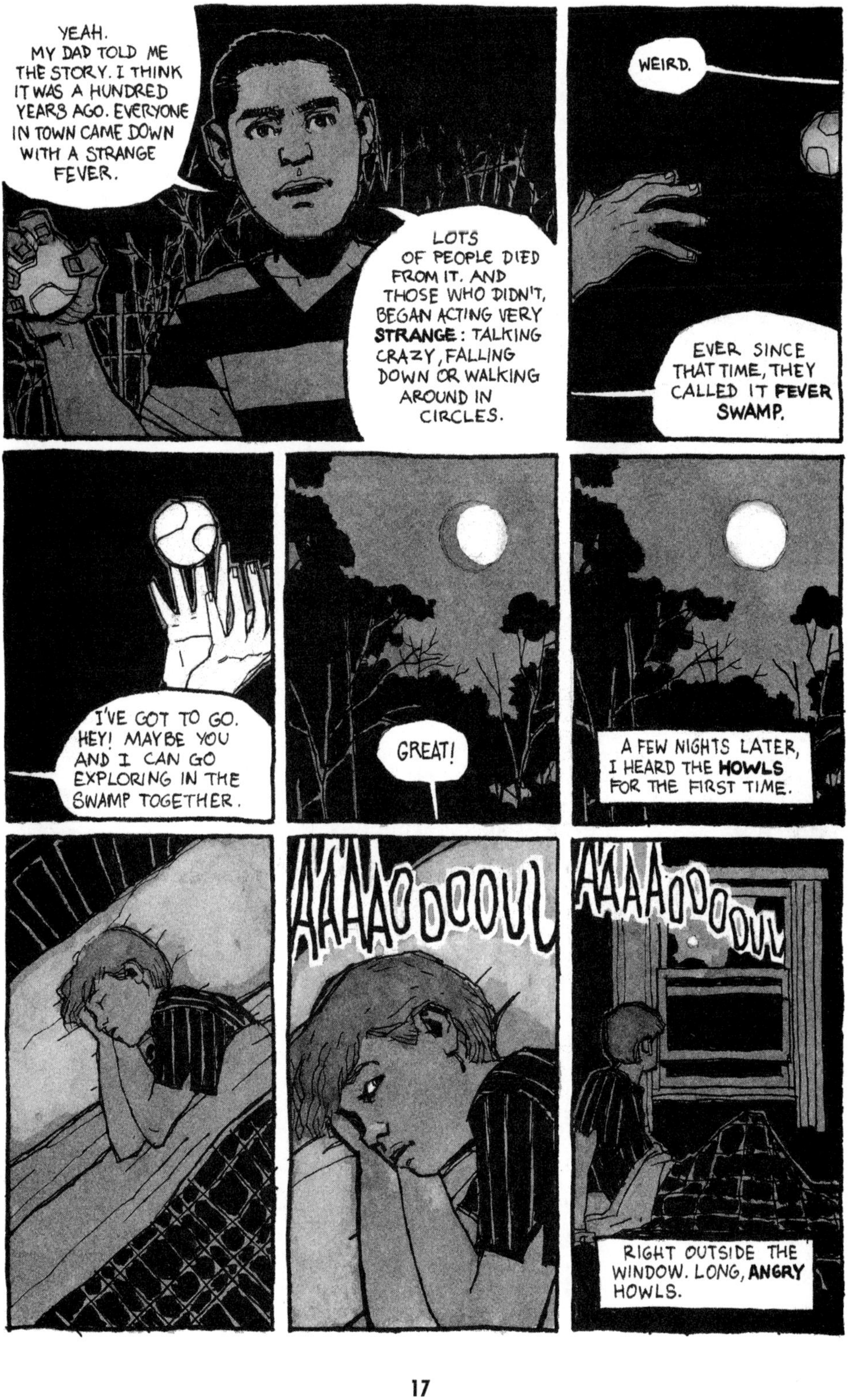
YEAH. MY DAD TOLD ME THE STORY. I THINK IT WAS A HUNDRED YEARS AGO. EVERYONE IN TOWN CAME DOWN WITH A STRANGE FEVER.
LOTS OF PEOPLE DIED FROM IT. AND THOSE WHO DIDN'T, BEGAN ACTING VERY **STRANGE**: TALKING CRAZY, FALLING DOWN OR WALKING AROUND IN CIRCLES.
WEIRD.
EVER SINCE THAT TIME, THEY CALLED IT **FEVER SWAMP**.
I'VE GOT TO GO. HEY! MAYBE YOU AND I CAN GO EXPLORING IN THE SWAMP TOGETHER.
GREAT!
A FEW NIGHTS LATER, I HEARD THE **HOWLS** FOR THE FIRST TIME.
AAAAOOOOUL
AAAAOOOOUL
RIGHT OUTSIDE THE WINDOW. LONG, **ANGRY** HOWLS.

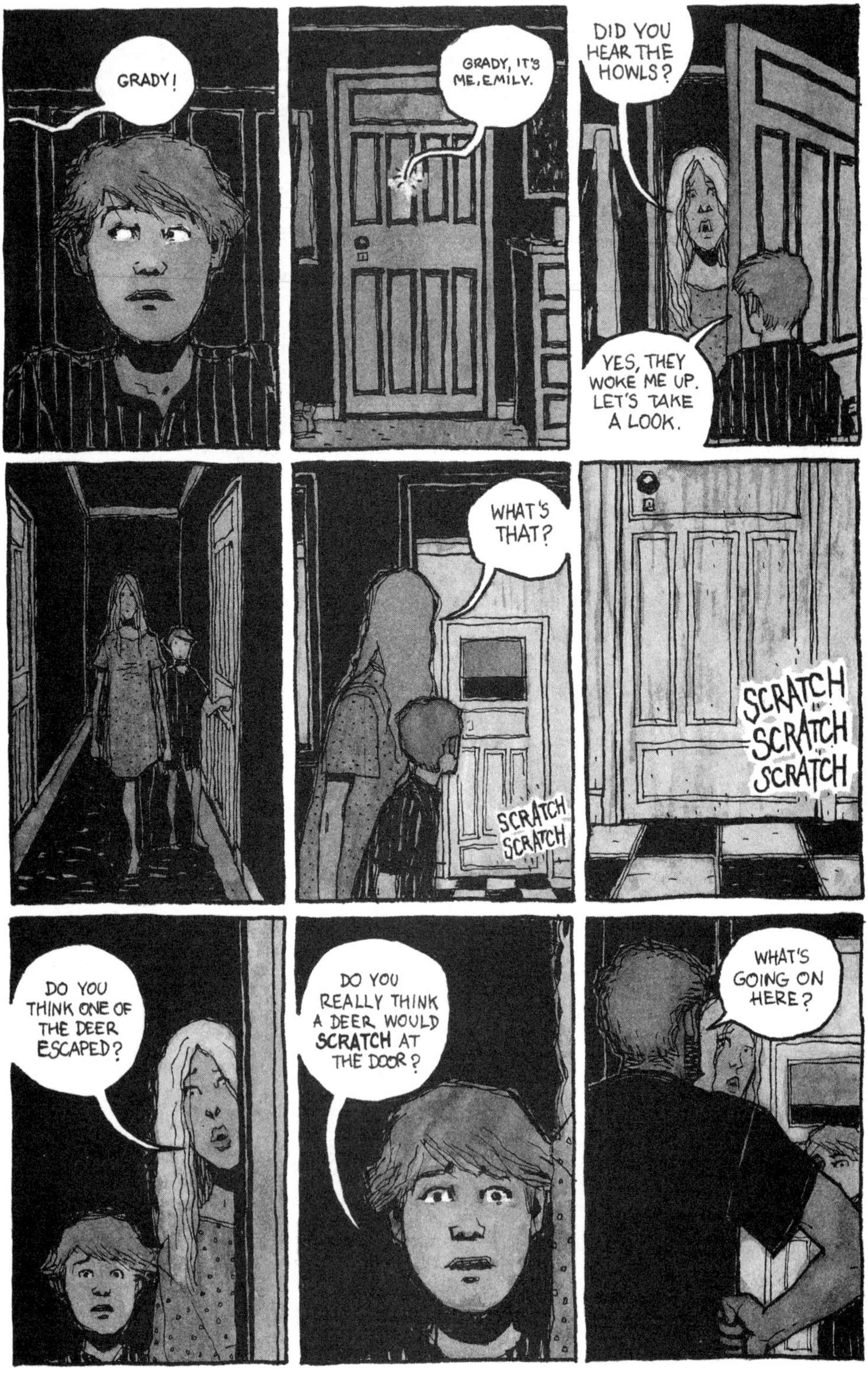
GRADY!
GRADY, IT'S ME, EMILY.
DID YOU HEAR THE HOWLS?
YES, THEY WOKE ME UP. LET'S TAKE A LOOK.
WHAT'S THAT?
SCRATCH SCRATCH
SCRATCH SCRATCH SCRATCH
DO YOU THINK ONE OF THE DEER ESCAPED?
DO YOU REALLY THINK A DEER WOULD SCRATCH AT THE DOOR?
WHAT'S GOING ON HERE?

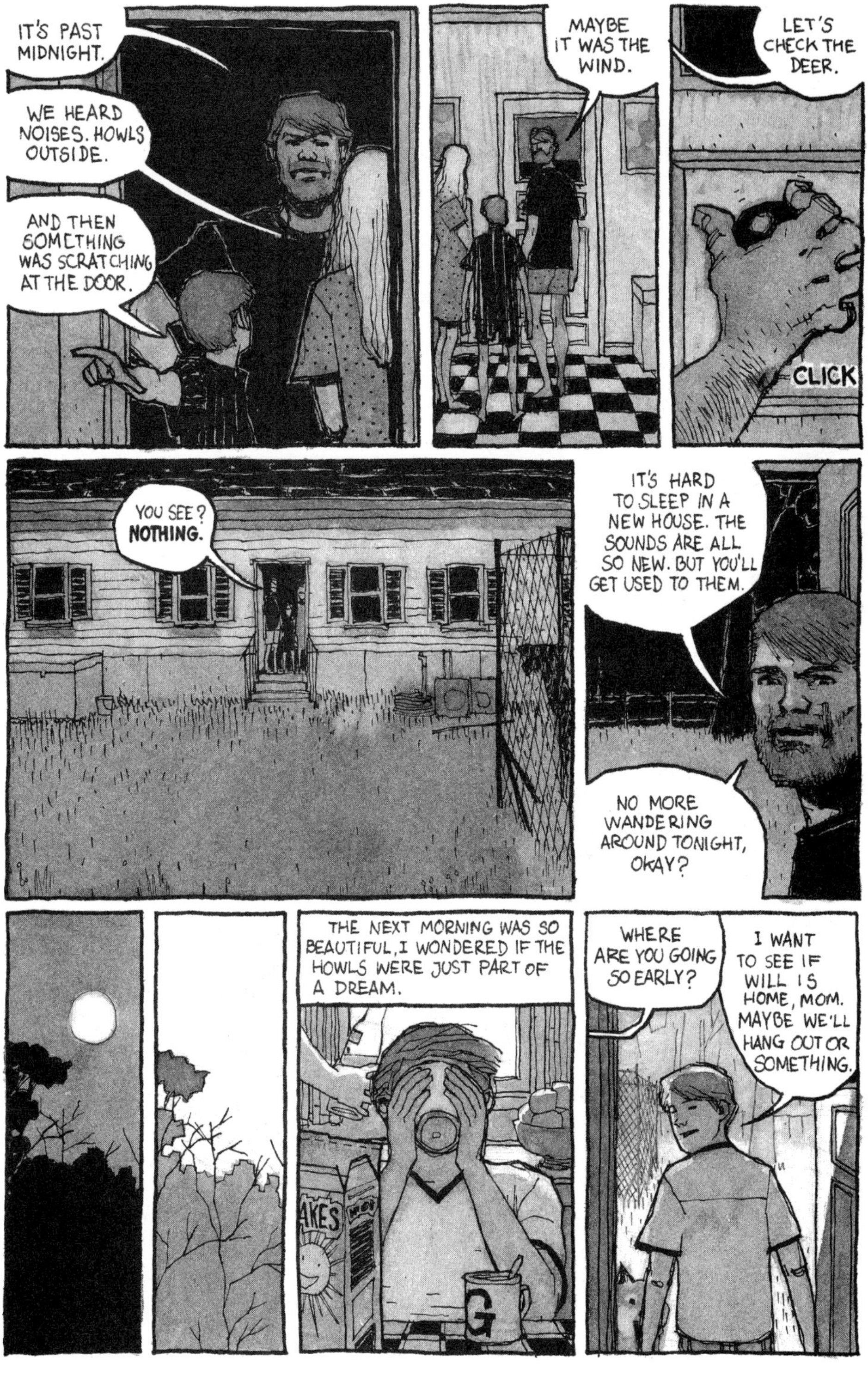
IT'S PAST MIDNIGHT.
WE HEARD NOISES. HOWLS OUTSIDE.
AND THEN SOMETHING WAS SCRATCHING AT THE DOOR.
MAYBE IT WAS THE WIND.
LET'S CHECK THE DEER.
CLICK
YOU SEE? **NOTHING.**
IT'S HARD TO SLEEP IN A NEW HOUSE. THE SOUNDS ARE ALL SO NEW. BUT YOU'LL GET USED TO THEM.
NO MORE WANDERING AROUND TONIGHT, OKAY?
THE NEXT MORNING WAS SO BEAUTIFUL, I WONDERED IF THE HOWLS WERE JUST PART OF A DREAM.
WHERE ARE YOU GOING SO EARLY?
I WANT TO SEE IF WILL IS HOME, MOM. MAYBE WE'LL HANG OUT OR SOMETHING.

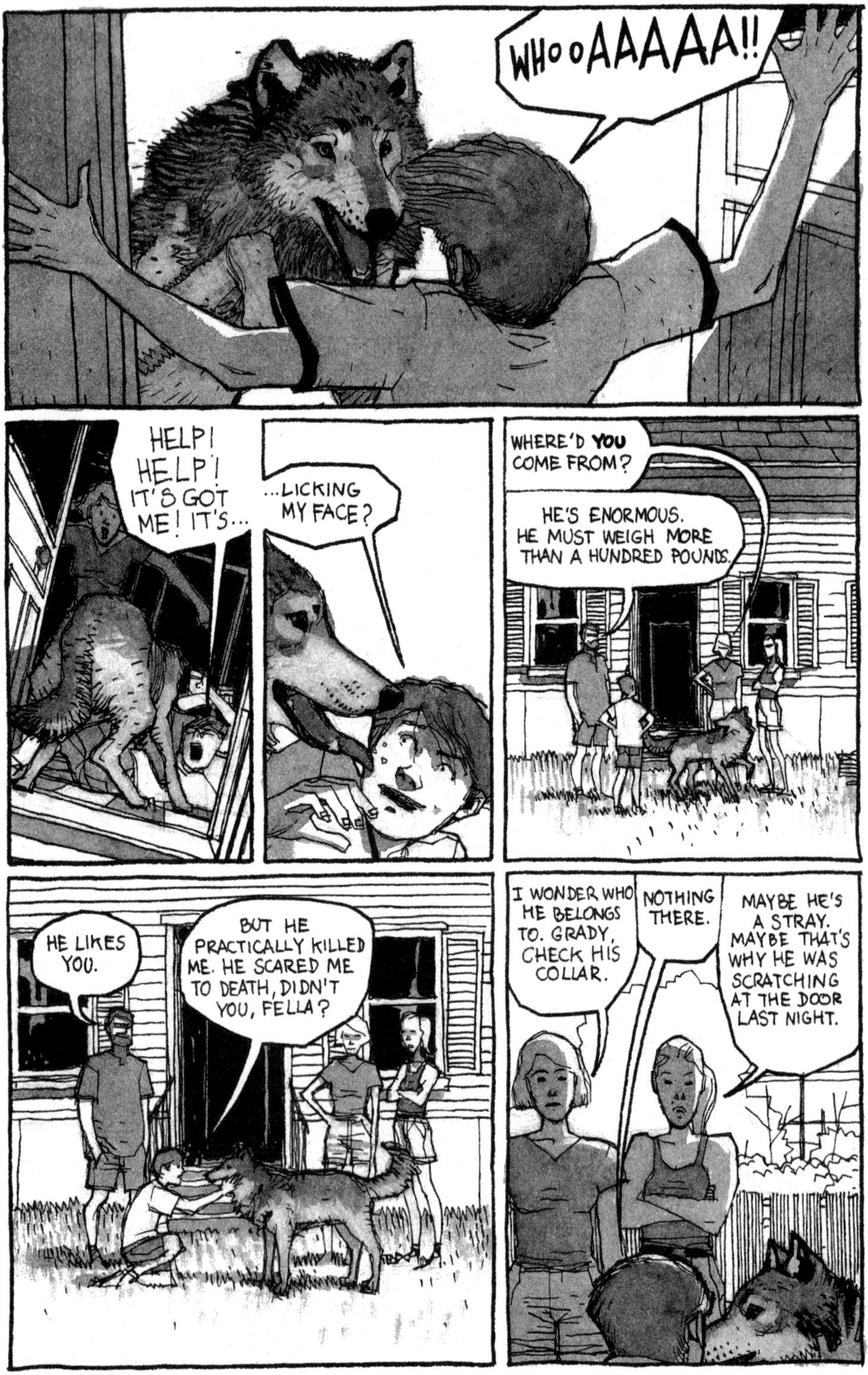
WHOOAAAAA!!
HELP! HELP! IT'S GOT ME! IT'S...
...LICKING MY FACE?
WHERE'D YOU COME FROM?
HE'S ENORMOUS. HE MUST WEIGH MORE THAN A HUNDRED POUNDS.
HE LIKES YOU.
BUT HE PRACTICALLY KILLED ME. HE SCARED ME TO DEATH, DIDN'T YOU, FELLA?
I WONDER WHO HE BELONGS TO. GRADY, CHECK HIS COLLAR.
NOTHING THERE.
MAYBE HE'S A STRAY. MAYBE THAT'S WHY HE WAS SCRATCHING AT THE DOOR LAST NIGHT.

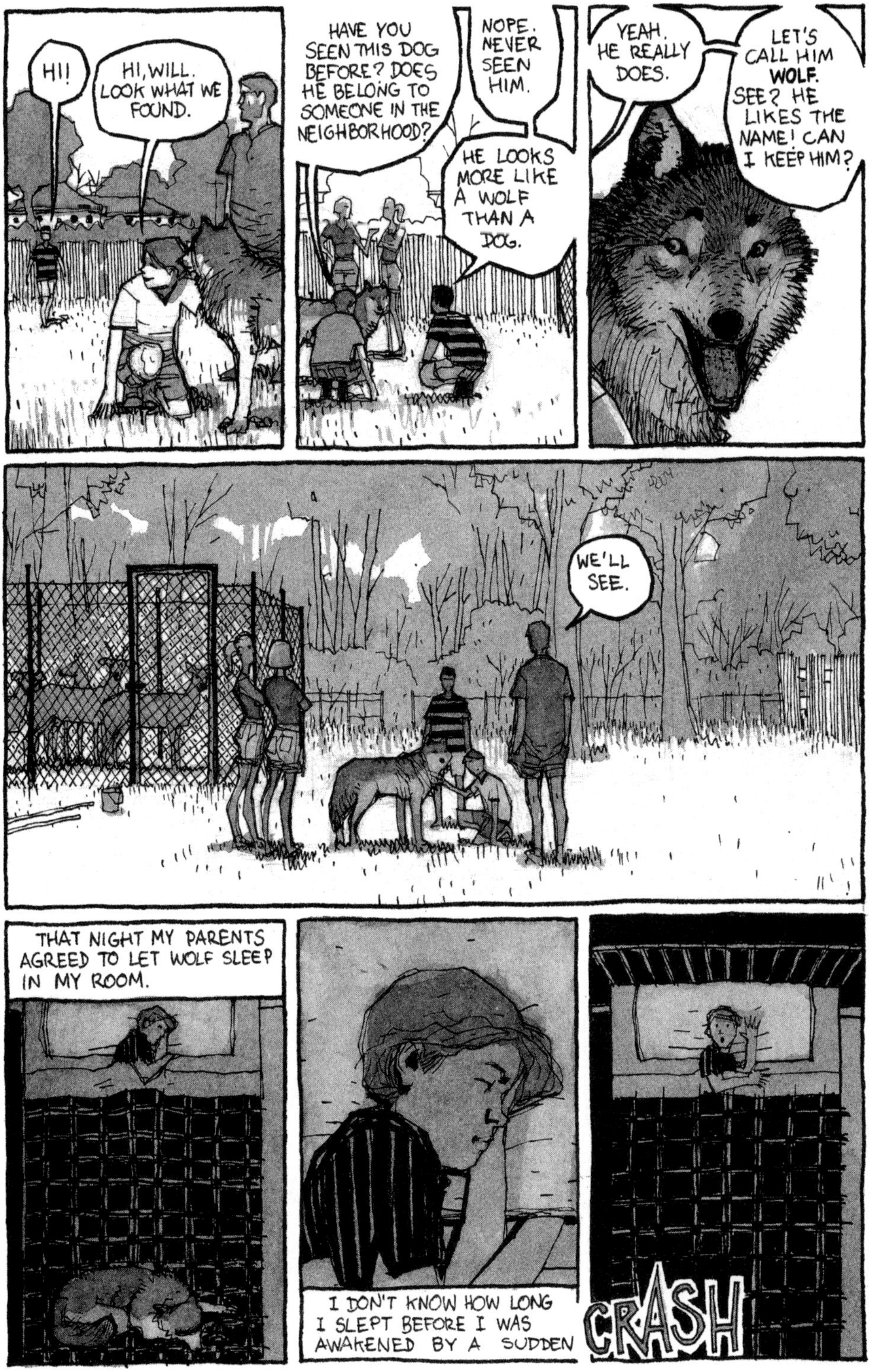
HI!
HI, WILL. LOOK WHAT WE FOUND.
HAVE YOU SEEN THIS DOG BEFORE? DOES HE BELONG TO SOMEONE IN THE NEIGHBORHOOD?
NOPE. NEVER SEEN HIM.
HE LOOKS MORE LIKE A WOLF THAN A DOG.
YEAH. HE REALLY DOES.
LET'S CALL HIM WOLF. SEE? HE LIKES THE NAME! CAN I KEEP HIM?
WE'LL SEE.
THAT NIGHT MY PARENTS AGREED TO LET WOLF SLEEP IN MY ROOM.
I DON'T KNOW HOW LONG I SLEPT BEFORE I WAS AWAKENED BY A SUDDEN
CRASH

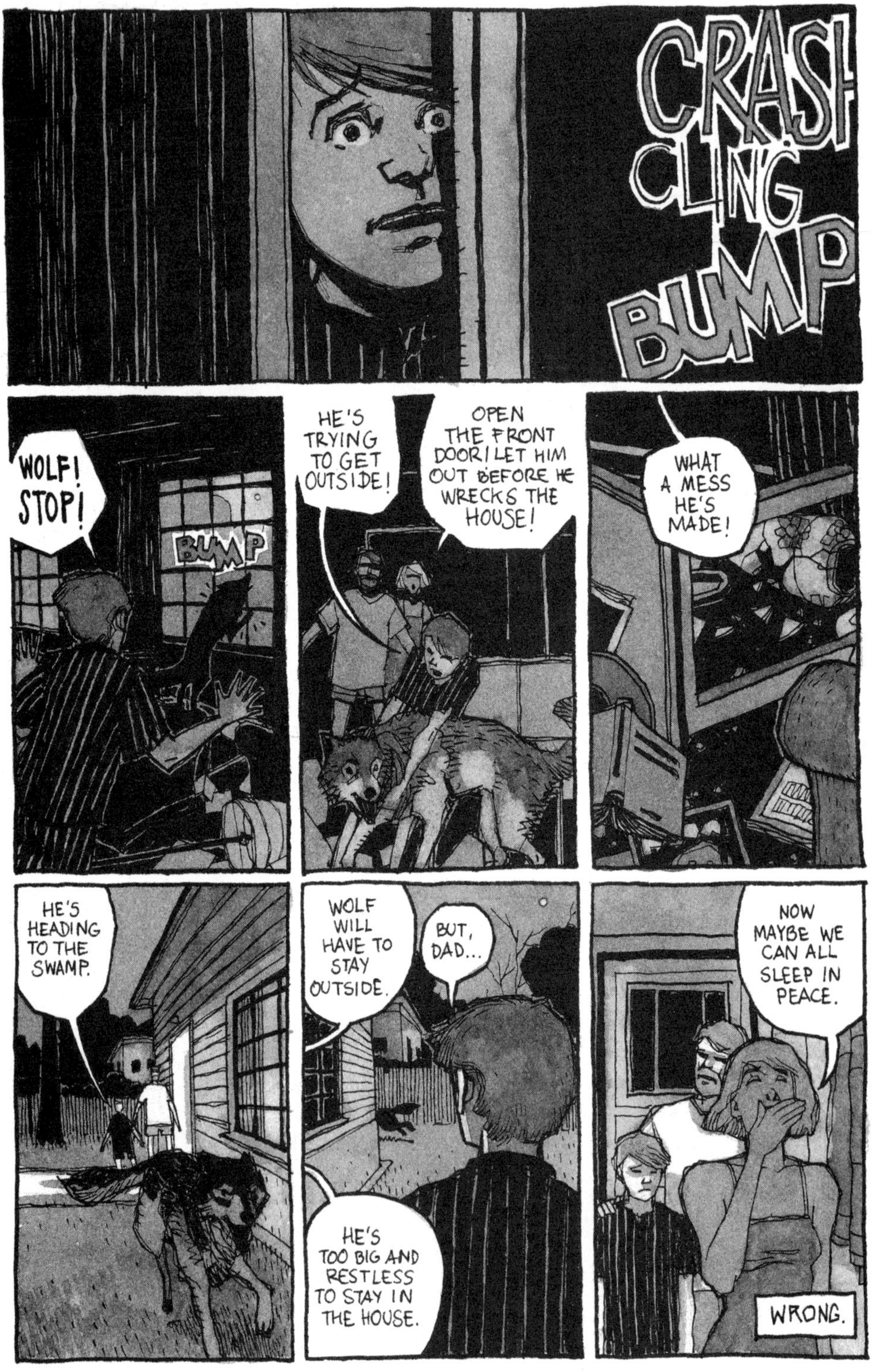
CRASH
CLING
BUMP
WOLF! STOP!
BUMP
HE'S TRYING TO GET OUTSIDE!
OPEN THE FRONT DOOR! LET HIM OUT BEFORE HE WRECKS THE HOUSE!
WHAT A MESS HE'S MADE!
HE'S HEADING TO THE SWAMP.
WOLF WILL HAVE TO STAY OUTSIDE.
BUT, DAD...
HE'S TOO BIG AND RESTLESS TO STAY IN THE HOUSE.
NOW MAYBE WE CAN ALL SLEEP IN PEACE.
WRONG.

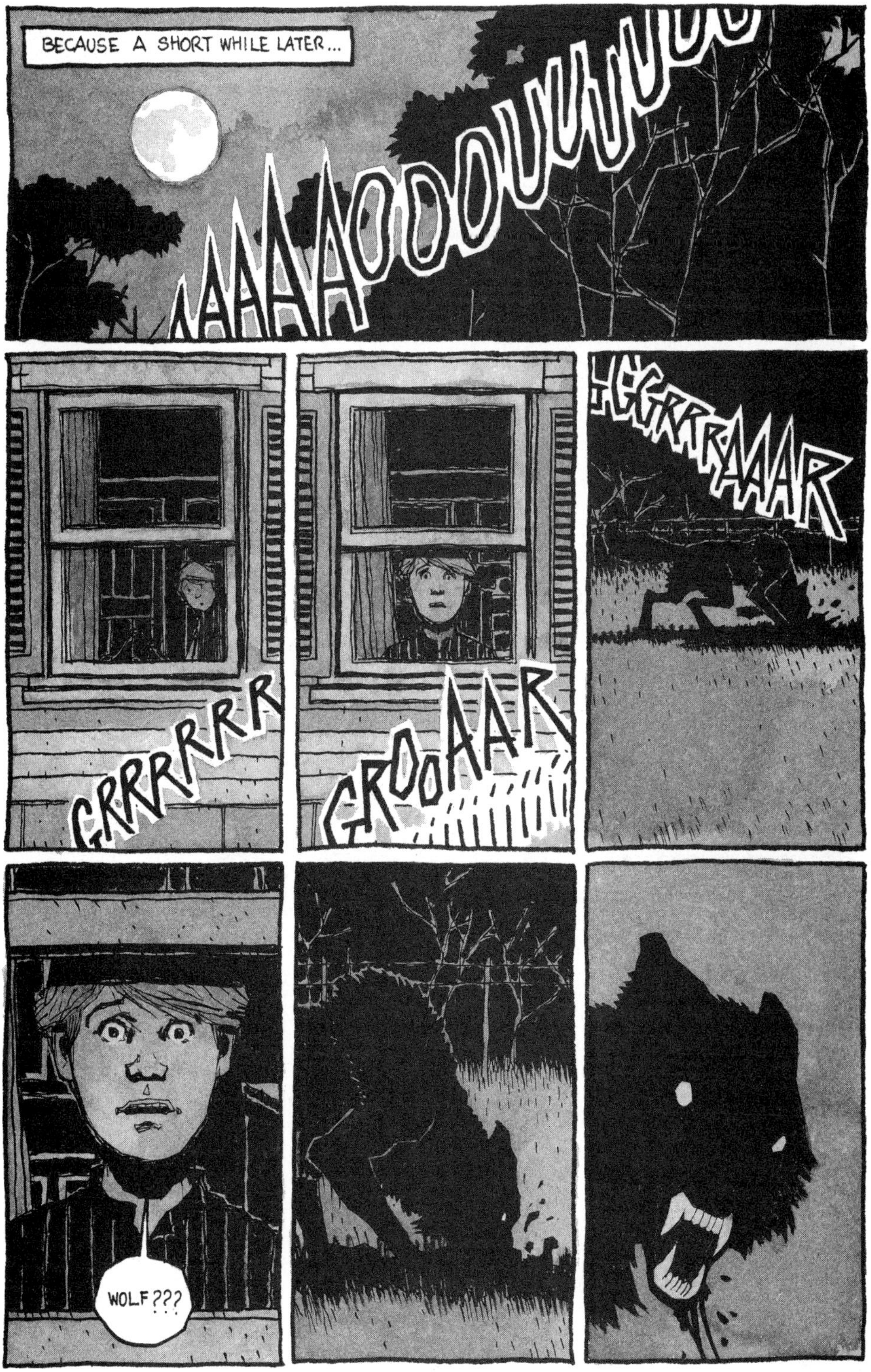
BECAUSE A SHORT WHILE LATER...
GRRRRRR
GROOAAR
WOLF???

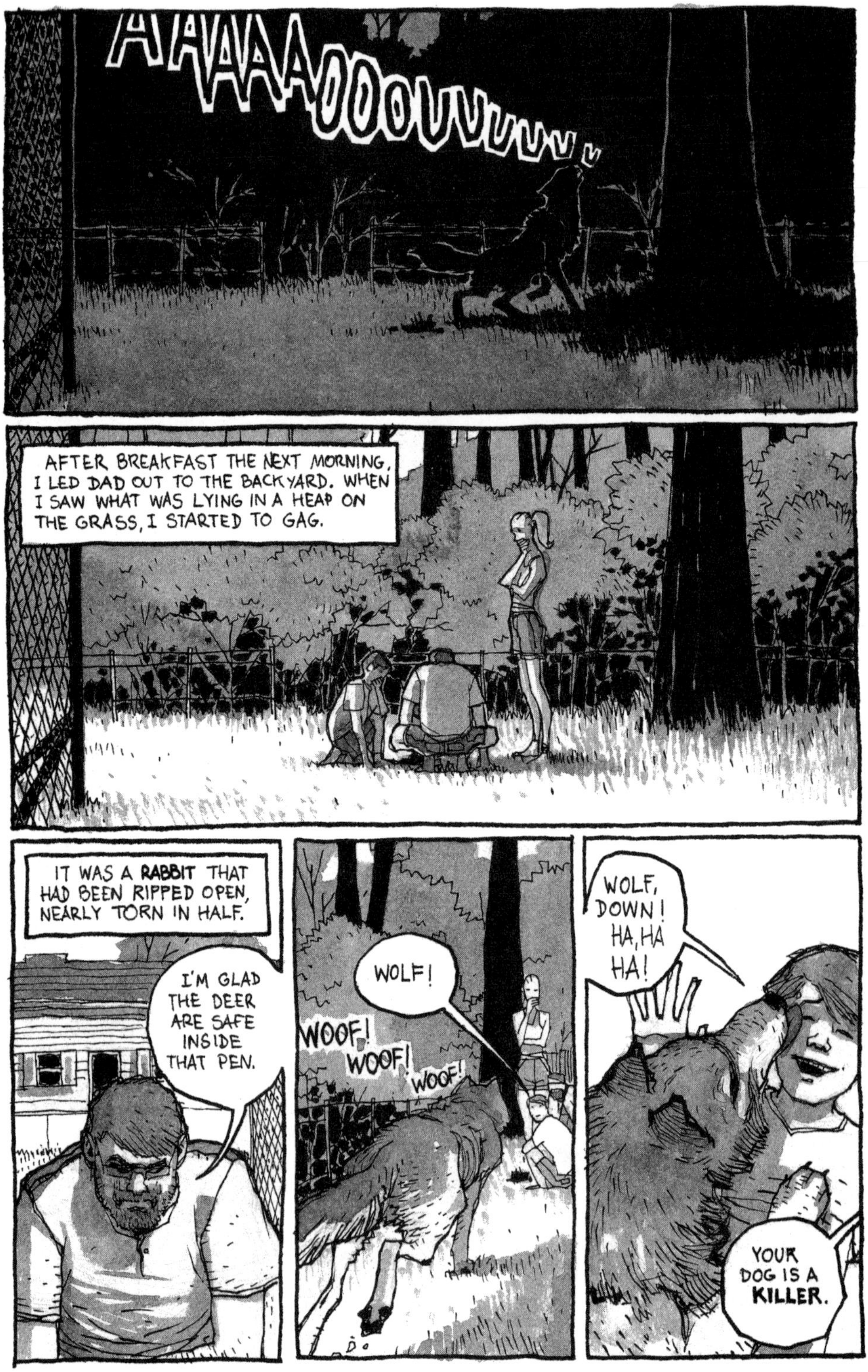
AAAAOOOUVUUUVVV
AFTER BREAKFAST THE NEXT MORNING, I LED DAD OUT TO THE BACKYARD. WHEN I SAW WHAT WAS LYING IN A HEAP ON THE GRASS, I STARTED TO GAG.
IT WAS A RABBIT THAT HAD BEEN RIPPED OPEN, NEARLY TORN IN HALF.
I'M GLAD THE DEER ARE SAFE INSIDE THAT PEN.
WOLF!
WOOF! WOOF! WOOF!
WOLF, DOWN! HA, HA HA!
YOUR DOG IS A KILLER.

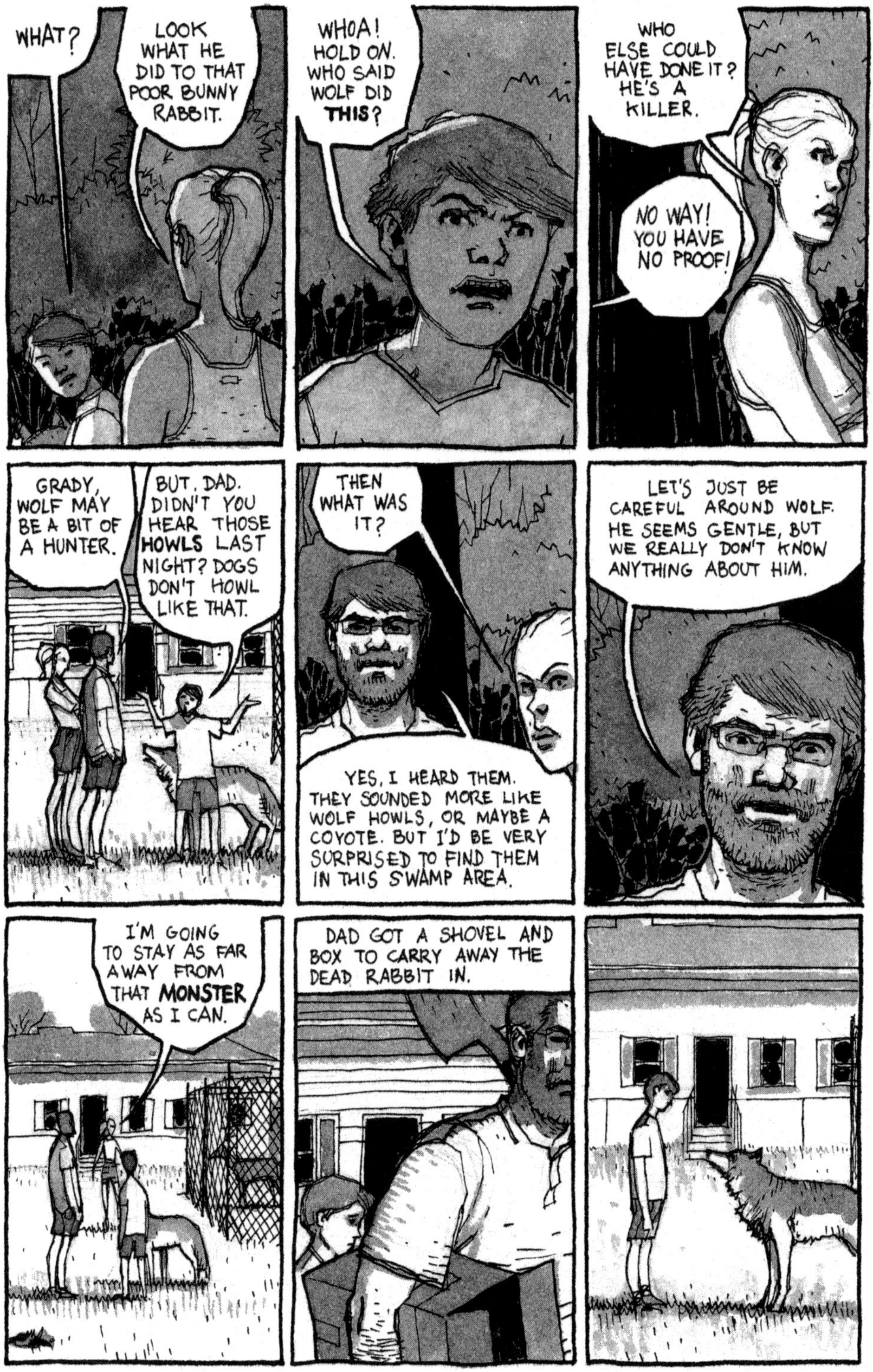
WHAT?
LOOK WHAT HE DID TO THAT POOR BUNNY RABBIT.
WHOA! HOLD ON. WHO SAID WOLF DID THIS?
WHO ELSE COULD HAVE DONE IT? HE'S A KILLER.
NO WAY! YOU HAVE NO PROOF!
GRADY, WOLF MAY BE A BIT OF A HUNTER.
BUT, DAD. DIDN'T YOU HEAR THOSE HOWLS LAST NIGHT? DOGS DON'T HOWL LIKE THAT.
THEN WHAT WAS IT?
YES, I HEARD THEM. THEY SOUNDED MORE LIKE WOLF HOWLS, OR MAYBE A COYOTE. BUT I'D BE VERY SURPRISED TO FIND THEM IN THIS SWAMP AREA.
LET'S JUST BE CAREFUL AROUND WOLF. HE SEEMS GENTLE, BUT WE REALLY DON'T KNOW ANYTHING ABOUT HIM.
I'M GOING TO STAY AS FAR AWAY FROM THAT MONSTER AS I CAN.
DAD GOT A SHOVEL AND BOX TO CARRY AWAY THE DEAD RABBIT IN.

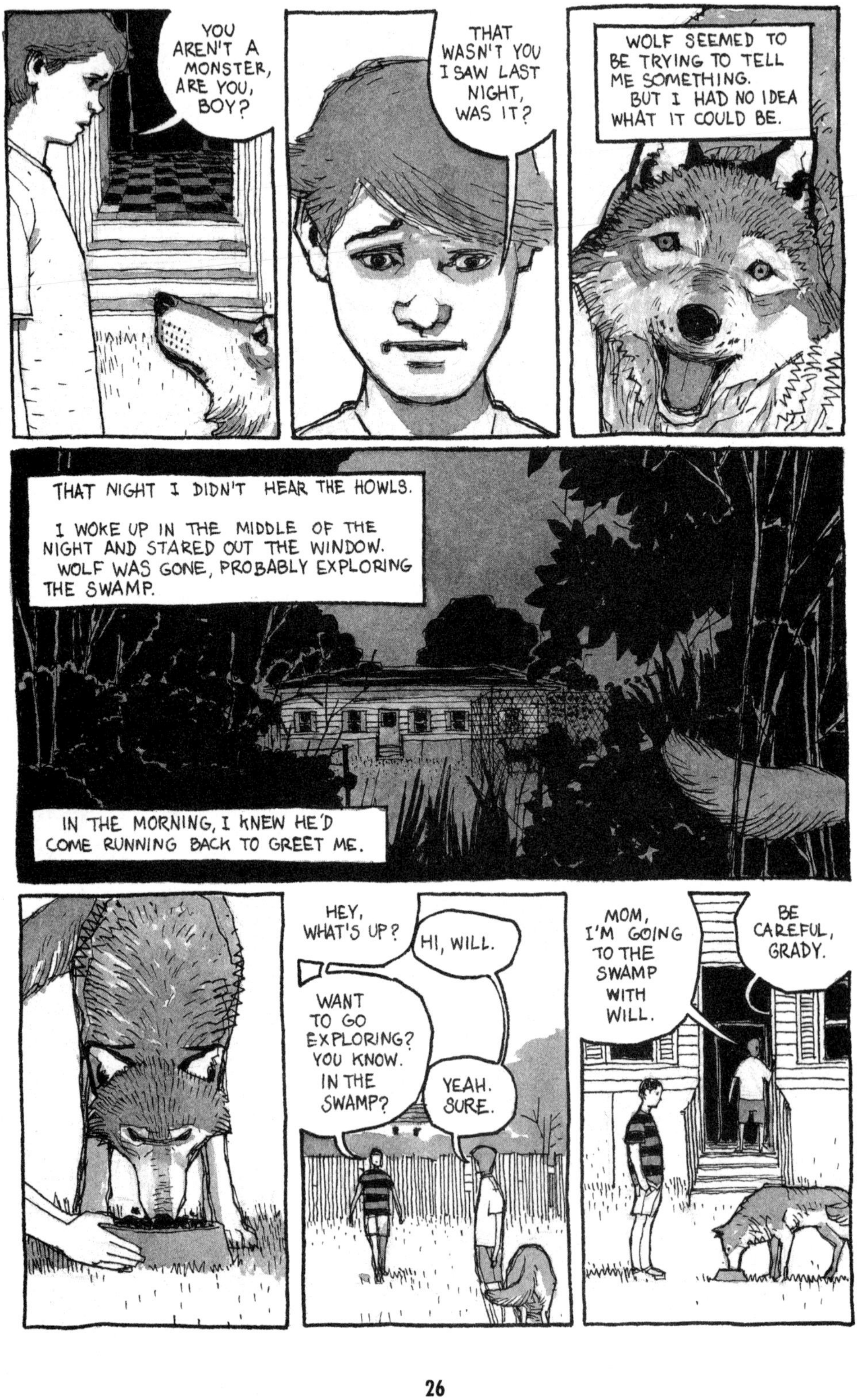
YOU AREN'T A MONSTER, ARE YOU, BOY?
THAT WASN'T YOU I SAW LAST NIGHT, WAS IT?
WOLF SEEMED TO BE TRYING TO TELL ME SOMETHING.
BUT I HAD NO IDEA WHAT IT COULD BE.
THAT NIGHT I DIDN'T HEAR THE HOWLS.
I WOKE UP IN THE MIDDLE OF THE NIGHT AND STARED OUT THE WINDOW.
WOLF WAS GONE, PROBABLY EXPLORING THE SWAMP.
IN THE MORNING, I KNEW HE'D COME RUNNING BACK TO GREET ME.
HEY, WHAT'S UP?
HI, WILL.
WANT TO GO EXPLORING? YOU KNOW. IN THE SWAMP?
YEAH. SURE.
MOM, I'M GOING TO THE SWAMP WITH WILL.
BE CAREFUL, GRADY.

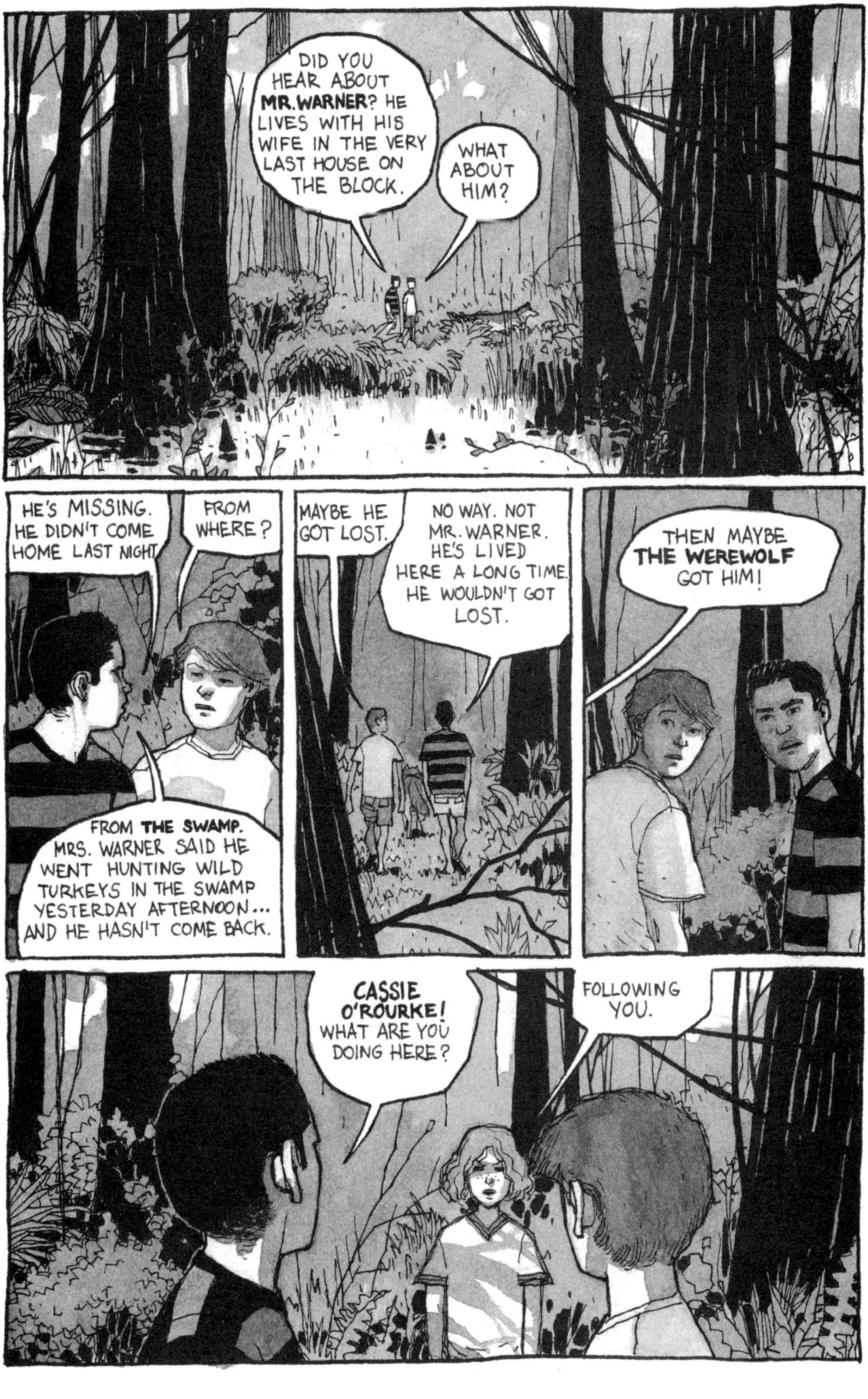
DID YOU HEAR ABOUT **MR. WARNER**? HE LIVES WITH HIS WIFE IN THE VERY LAST HOUSE ON THE BLOCK.
WHAT ABOUT HIM?
HE'S MISSING. HE DIDN'T COME HOME LAST NIGHT.
FROM WHERE?
FROM **THE SWAMP.** MRS. WARNER SAID HE WENT HUNTING WILD TURKEYS IN THE SWAMP YESTERDAY AFTERNOON... AND HE HASN'T COME BACK.
MAYBE HE GOT LOST.
NO WAY. NOT MR. WARNER. HE'S LIVED HERE A LONG TIME. HE WOULDN'T GOT LOST.
THEN MAYBE **THE WEREWOLF** GOT HIM!
CASSIE O'ROURKE! WHAT ARE YOU DOING HERE?
FOLLOWING YOU.

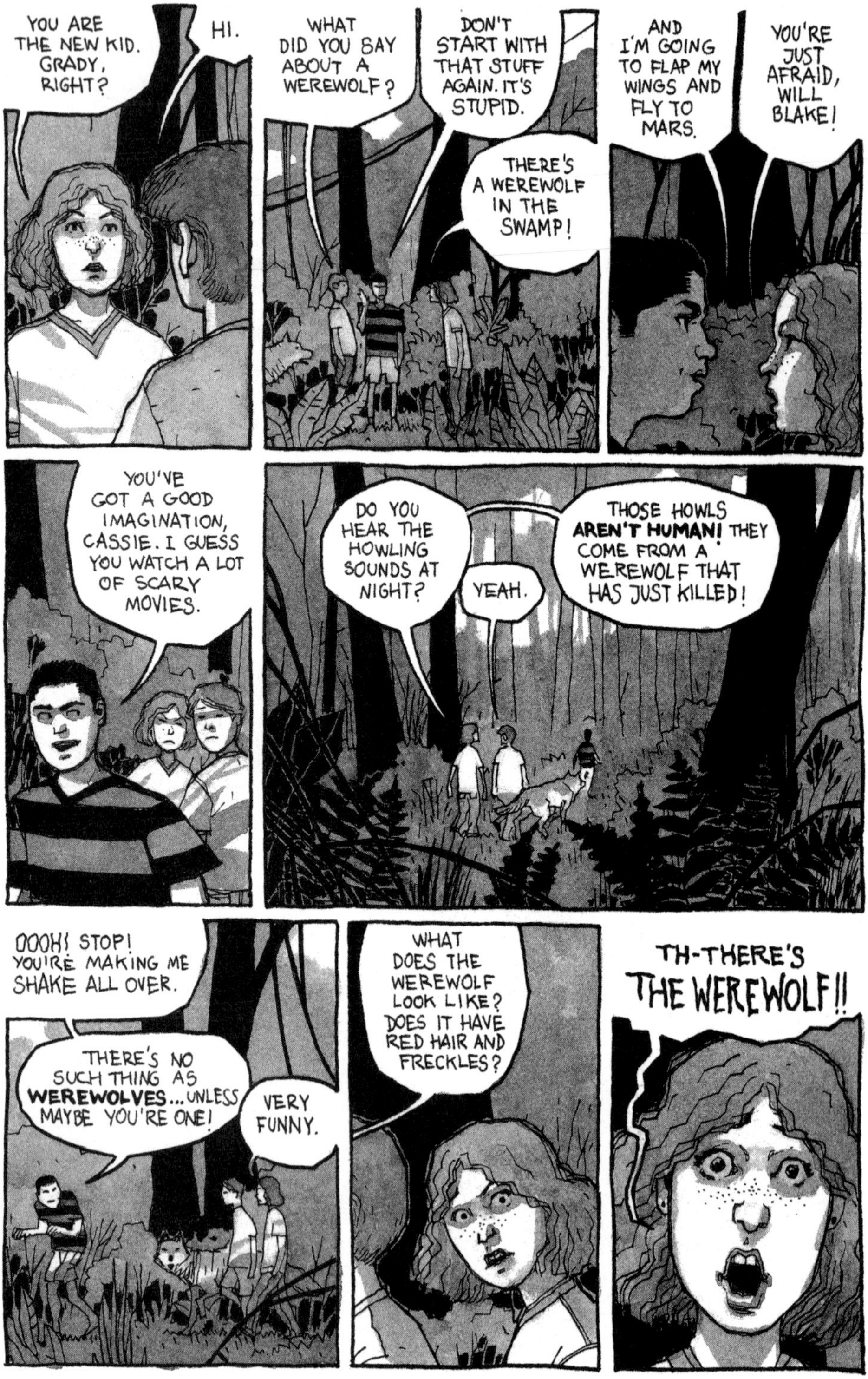
YOU ARE THE NEW KID. GRADY, RIGHT?
HI.
WHAT DID YOU SAY ABOUT A WEREWOLF?
DON'T START WITH THAT STUFF AGAIN. IT'S STUPID.
THERE'S A WEREWOLF IN THE SWAMP!
AND I'M GOING TO FLAP MY WINGS AND FLY TO MARS.
YOU'RE JUST AFRAID, WILL BLAKE!
YOU'VE GOT A GOOD IMAGINATION, CASSIE. I GUESS YOU WATCH A LOT OF SCARY MOVIES.
DO YOU HEAR THE HOWLING SOUNDS AT NIGHT?
YEAH.
THOSE HOWLS AREN'T HUMAN! THEY COME FROM A WEREWOLF THAT HAS JUST KILLED!
OOOH! STOP! YOU'RE MAKING ME SHAKE ALL OVER.
THERE'S NO SUCH THING AS WEREWOLVES... UNLESS MAYBE YOU'RE ONE!
VERY FUNNY.
WHAT DOES THE WEREWOLF LOOK LIKE? DOES IT HAVE RED HAIR AND FRECKLES?
TH-THERE'S THE WEREWOLF!!

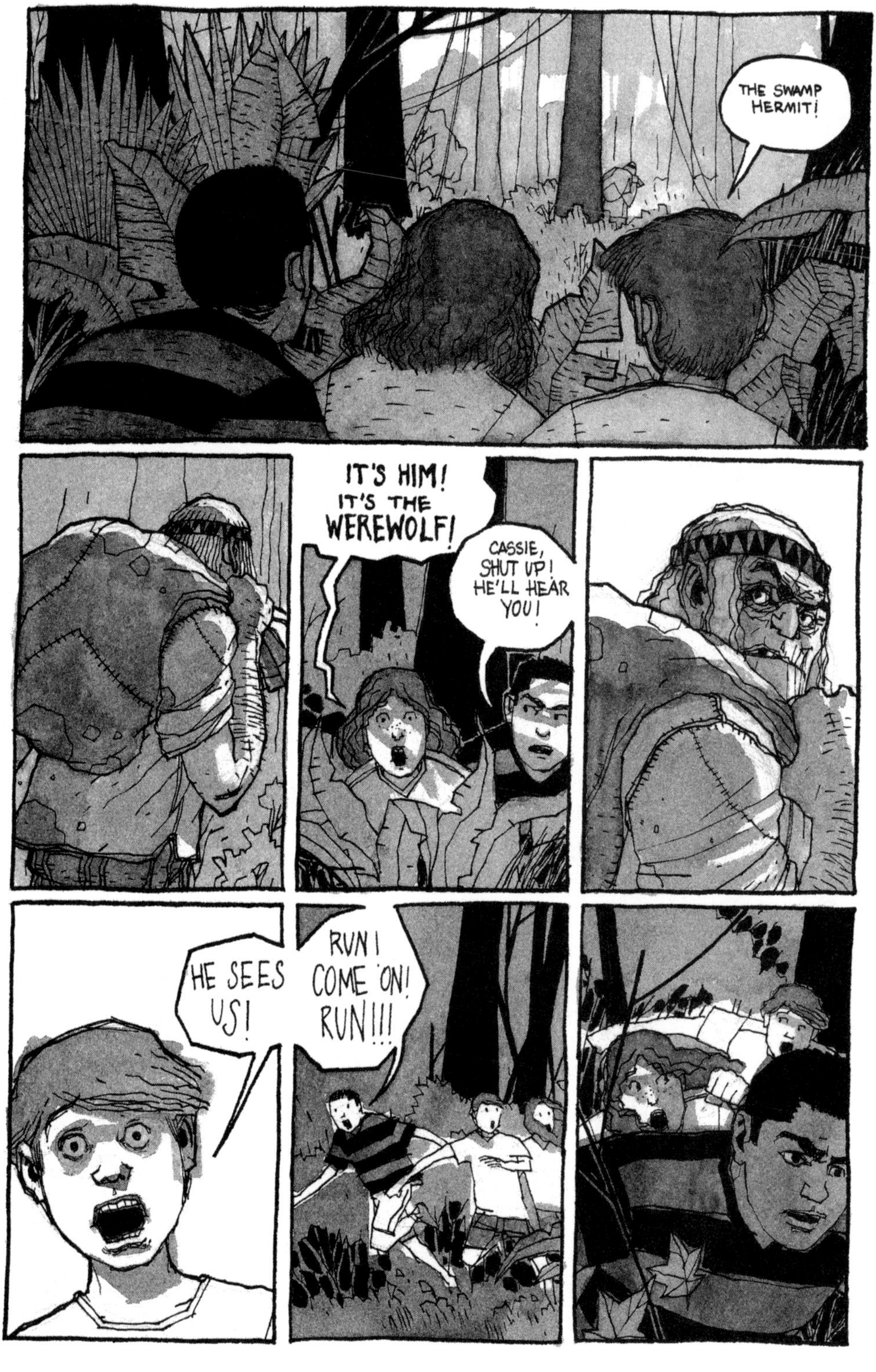
THE SWAMP HERMIT!
IT'S HIM! IT'S THE WEREWOLF!
CASSIE, SHUT UP! HE'LL HEAR YOU!
HE SEES US!
RUN! COME ON! RUN!!!

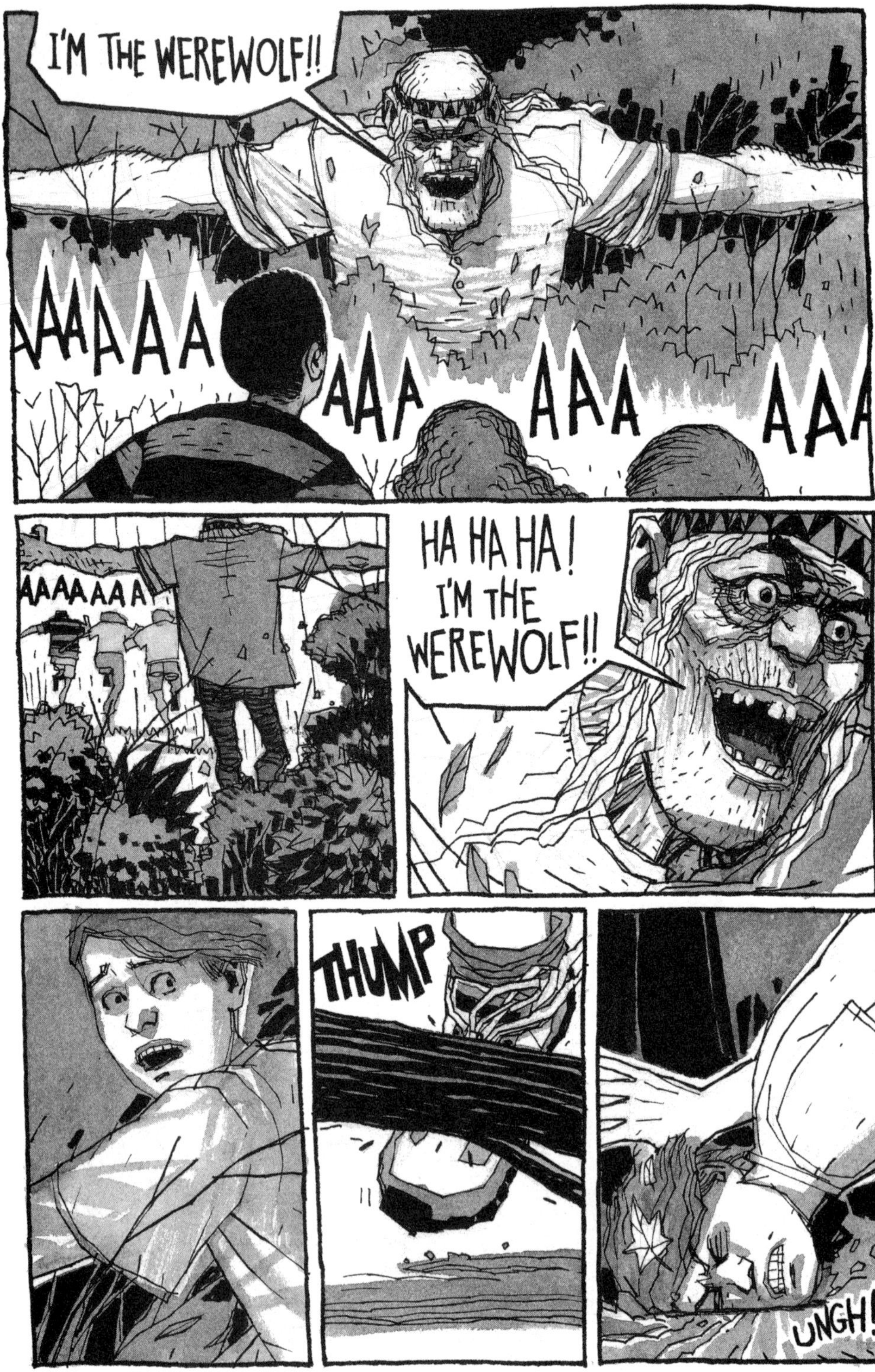
I'M THE WEREWOLF!!
AAAAAA AAA AAA AAA
AAAAAAA
HA HA HA! I'M THE WEREWOLF!!
THUMP
UNGH!

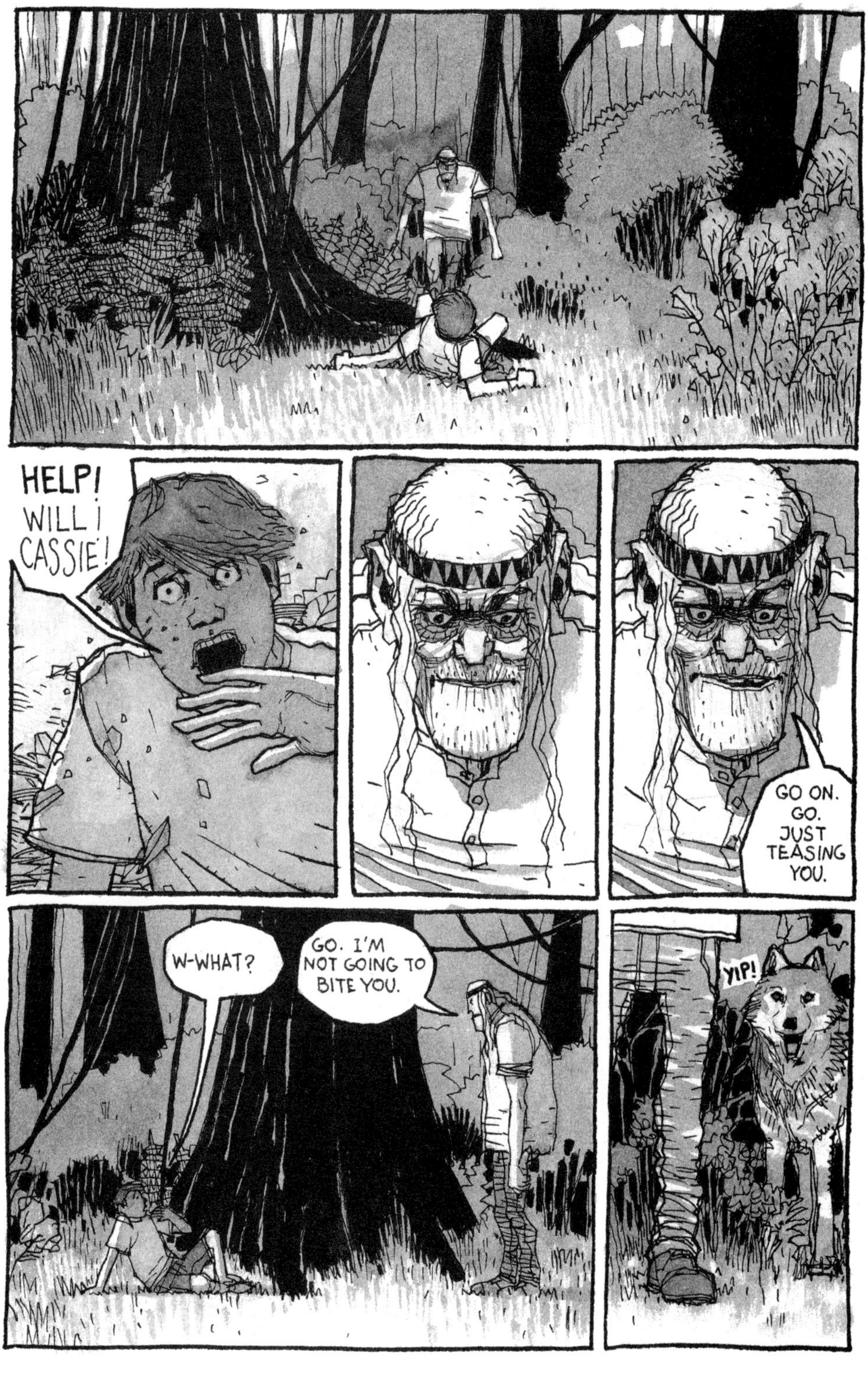
HELP! WILL! CASSIE!
GO ON. GO. JUST TEASING YOU.
W-WHAT?
GO. I'M NOT GOING TO BITE YOU.
YIP!

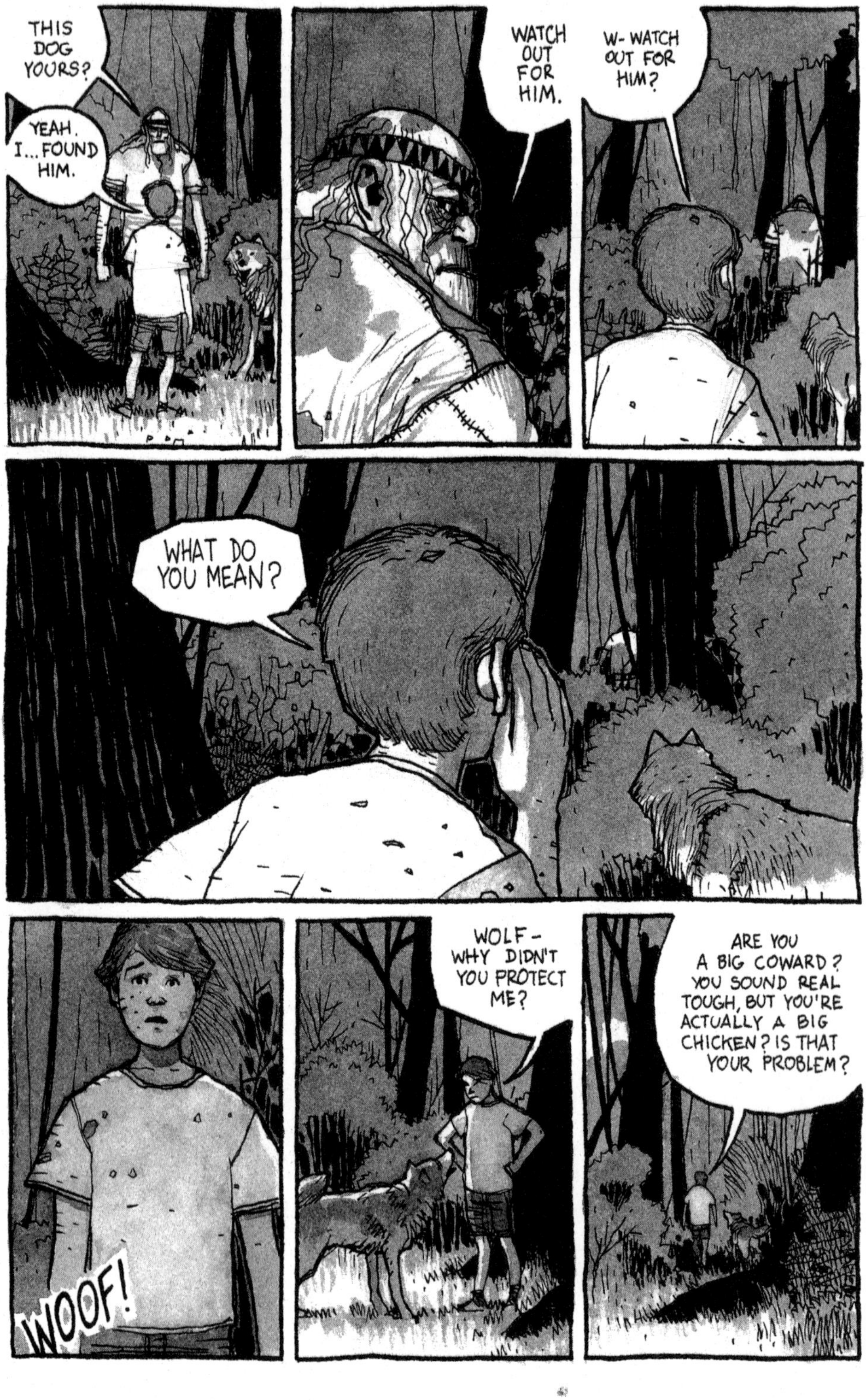
THIS DOG YOURS?
YEAH. I... FOUND HIM.
WATCH OUT FOR HIM.
W- WATCH OUT FOR HIM?
WHAT DO YOU MEAN?
WOOF!
WOLF - WHY DIDN'T YOU PROTECT ME?
ARE YOU A BIG COWARD? YOU SOUND REAL TOUGH, BUT YOU'RE ACTUALLY A BIG CHICKEN? IS THAT YOUR PROBLEM?

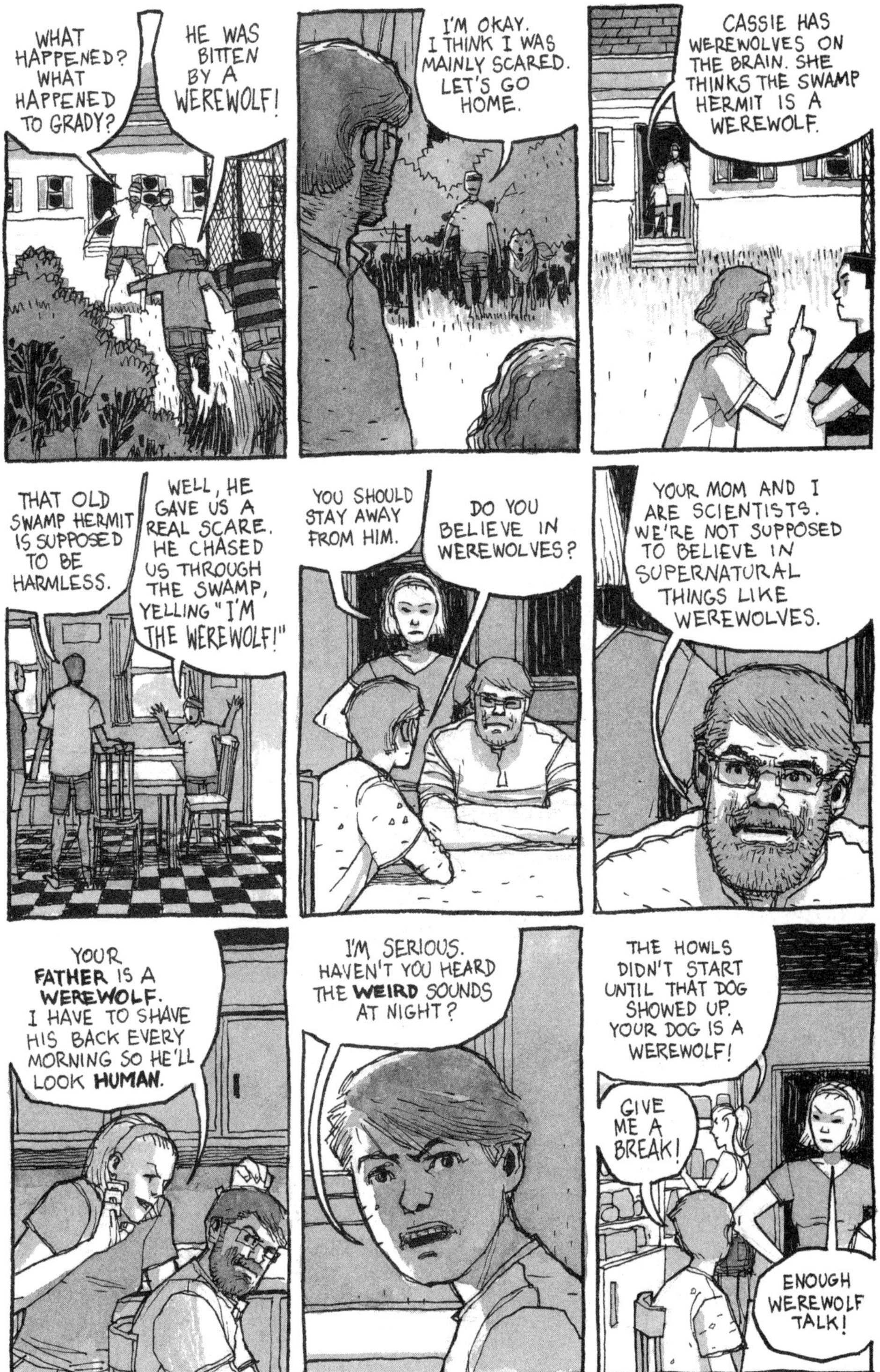
WHAT HAPPENED? WHAT HAPPENED TO GRADY?
HE WAS BITTEN BY A WEREWOLF!
I'M OKAY. I THINK I WAS MAINLY SCARED. LET'S GO HOME.
CASSIE HAS WEREWOLVES ON THE BRAIN. SHE THINKS THE SWAMP HERMIT IS A WEREWOLF.
THAT OLD SWAMP HERMIT IS SUPPOSED TO BE HARMLESS.
WELL, HE GAVE US A REAL SCARE. HE CHASED US THROUGH THE SWAMP, YELLING "I'M THE WEREWOLF!"
YOU SHOULD STAY AWAY FROM HIM.
DO YOU BELIEVE IN WEREWOLVES?
YOUR MOM AND I ARE SCIENTISTS. WE'RE NOT SUPPOSED TO BELIEVE IN SUPERNATURAL THINGS LIKE WEREWOLVES.
YOUR **FATHER** IS A **WEREWOLF**. I HAVE TO SHAVE HIS BACK EVERY MORNING SO HE'LL LOOK **HUMAN**.
I'M SERIOUS. HAVEN'T YOU HEARD THE **WEIRD** SOUNDS AT NIGHT?
THE HOWLS DIDN'T START UNTIL THAT DOG SHOWED UP. YOUR DOG IS A WEREWOLF!
GIVE ME A BREAK!
ENOUGH WEREWOLF TALK!

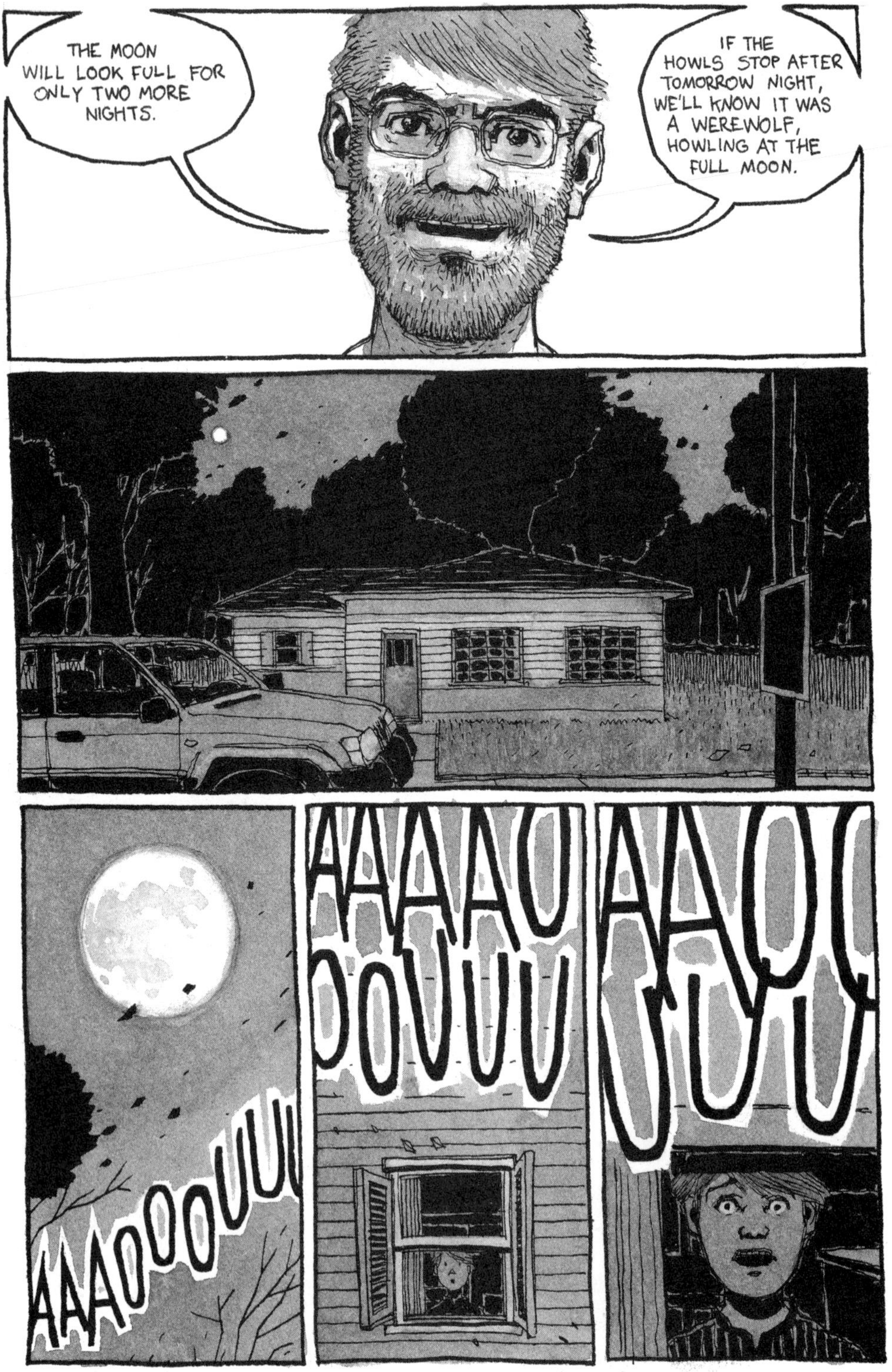
THE MOON WILL LOOK FULL FOR ONLY TWO MORE NIGHTS.
IF THE HOWLS STOP AFTER TOMORROW NIGHT, WE'LL KNOW IT WAS A WEREWOLF, HOWLING AT THE FULL MOON.
AAAOOOUUU
AAAAOOUUU

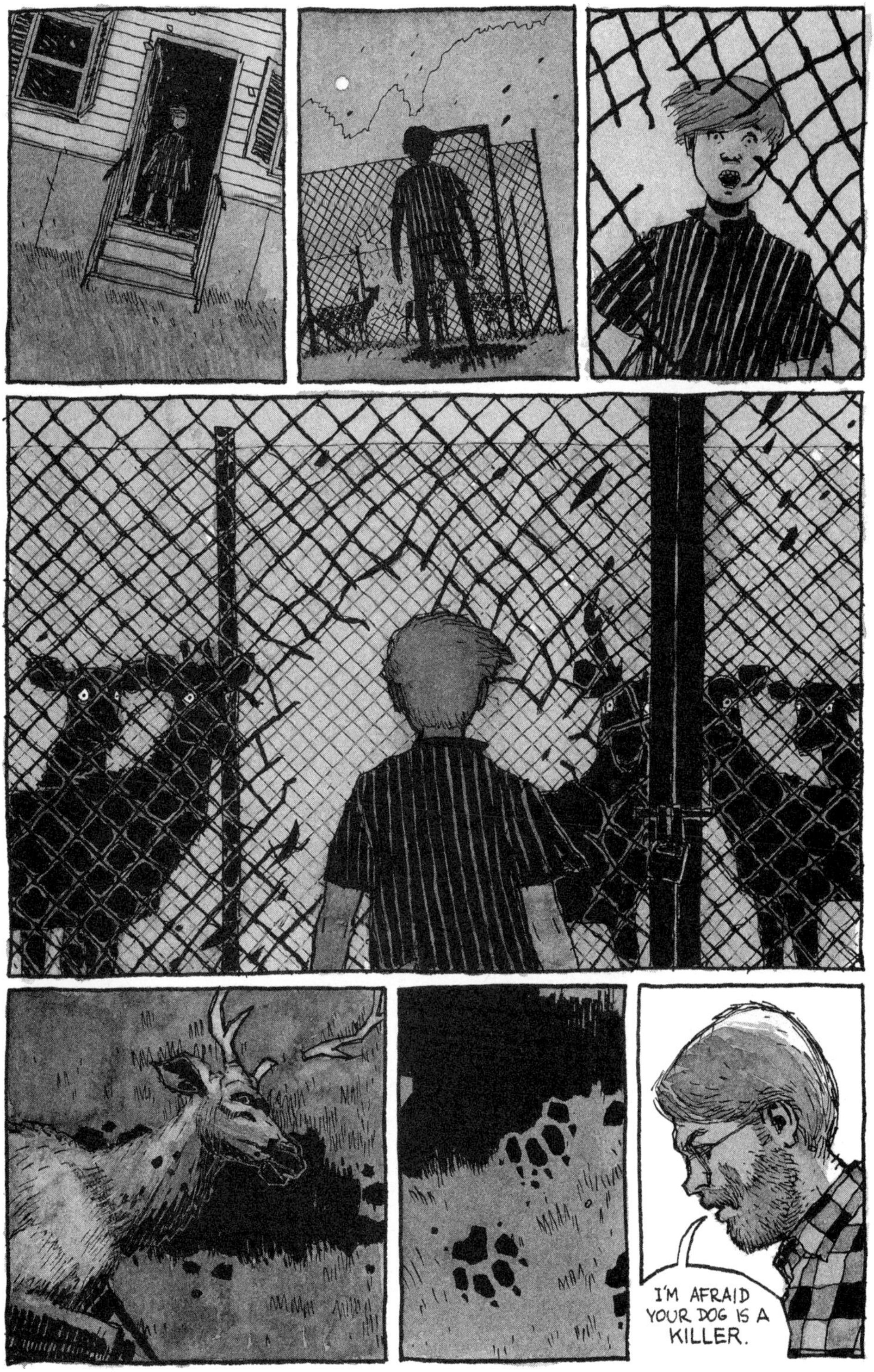
I'M AFRAID YOUR DOG IS A KILLER.

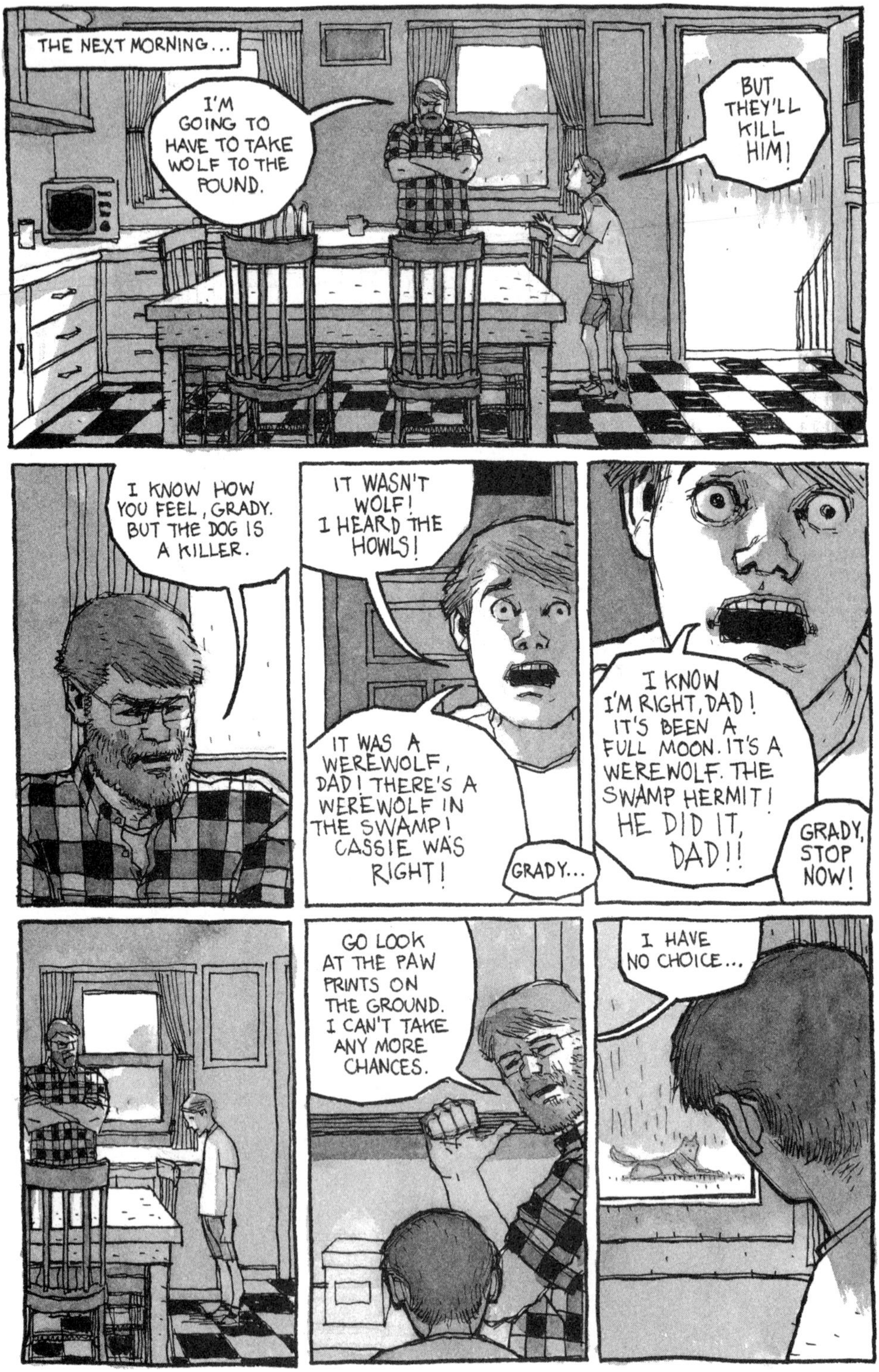
THE NEXT MORNING...
I'M GOING TO HAVE TO TAKE WOLF TO THE POUND.
BUT THEY'LL KILL HIM!
I KNOW HOW YOU FEEL, GRADY. BUT THE DOG IS A KILLER.
IT WASN'T WOLF! I HEARD THE HOWLS!
IT WAS A WEREWOLF, DAD! THERE'S A WEREWOLF IN THE SWAMP! CASSIE WAS RIGHT!
GRADY...
I KNOW I'M RIGHT, DAD! IT'S BEEN A FULL MOON. IT'S A WEREWOLF. THE SWAMP HERMIT! HE DID IT, DAD!!
GRADY, STOP NOW!
GO LOOK AT THE PAW PRINTS ON THE GROUND. I CAN'T TAKE ANY MORE CHANCES.
I HAVE NO CHOICE...

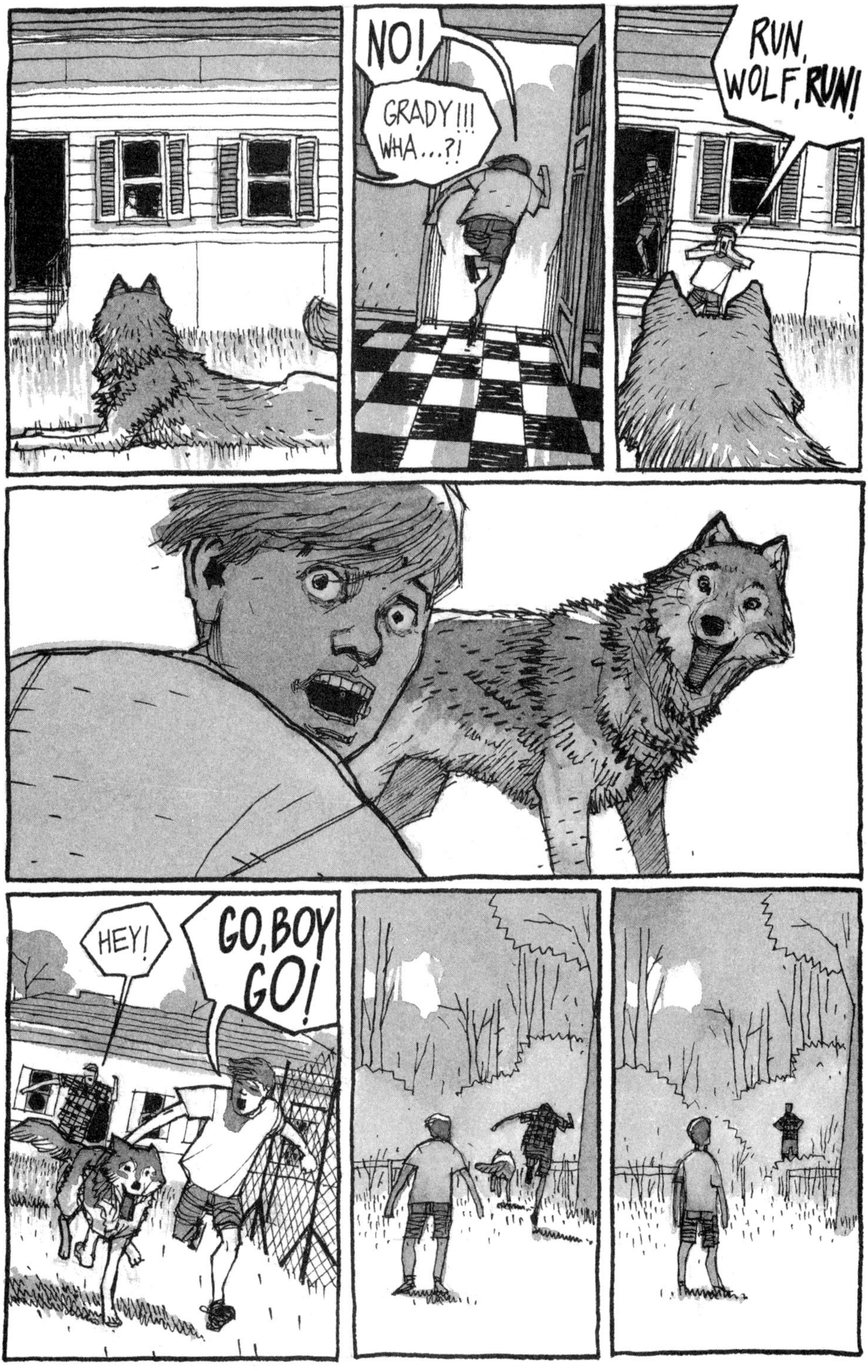
NO!
GRADY!!! WHA...?!
RUN, WOLF, RUN!
HEY!
GO, BOY GO!

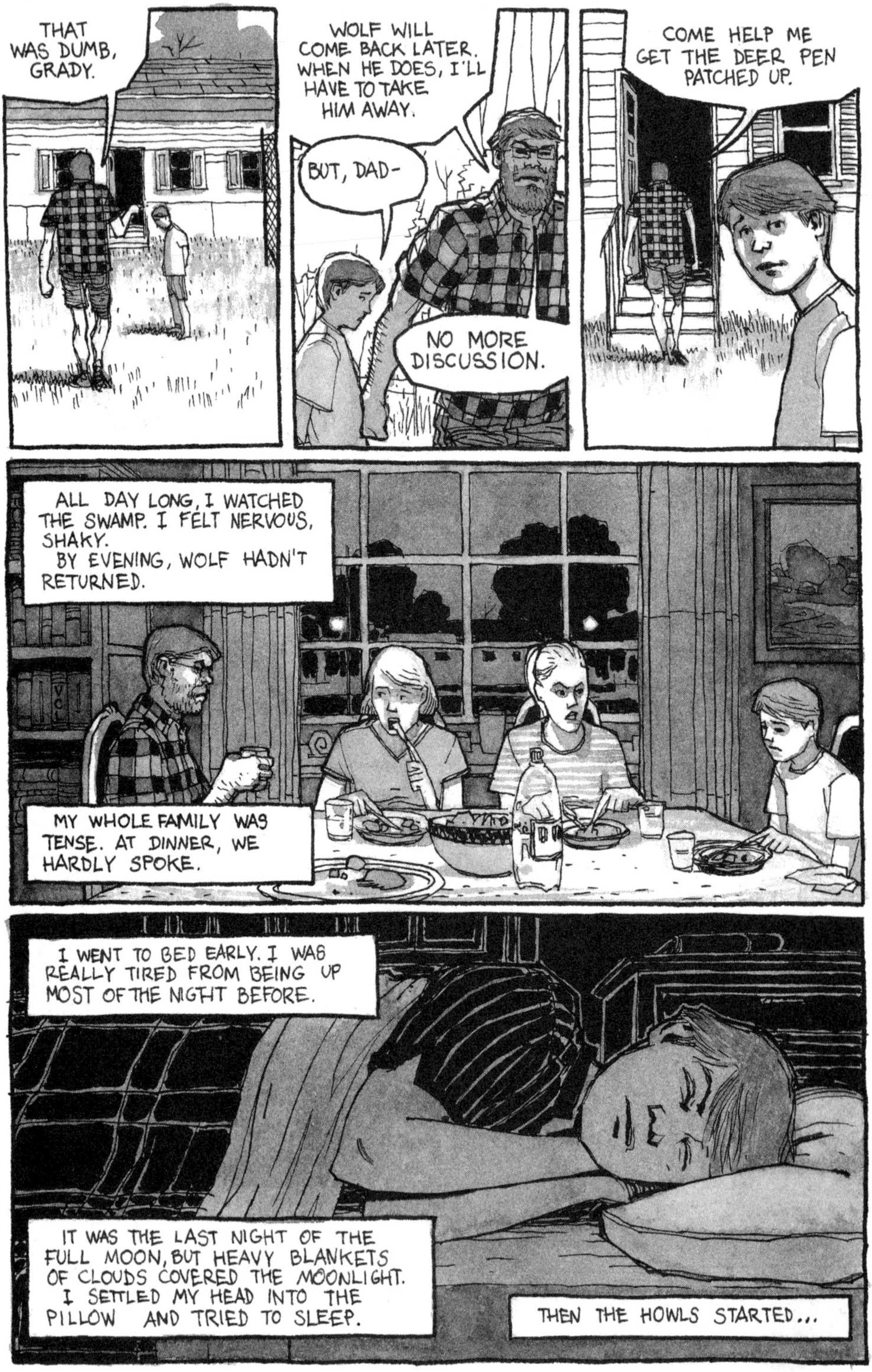
THAT WAS DUMB, GRADY.
WOLF WILL COME BACK LATER. WHEN HE DOES, I'LL HAVE TO TAKE HIM AWAY.
BUT, DAD-
NO MORE DISCUSSION.
COME HELP ME GET THE DEER PEN PATCHED UP.
ALL DAY LONG, I WATCHED THE SWAMP. I FELT NERVOUS, SHAKY.
BY EVENING, WOLF HADN'T RETURNED.
MY WHOLE FAMILY WAS TENSE. AT DINNER, WE HARDLY SPOKE.
I WENT TO BED EARLY. I WAS REALLY TIRED FROM BEING UP MOST OF THE NIGHT BEFORE.
IT WAS THE LAST NIGHT OF THE FULL MOON, BUT HEAVY BLANKETS OF CLOUDS COVERED THE MOONLIGHT.
I SETTLED MY HEAD INTO THE PILLOW AND TRIED TO SLEEP.
THEN THE HOWLS STARTED...

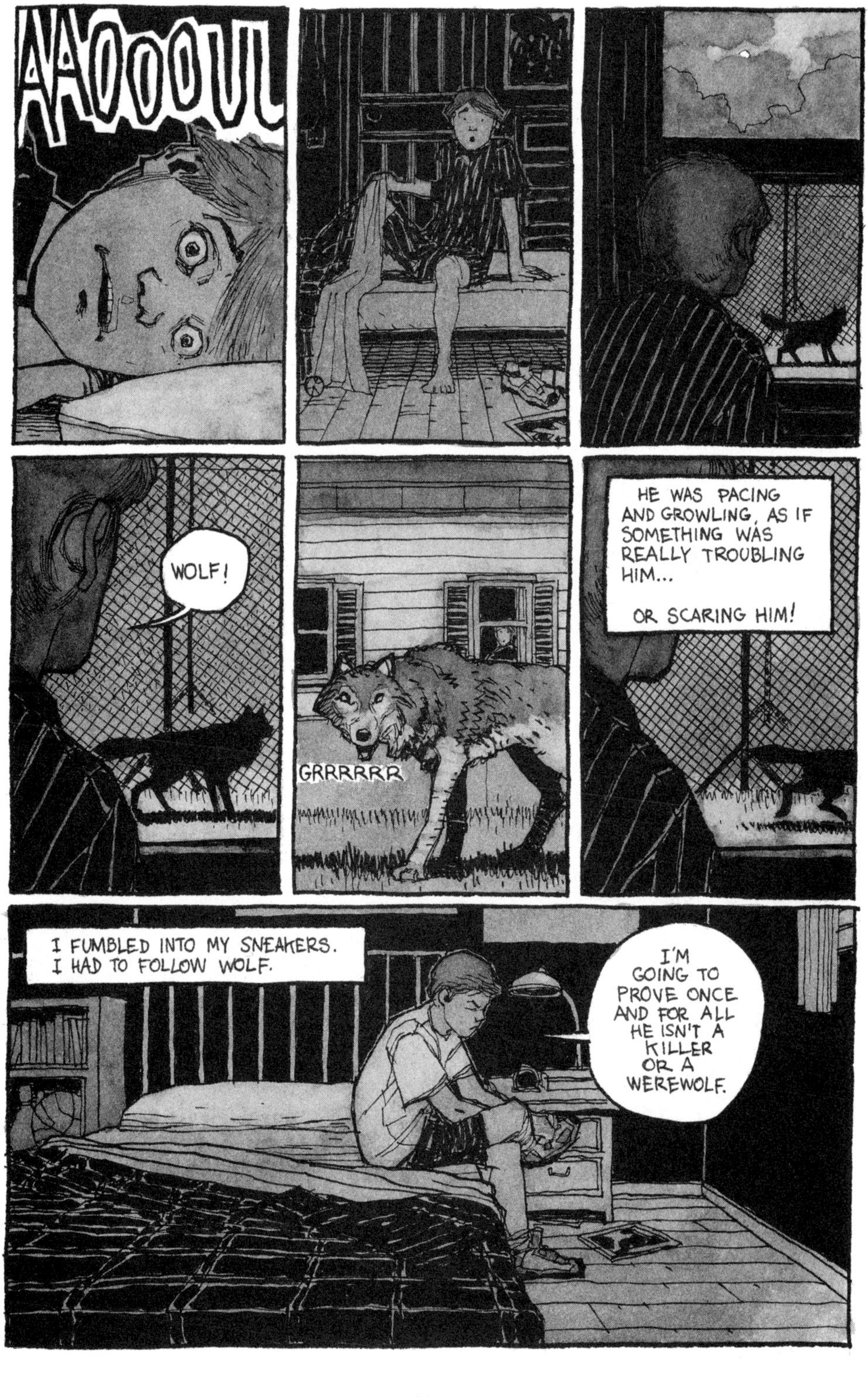
AAOOOUL
WOLF!
GRRRRRR
HE WAS PACING AND GROWLING, AS IF SOMETHING WAS REALLY TROUBLING HIM...
OR SCARING HIM!
I FUMBLED INTO MY SNEAKERS. I HAD TO FOLLOW WOLF.
I'M GOING TO PROVE ONCE AND FOR ALL HE ISN'T A KILLER OR A WEREWOLF.

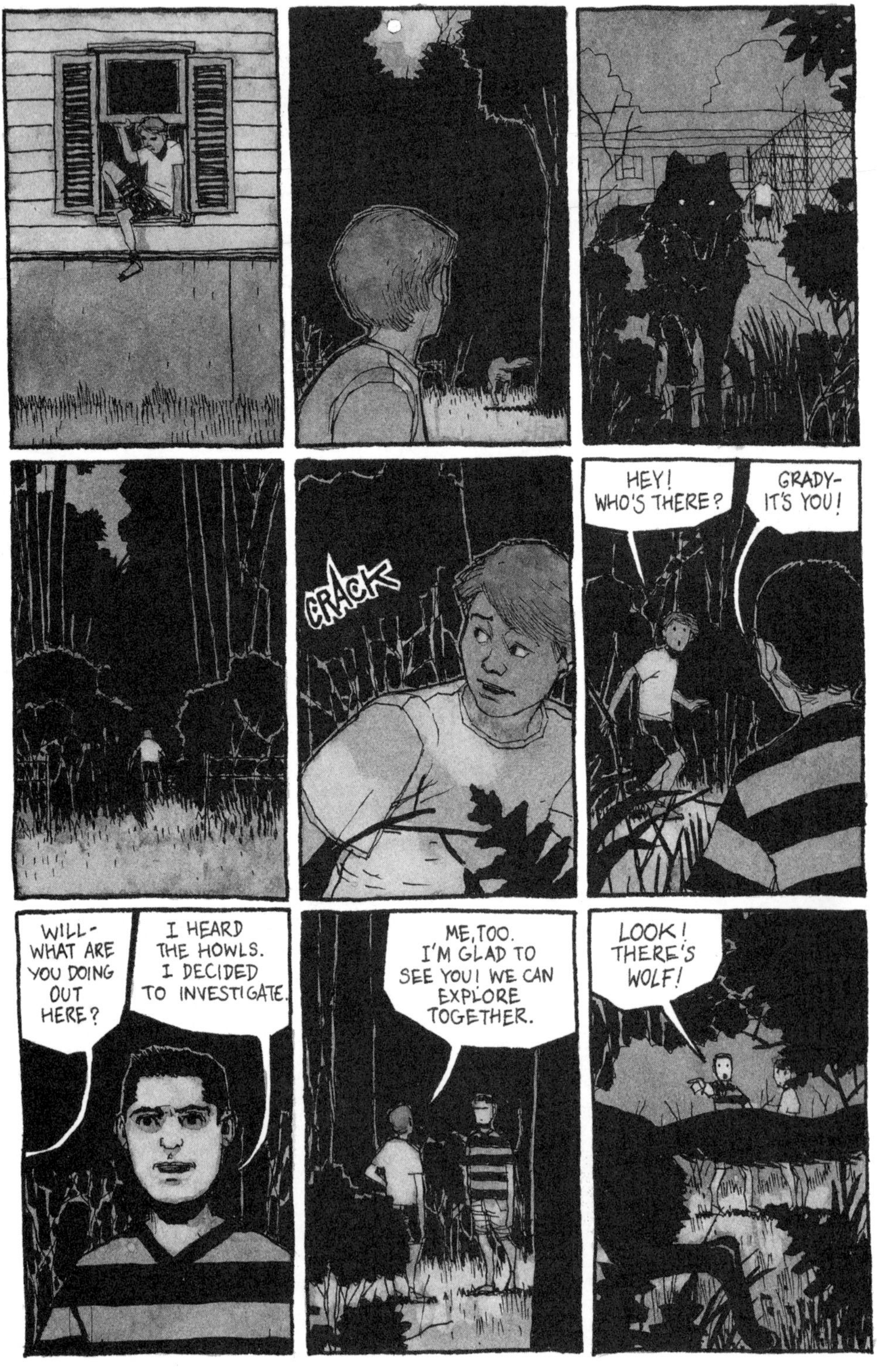
CRACK
HEY! WHO'S THERE?
GRADY- IT'S YOU!
WILL- WHAT ARE YOU DOING OUT HERE?
I HEARD THE HOWLS. I DECIDED TO INVESTIGATE.
ME, TOO. I'M GLAD TO SEE YOU! WE CAN EXPLORE TOGETHER.
LOOK! THERE'S WOLF!

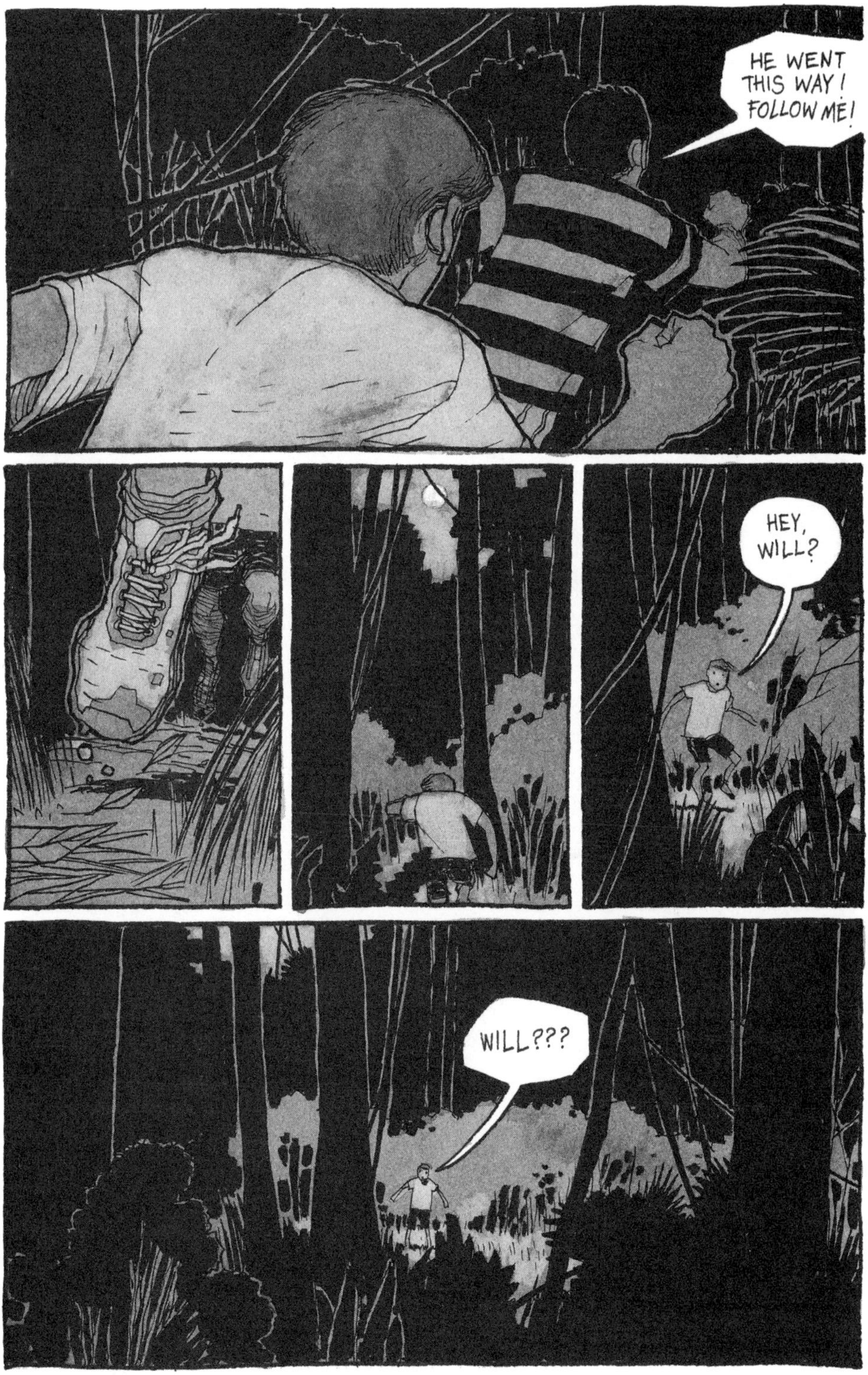
HE WENT THIS WAY! FOLLOW ME!
HEY, WILL?
WILL???

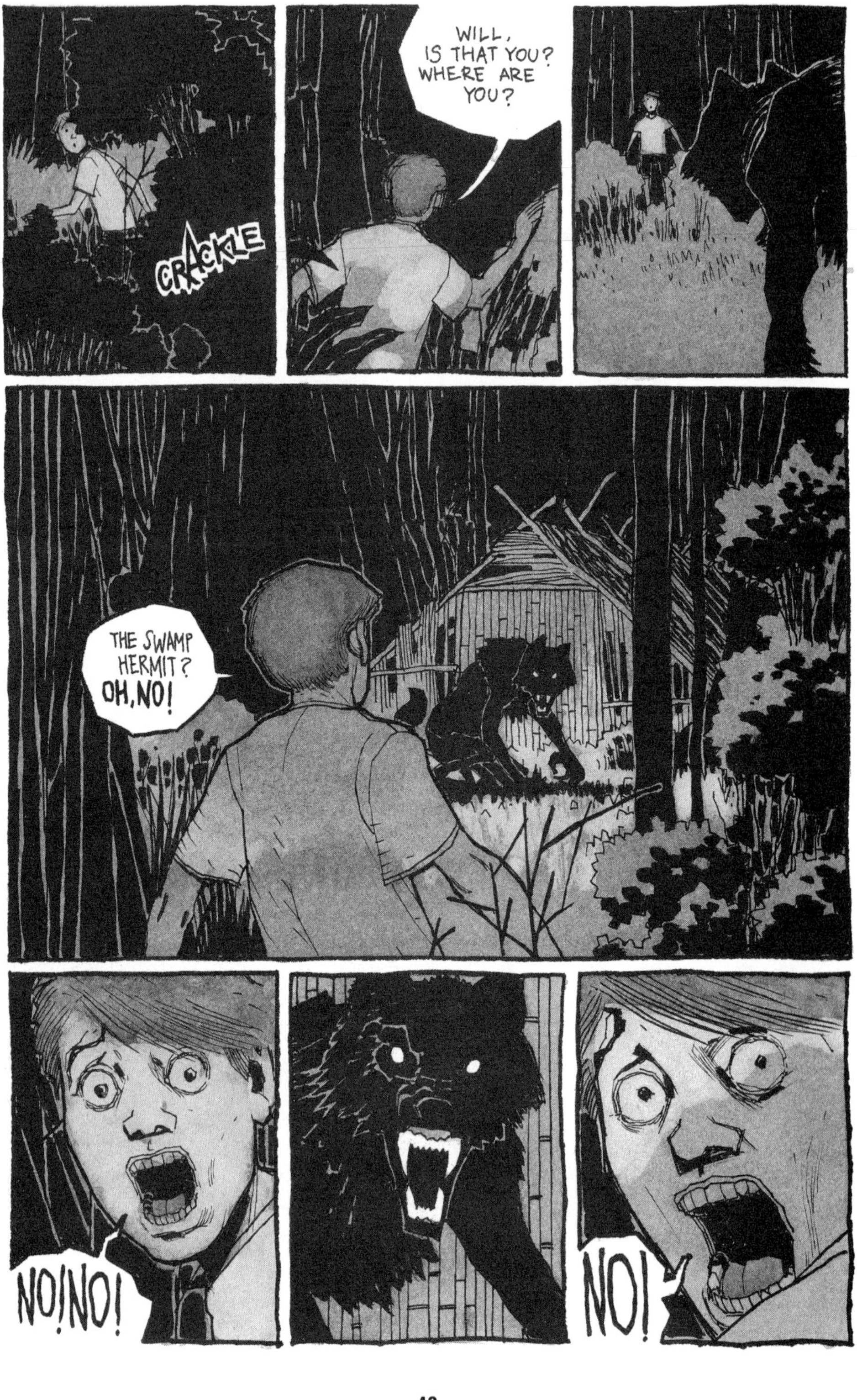
CRACKLE
WILL, IS THAT YOU? WHERE ARE YOU?
THE SWAMP HERMIT? OH, NO!
NO! NO!
NO!

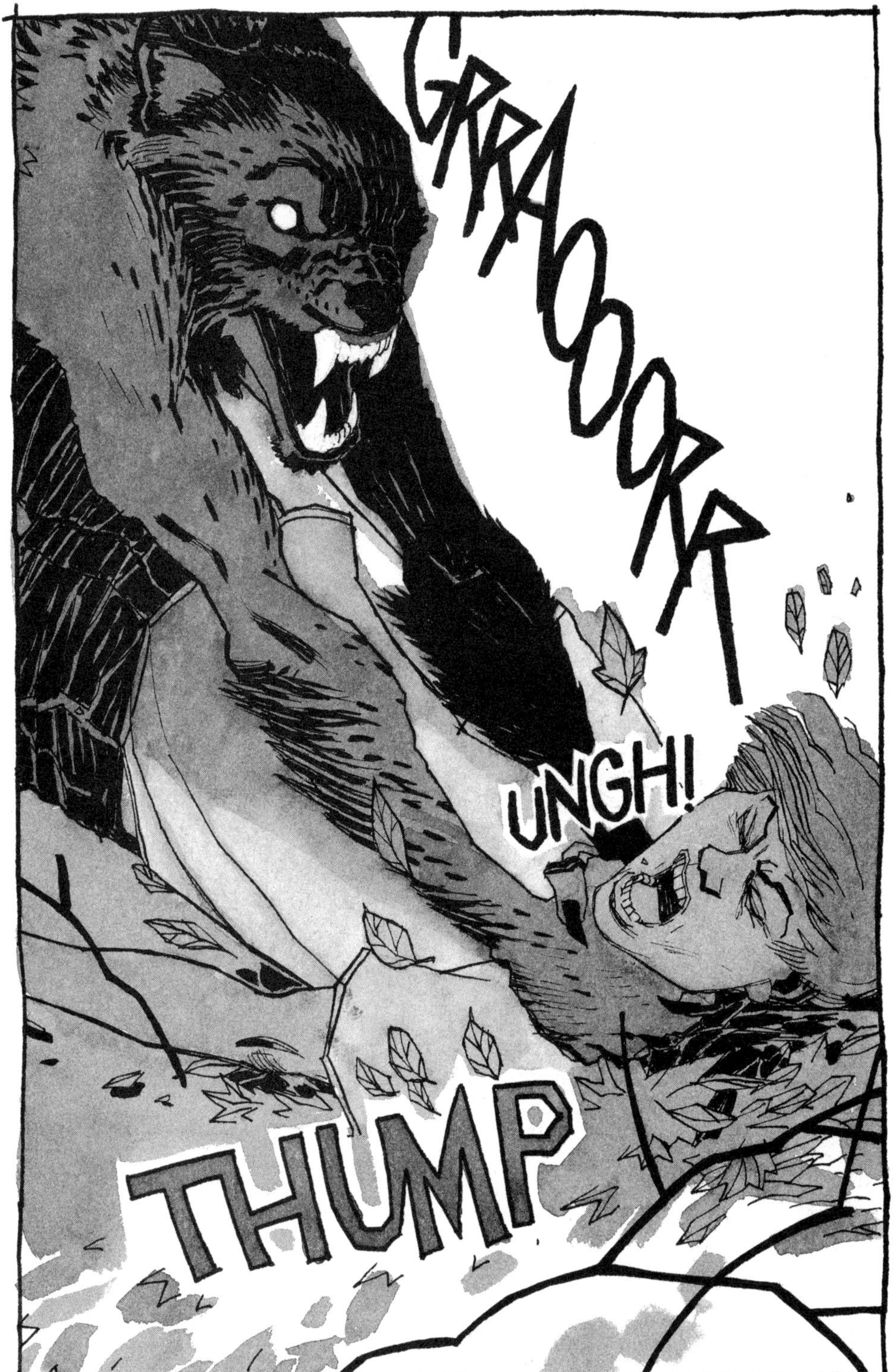
GRRAOOORR
UNGH!
THUMP

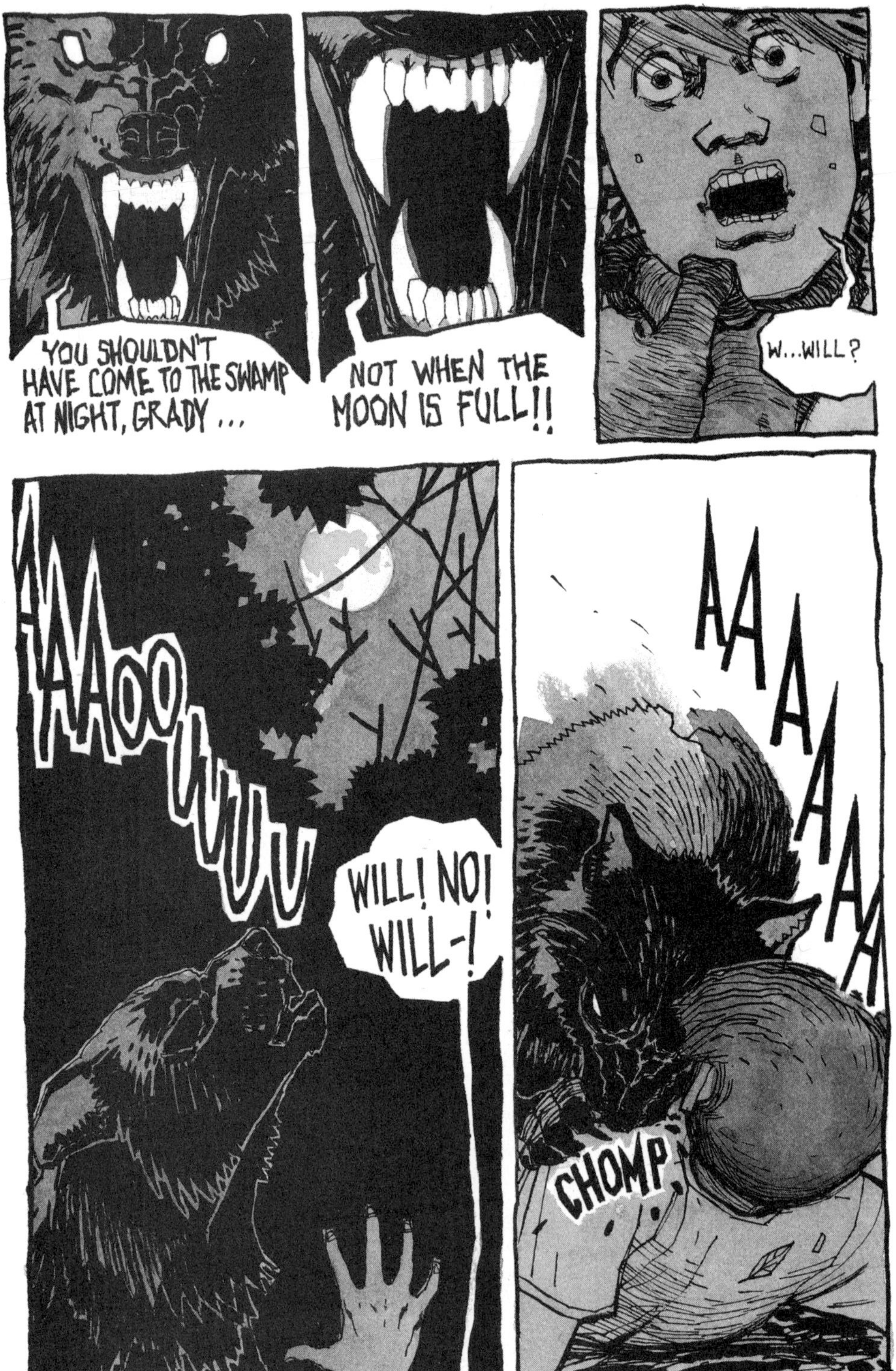
YOU SHOULDN'T HAVE COME TO THE SWAMP AT NIGHT, GRADY ...
NOT WHEN THE MOON IS FULL!!
W...WILL?
AAAOOUUUU
WILL! NO! WILL-!
AAAAAAAAA
CHOMP

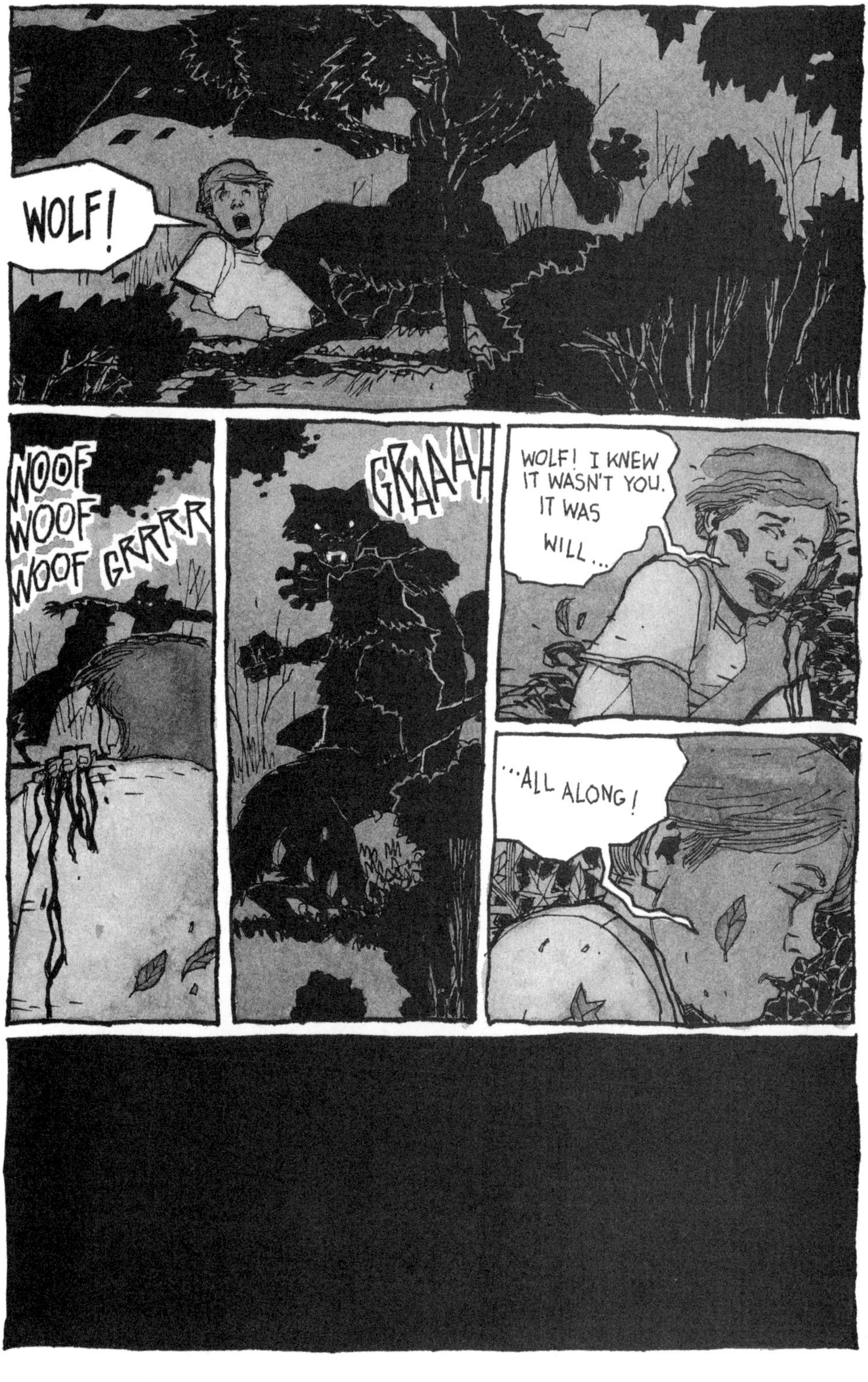
WOLF!
WOOF WOOF WOOF GRRRR
GRAAAH
WOLF! I KNEW IT WASN'T YOU. IT WAS WILL...
...ALL ALONG!

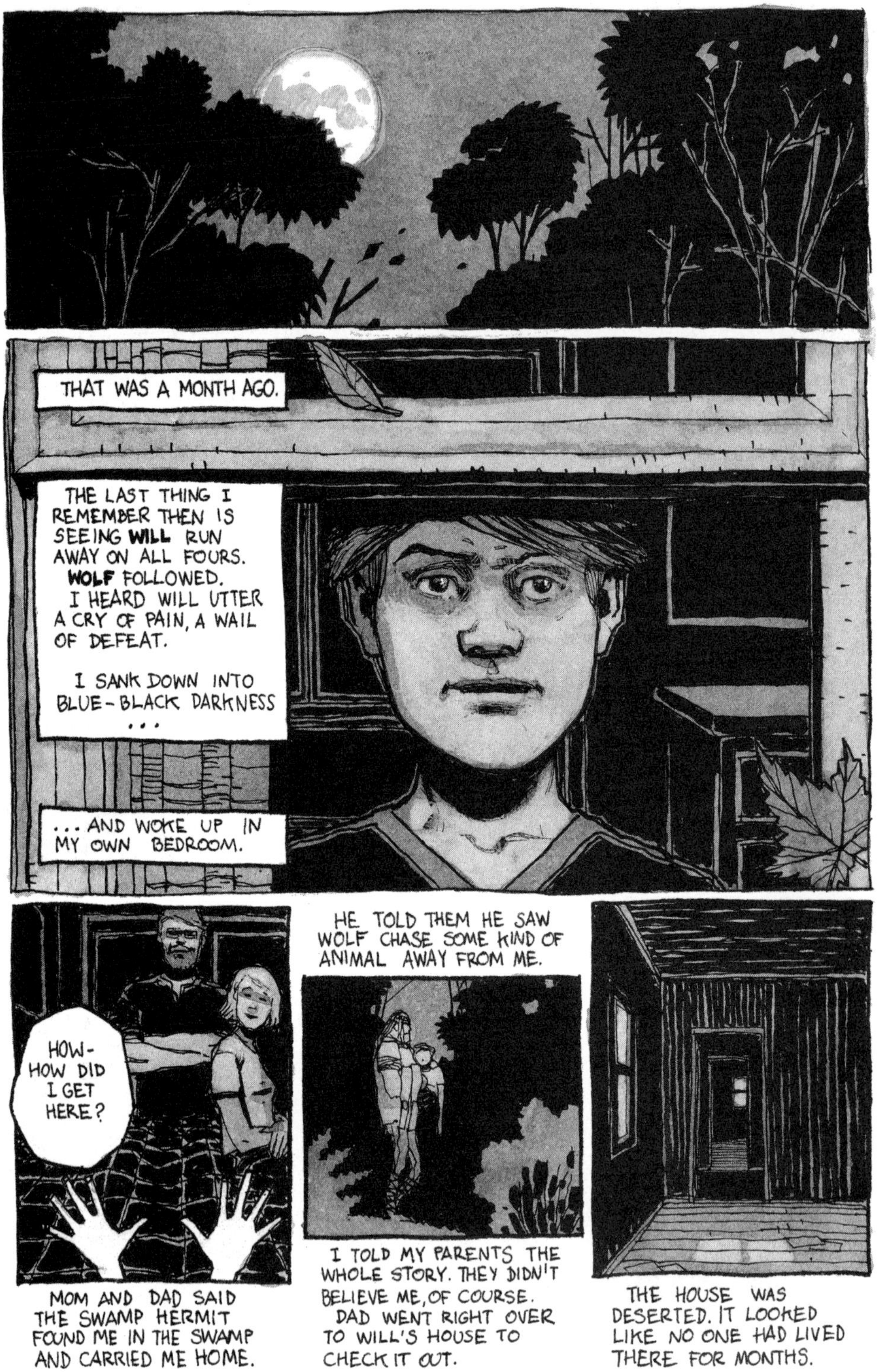
THAT WAS A MONTH AGO.
THE LAST THING I REMEMBER THEN IS SEEING WILL RUN AWAY ON ALL FOURS. WOLF FOLLOWED. I HEARD WILL UTTER A CRY OF PAIN, A WAIL OF DEFEAT.
I SANK DOWN INTO BLUE-BLACK DARKNESS ...
... AND WOKE UP IN MY OWN BEDROOM.
HOW- HOW DID I GET HERE?
MOM AND DAD SAID THE SWAMP HERMIT FOUND ME IN THE SWAMP AND CARRIED ME HOME.
HE TOLD THEM HE SAW WOLF CHASE SOME KIND OF ANIMAL AWAY FROM ME.
I TOLD MY PARENTS THE WHOLE STORY. THEY DIDN'T BELIEVE ME, OF COURSE. DAD WENT RIGHT OVER TO WILL'S HOUSE TO CHECK IT OUT.
THE HOUSE WAS DESERTED. IT LOOKED LIKE NO ONE HAD LIVED THERE FOR MONTHS.

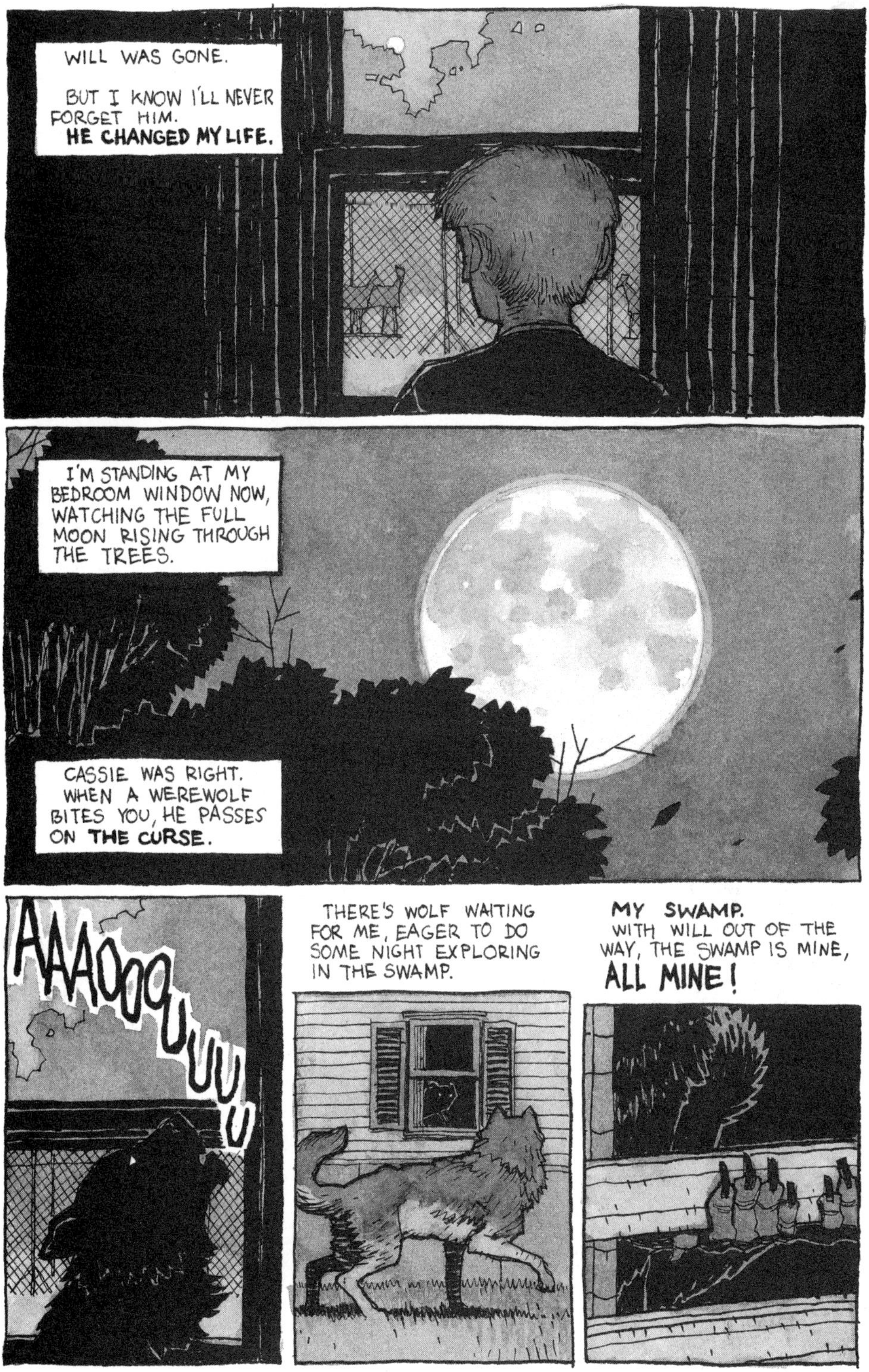
WILL WAS GONE.
BUT I KNOW I'LL NEVER FORGET HIM. HE CHANGED MY LIFE.
I'M STANDING AT MY BEDROOM WINDOW NOW, WATCHING THE FULL MOON RISING THROUGH THE TREES.
CASSIE WAS RIGHT. WHEN A WEREWOLF BITES YOU, HE PASSES ON THE CURSE.
AAAOOOUUUU
THERE'S WOLF WAITING FOR ME, EAGER TO DO SOME NIGHT EXPLORING IN THE SWAMP.
MY SWAMP.
WITH WILL OUT OF THE WAY, THE SWAMP IS MINE, ALL MINE!

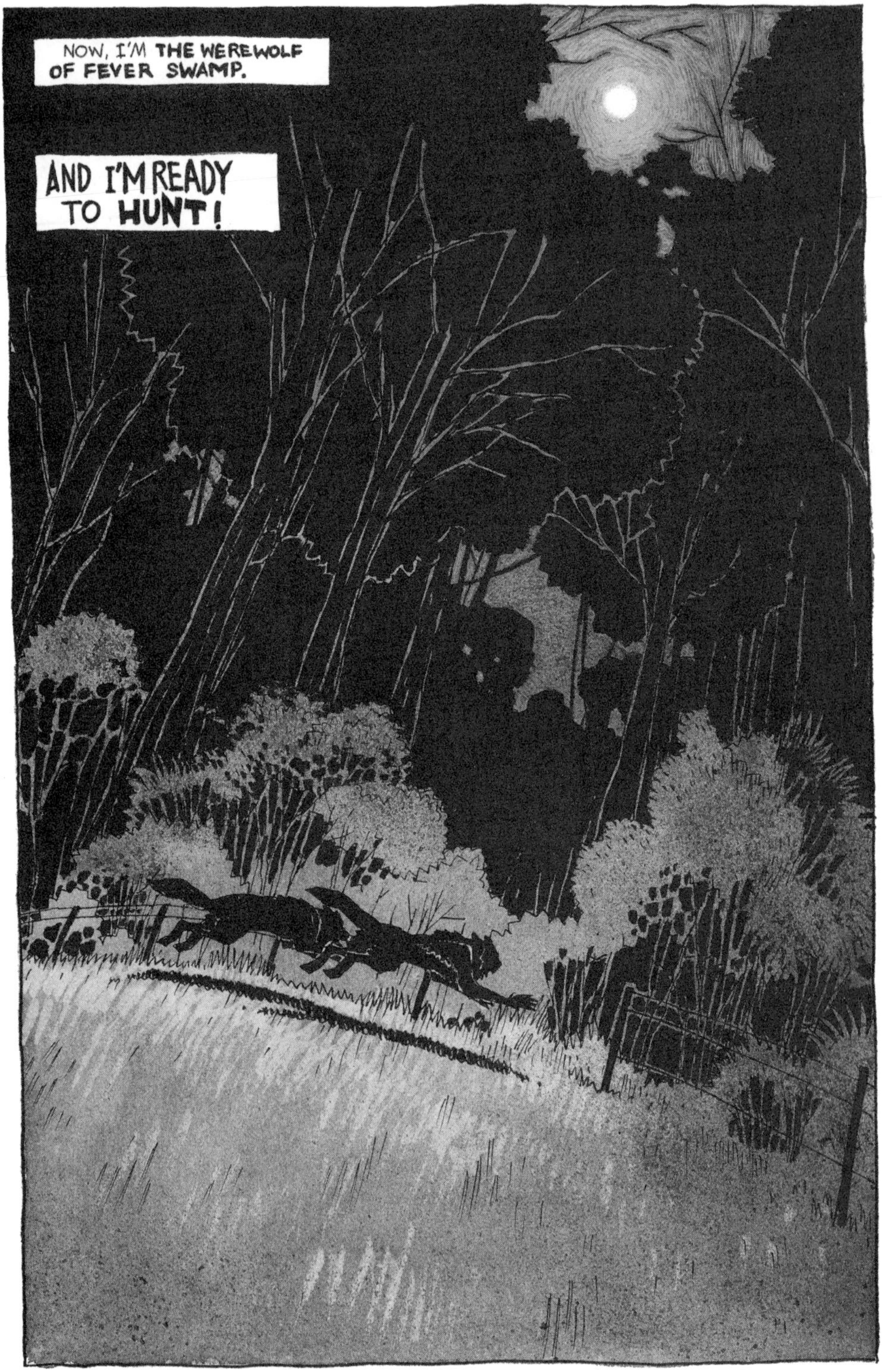
NOW, I'M THE WEREWOLF OF FEVER SWAMP.
AND I'M READY TO HUNT!

THE
SCARECROW
WALKS AT
MIDNIGHT

ADAPTED AND ILLUSTRATED BY

Greg Ruth

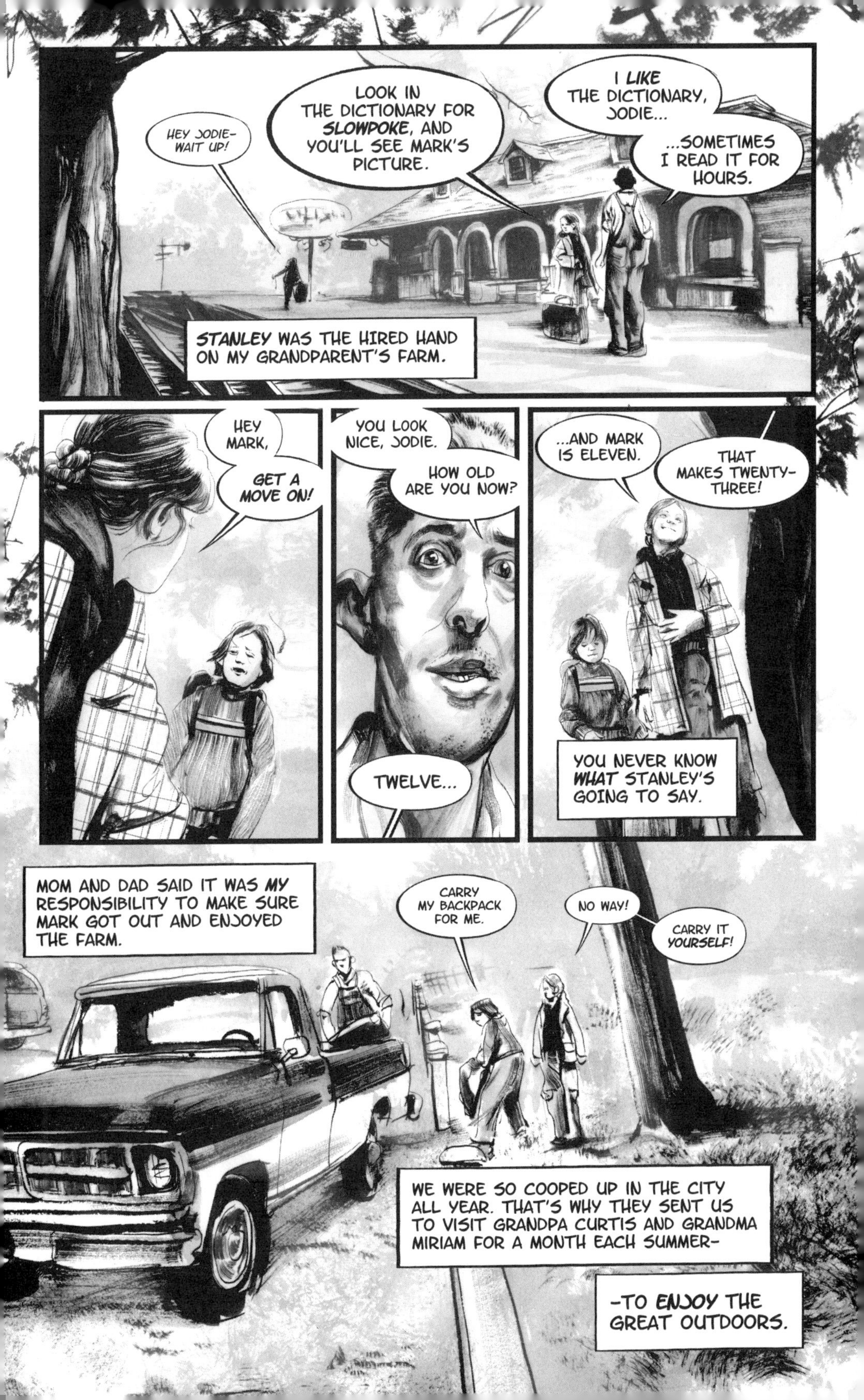
HEY JODIE-
WAIT UP!
LOOK IN THE DICTIONARY FOR SLOWPOKE, AND YOU'LL SEE MARK'S PICTURE.
I LIKE THE DICTIONARY, JODIE...
...SOMETIMES I READ IT FOR HOURS.
STANLEY WAS THE HIRED HAND ON MY GRANDPARENT'S FARM.
HEY MARK,
GET A MOVE ON!
YOU LOOK NICE, JODIE.
HOW OLD ARE YOU NOW?
TWELVE...
...AND MARK IS ELEVEN.
THAT MAKES TWENTY-THREE!
YOU NEVER KNOW WHAT STANLEY'S GOING TO SAY.
MOM AND DAD SAID IT WAS MY RESPONSIBILITY TO MAKE SURE MARK GOT OUT AND ENJOYED THE FARM.
CARRY MY BACKPACK FOR ME.
NO WAY!
CARRY IT YOURSELF!
WE WERE SO COOPED UP IN THE CITY ALL YEAR. THAT'S WHY THEY SENT US TO VISIT GRANDPA CURTIS AND GRANDMA MIRIAM FOR A MONTH EACH SUMMER-
-TO ENJOY THE GREAT OUTDOORS.

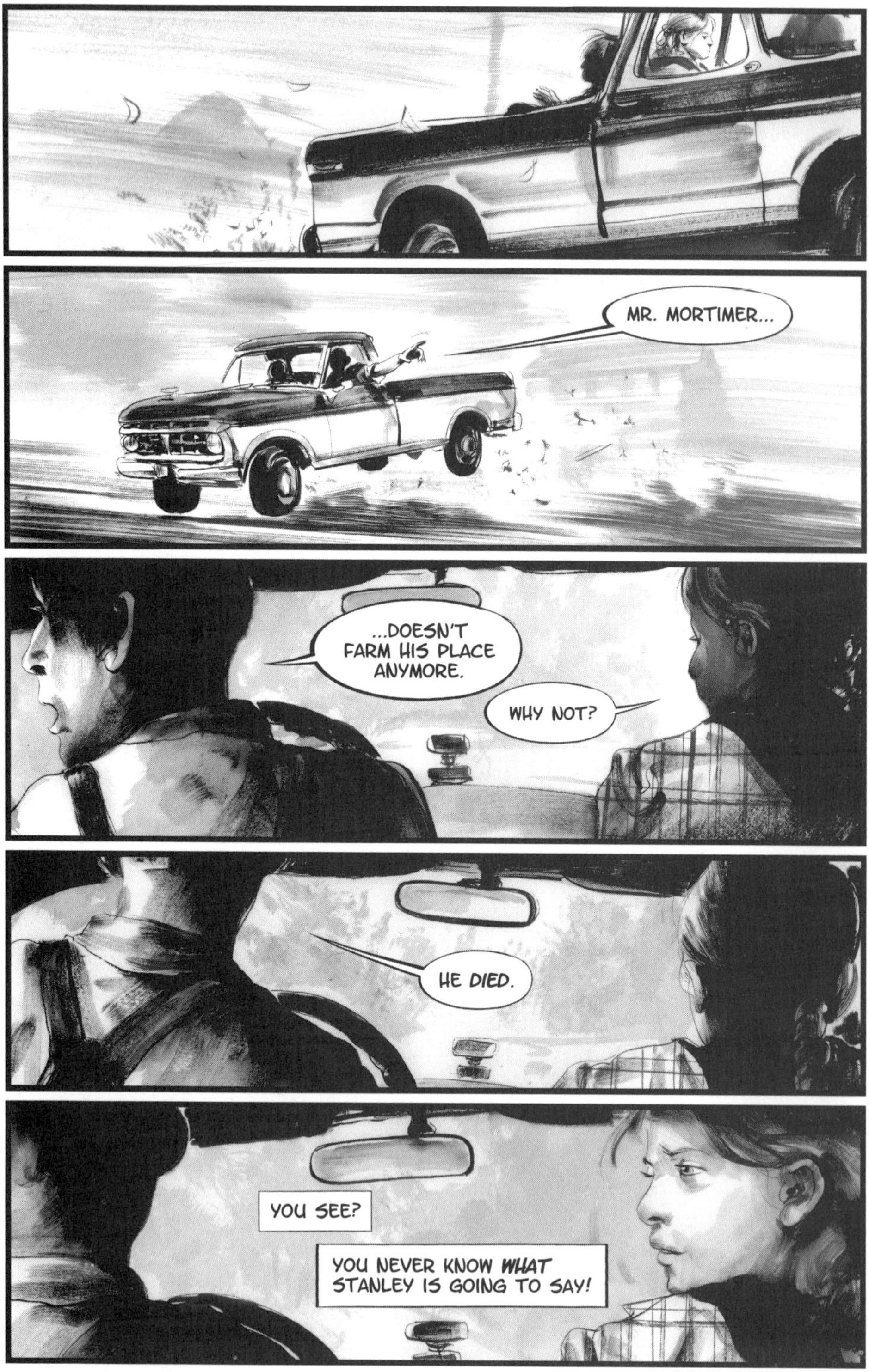
MR. MORTIMER...
...DOESN'T FARM HIS PLACE ANYMORE.
WHY NOT?
HE *DIED*.
YOU SEE?
YOU NEVER KNOW ***WHAT*** STANLEY IS GOING TO SAY!

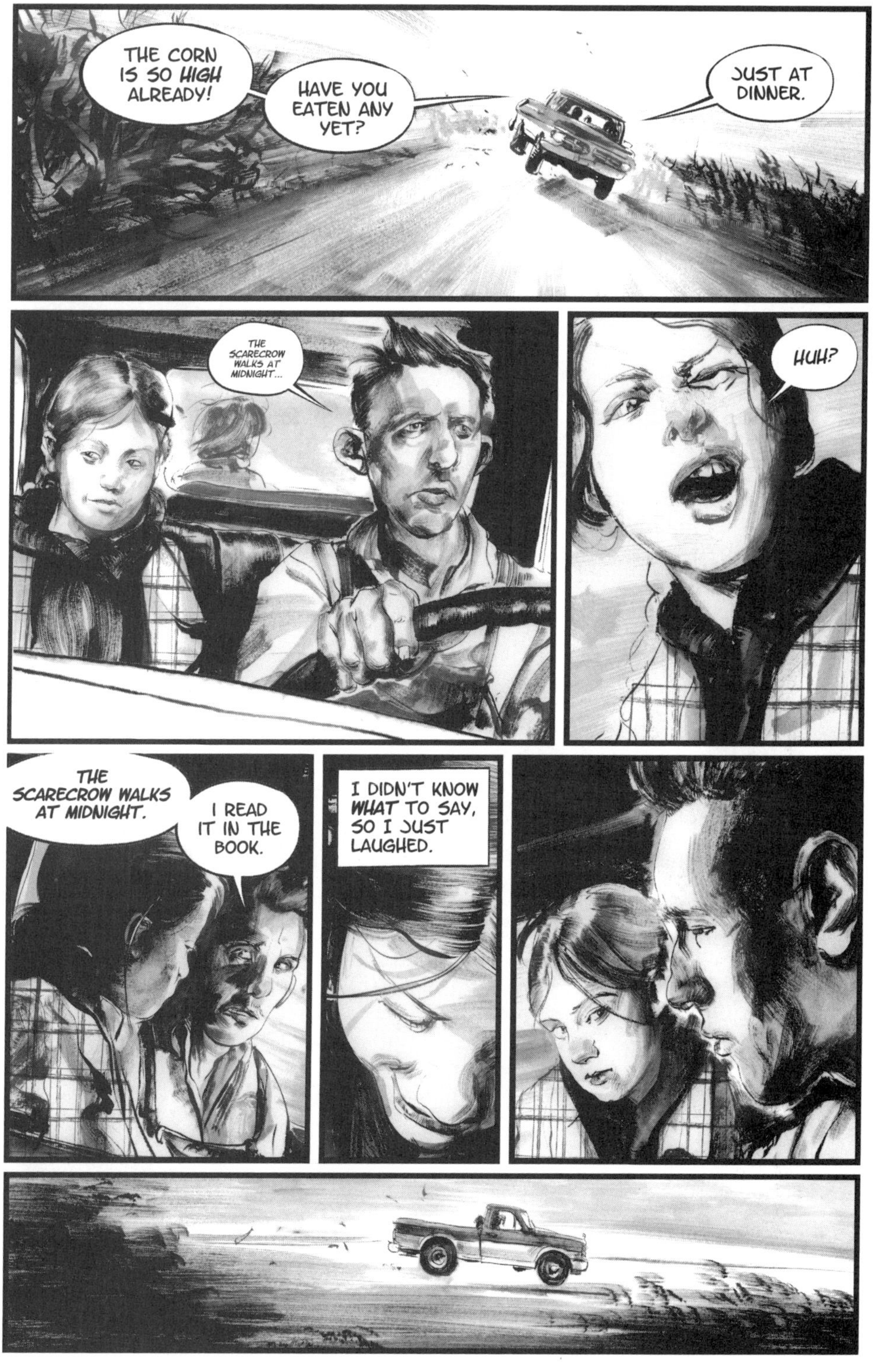
THE CORN IS SO HIGH ALREADY!
HAVE YOU EATEN ANY YET?
JUST AT DINNER.
THE SCARECROW WALKS AT MIDNIGHT...
HUH?
THE SCARECROW WALKS AT MIDNIGHT.
I READ IT IN THE BOOK.
I DIDN'T KNOW WHAT TO SAY, SO I JUST LAUGHED.

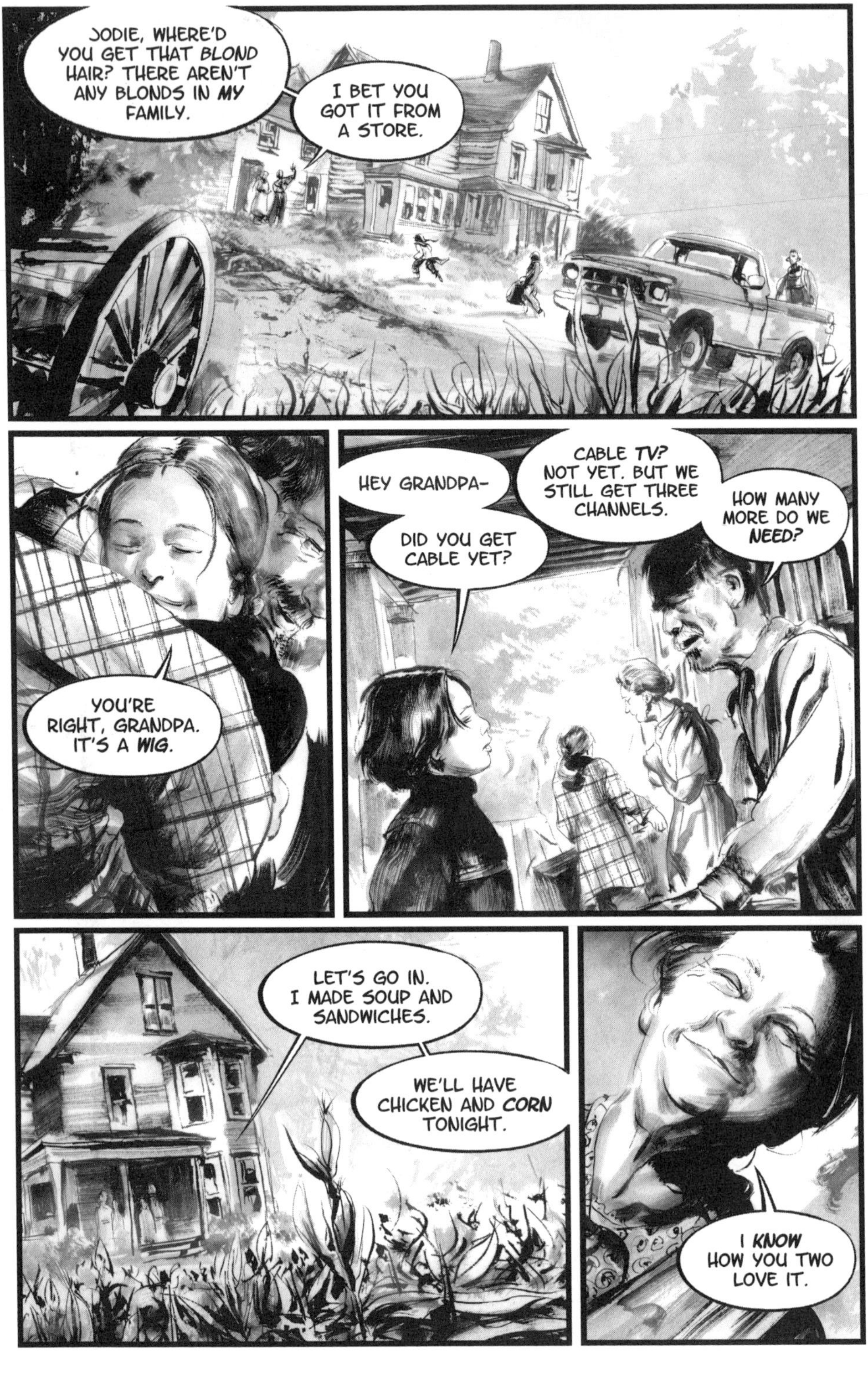
JODIE, WHERE'D YOU GET THAT BLOND HAIR? THERE AREN'T ANY BLONDS IN MY FAMILY.
I BET YOU GOT IT FROM A STORE.
YOU'RE RIGHT, GRANDPA. IT'S A WIG.
HEY GRANDPA-
DID YOU GET CABLE YET?
CABLE TV? NOT YET. BUT WE STILL GET THREE CHANNELS.
HOW MANY MORE DO WE NEED?
LET'S GO IN. I MADE SOUP AND SANDWICHES.
WE'LL HAVE CHICKEN AND CORN TONIGHT.
I KNOW HOW YOU TWO LOVE IT.

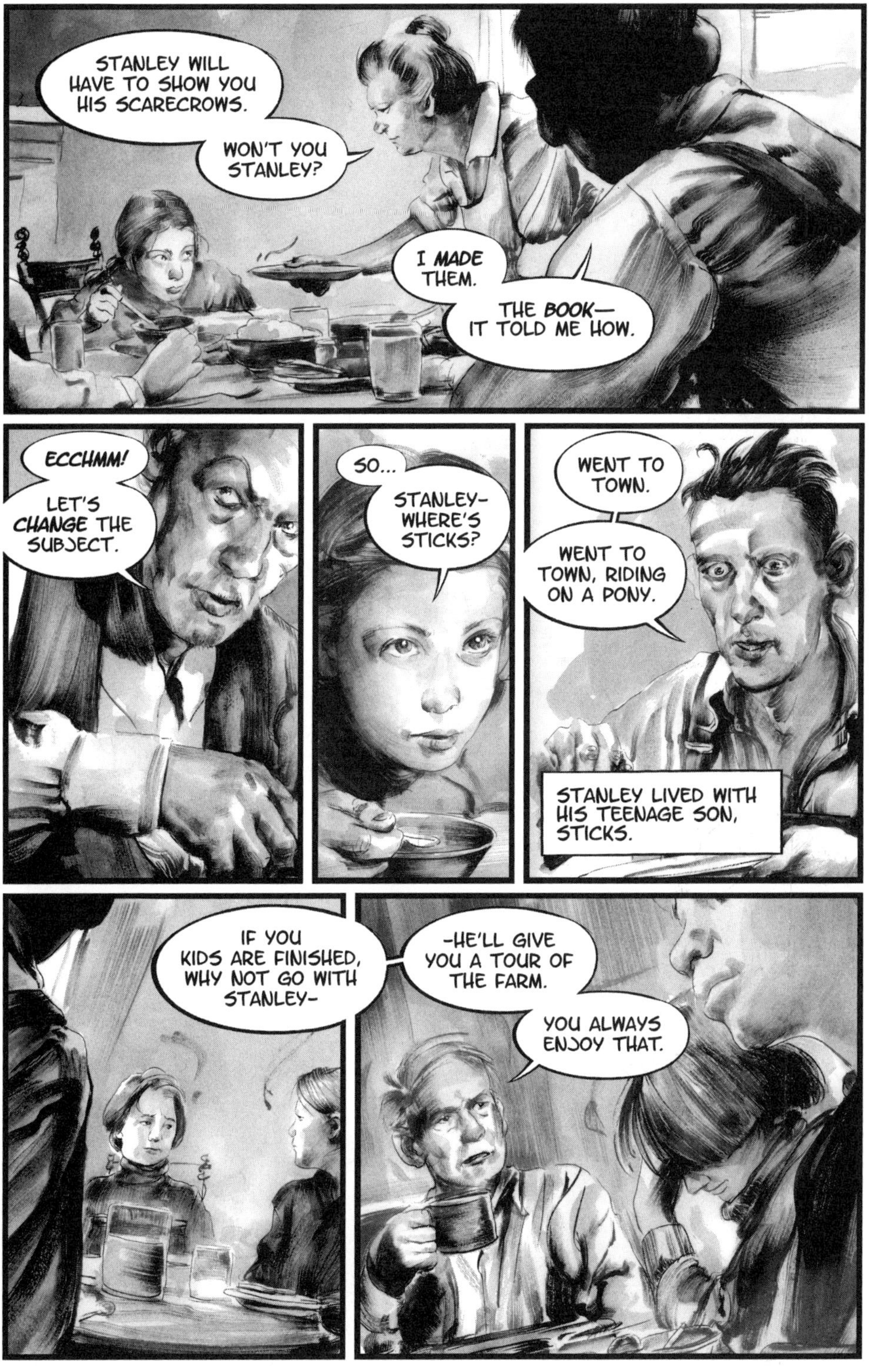
STANLEY WILL HAVE TO SHOW YOU HIS SCARECROWS.
WON'T YOU STANLEY?
I MADE THEM.
THE BOOK— IT TOLD ME HOW.
ECCHMM!
LET'S CHANGE THE SUBJECT.
SO...
STANLEY- WHERE'S STICKS?
WENT TO TOWN.
WENT TO TOWN, RIDING ON A PONY.
STANLEY LIVED WITH HIS TEENAGE SON, STICKS.
IF YOU KIDS ARE FINISHED, WHY NOT GO WITH STANLEY-
-HE'LL GIVE YOU A TOUR OF THE FARM.
YOU ALWAYS ENJOY THAT.

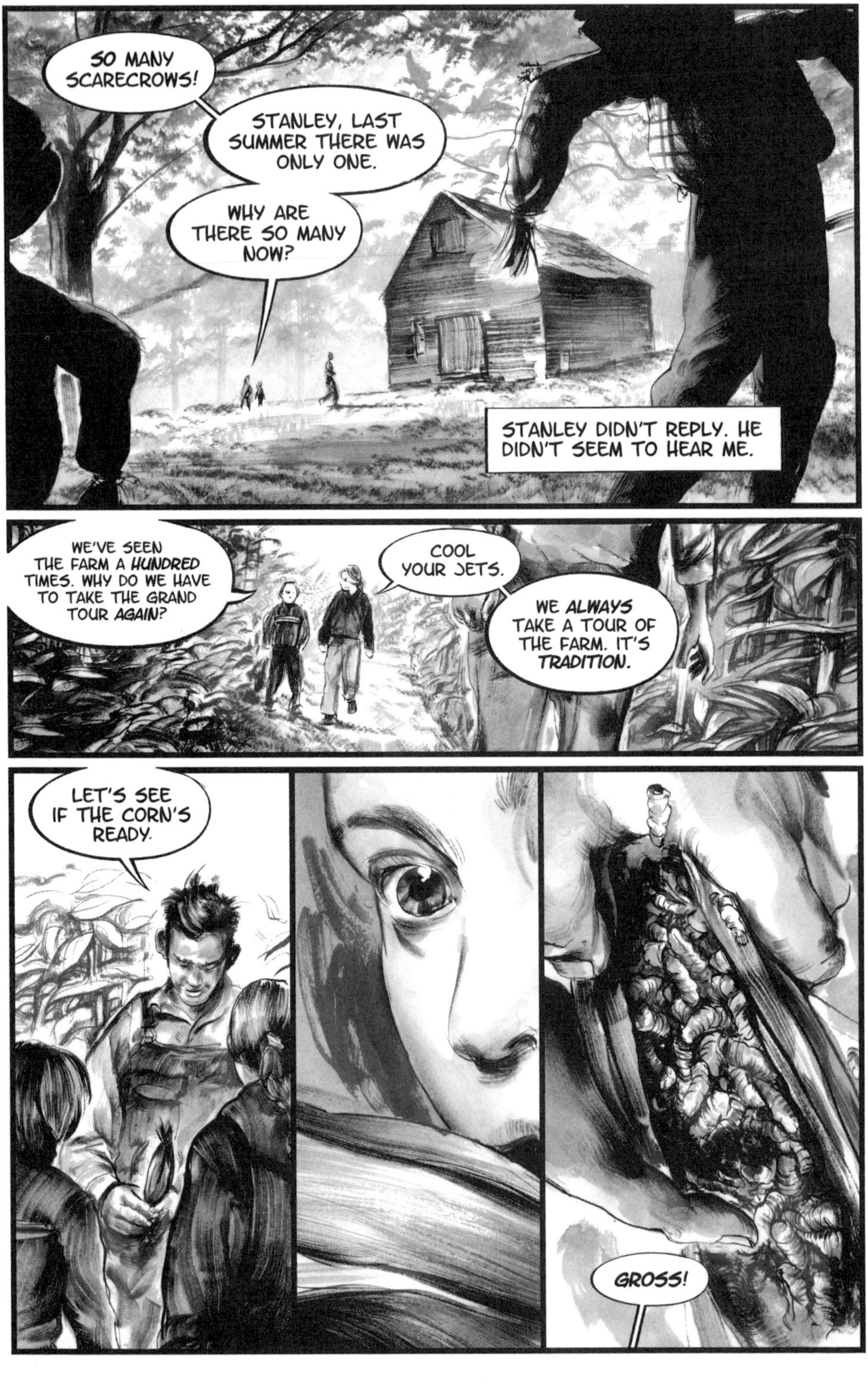
SO MANY SCARECROWS!
STANLEY, LAST SUMMER THERE WAS ONLY ONE.
WHY ARE THERE SO MANY NOW?
STANLEY DIDN'T REPLY. HE DIDN'T SEEM TO HEAR ME.
WE'VE SEEN THE FARM A HUNDRED TIMES. WHY DO WE HAVE TO TAKE THE GRAND TOUR AGAIN?
COOL YOUR JETS.
WE ALWAYS TAKE A TOUR OF THE FARM. IT'S TRADITION.
LET'S SEE IF THE CORN'S READY.
GROSS!

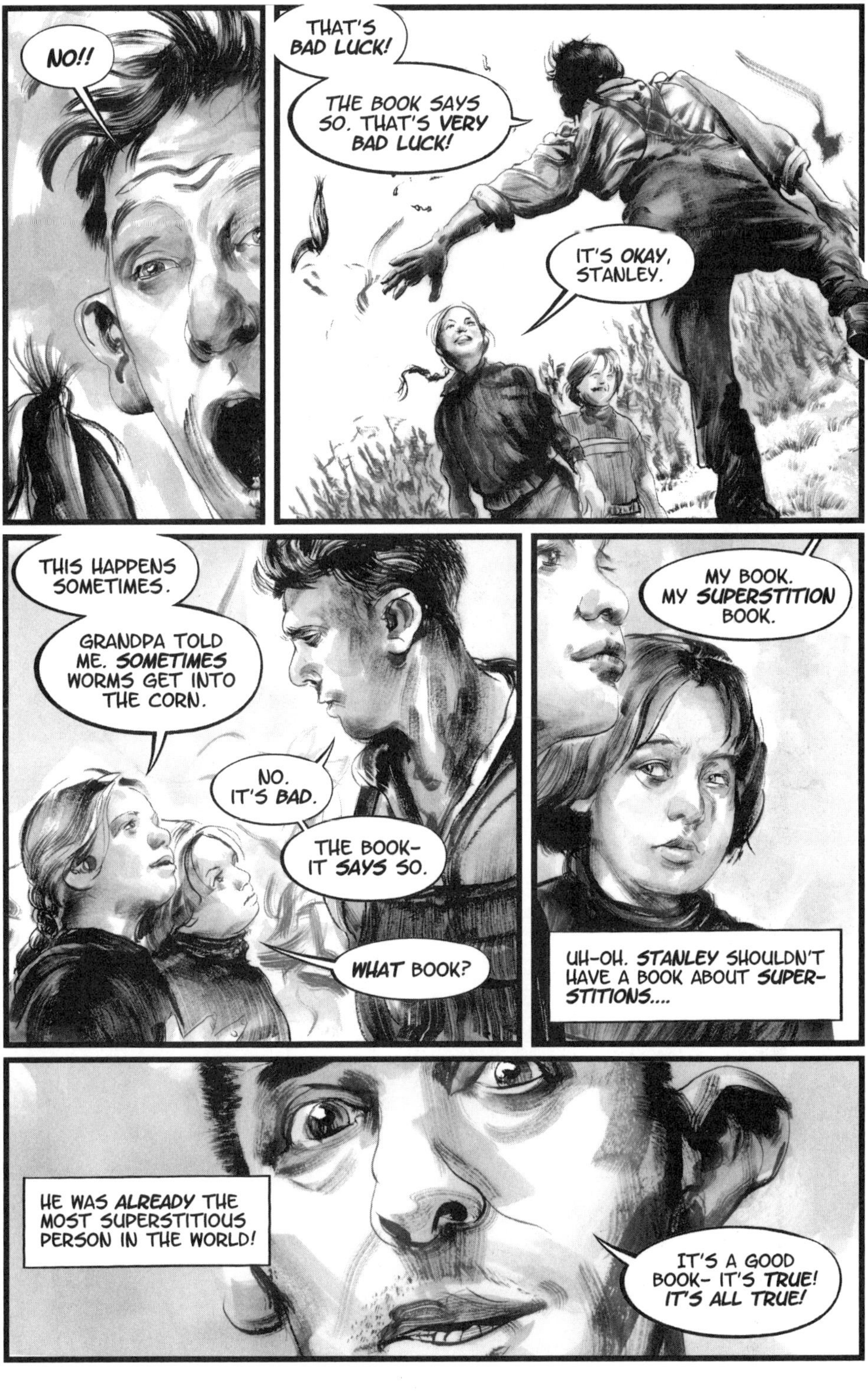
NO!!
THAT'S BAD LUCK!
THE BOOK SAYS SO. THAT'S VERY BAD LUCK!
IT'S OKAY, STANLEY.
THIS HAPPENS SOMETIMES.
GRANDPA TOLD ME. SOMETIMES WORMS GET INTO THE CORN.
NO. IT'S BAD.
THE BOOK- IT SAYS SO.
WHAT BOOK?
MY BOOK. MY SUPERSTITION BOOK.
UH-OH. STANLEY SHOULDN'T HAVE A BOOK ABOUT SUPER-STITIONS....
HE WAS ALREADY THE MOST SUPERSTITIOUS PERSON IN THE WORLD!
IT'S A GOOD BOOK- IT'S TRUE! IT'S ALL TRUE!

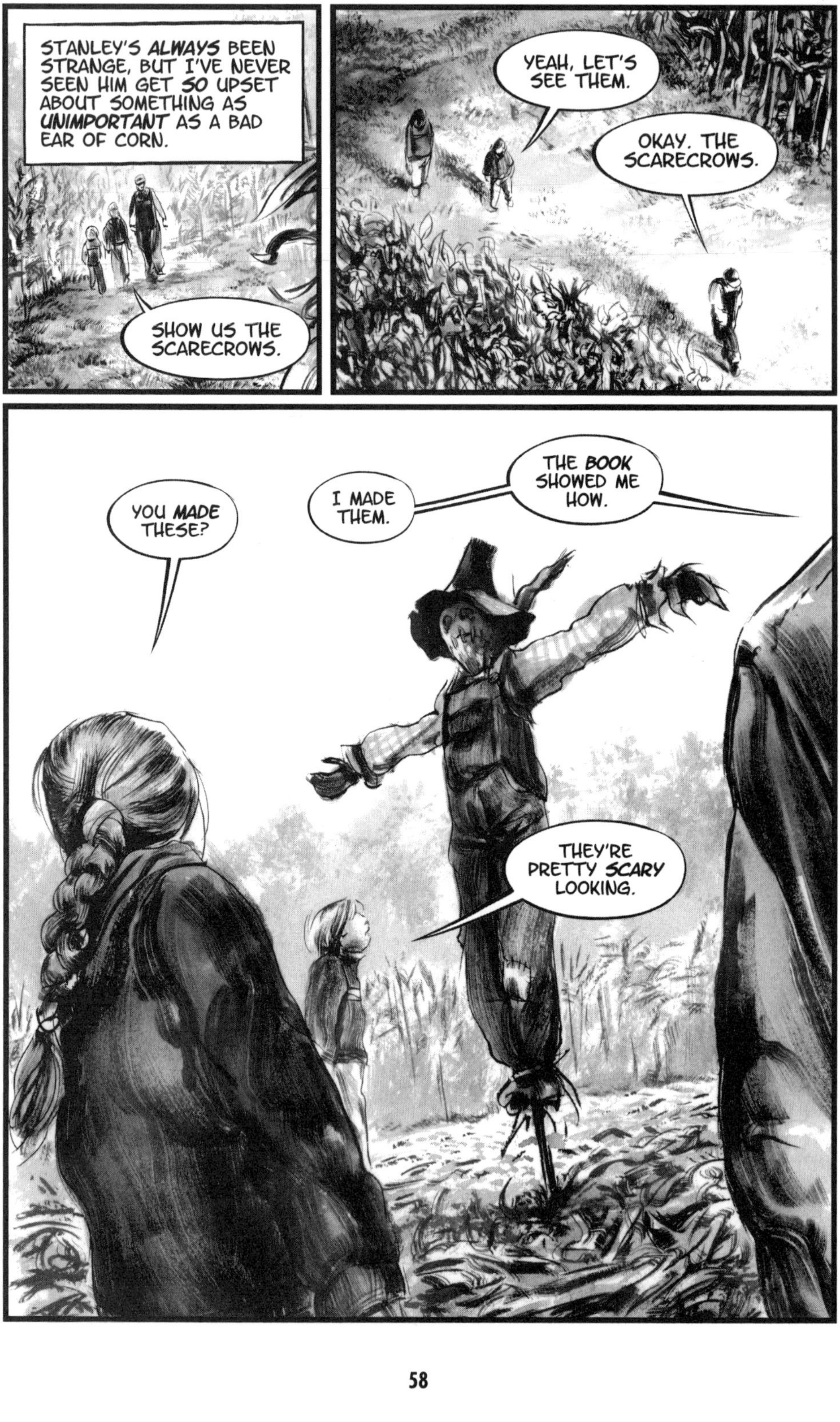
STANLEY'S ALWAYS BEEN STRANGE, BUT I'VE NEVER SEEN HIM GET SO UPSET ABOUT SOMETHING AS UNIMPORTANT AS A BAD EAR OF CORN.
SHOW US THE SCARECROWS.
YEAH, LET'S SEE THEM.
OKAY. THE SCARECROWS.
YOU MADE THESE?
I MADE THEM.
THE BOOK SHOWED ME HOW.
THEY'RE PRETTY SCARY LOOKING.

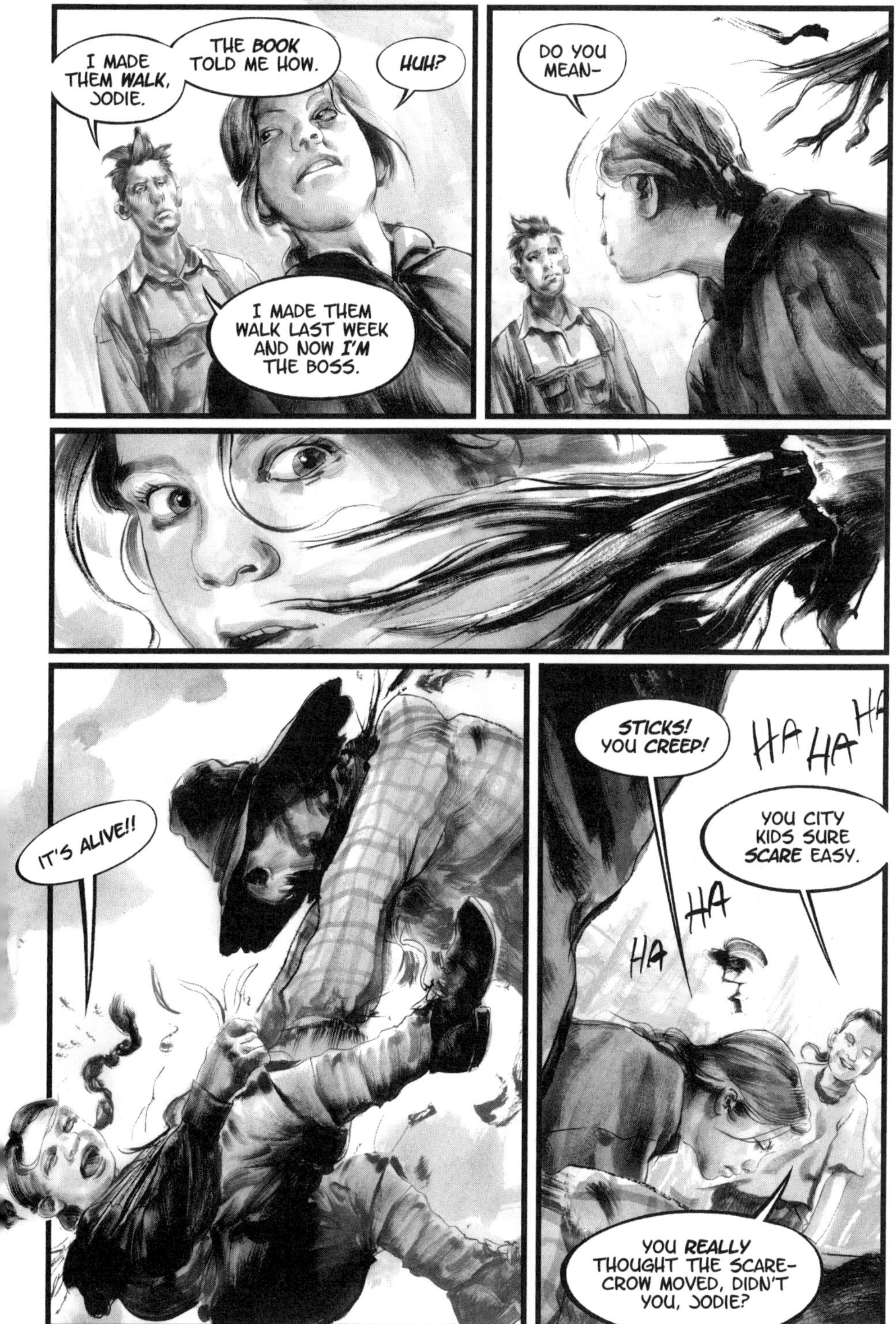
I MADE THEM WALK, JODIE.
THE BOOK TOLD ME HOW.
HUH?
I MADE THEM WALK LAST WEEK AND NOW I'M THE BOSS.
DO YOU MEAN-
IT'S ALIVE!!
STICKS! YOU CREEP!
HA HA HA
YOU CITY KIDS SURE SCARE EASY.
HA HA
YOU REALLY THOUGHT THE SCARE-CROW MOVED, DIDN'T YOU, JODIE?

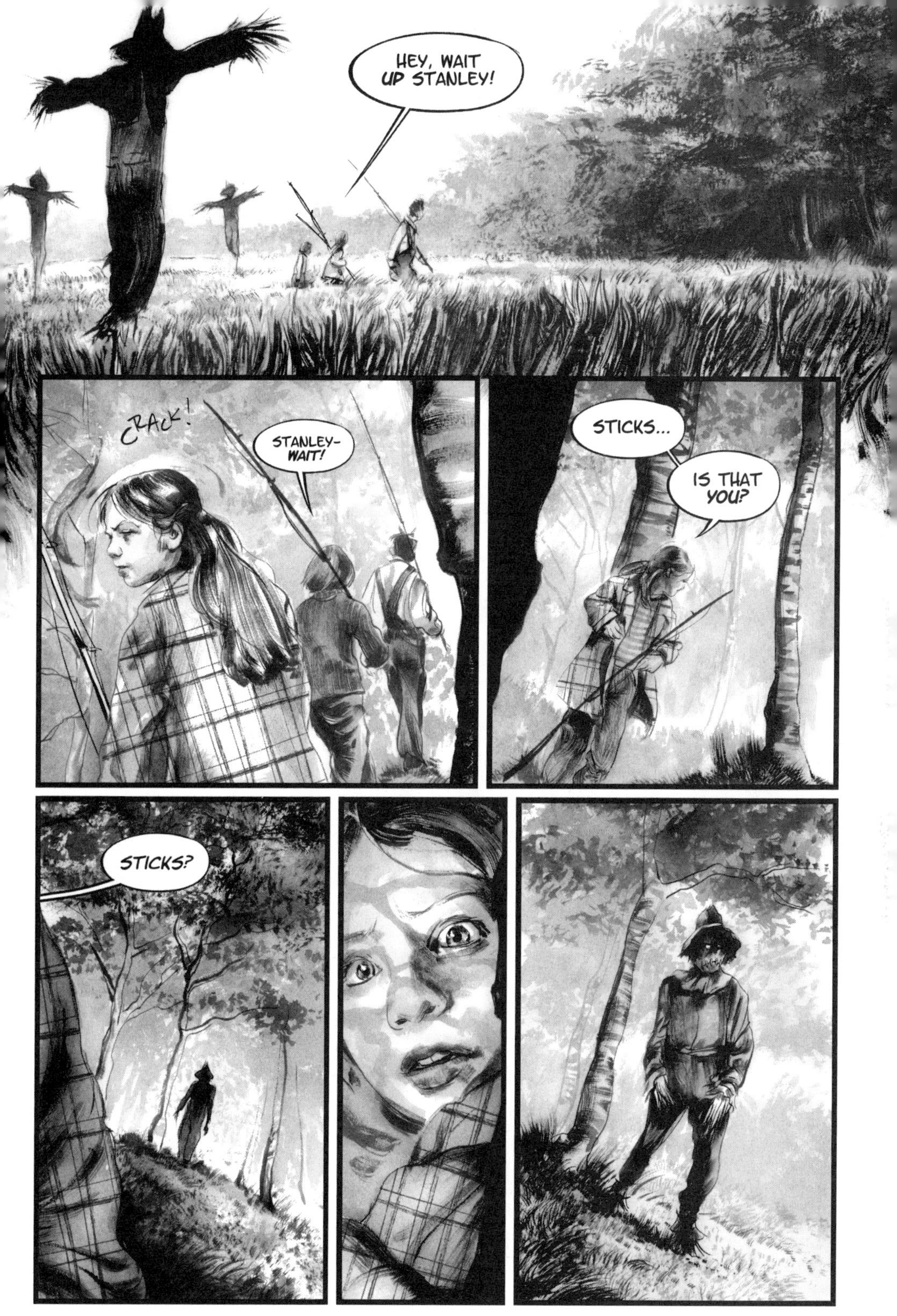
HEY, WAIT UP STANLEY!
CRACK!
STANLEY- WAIT!
STICKS...
IS THAT YOU?
STICKS?

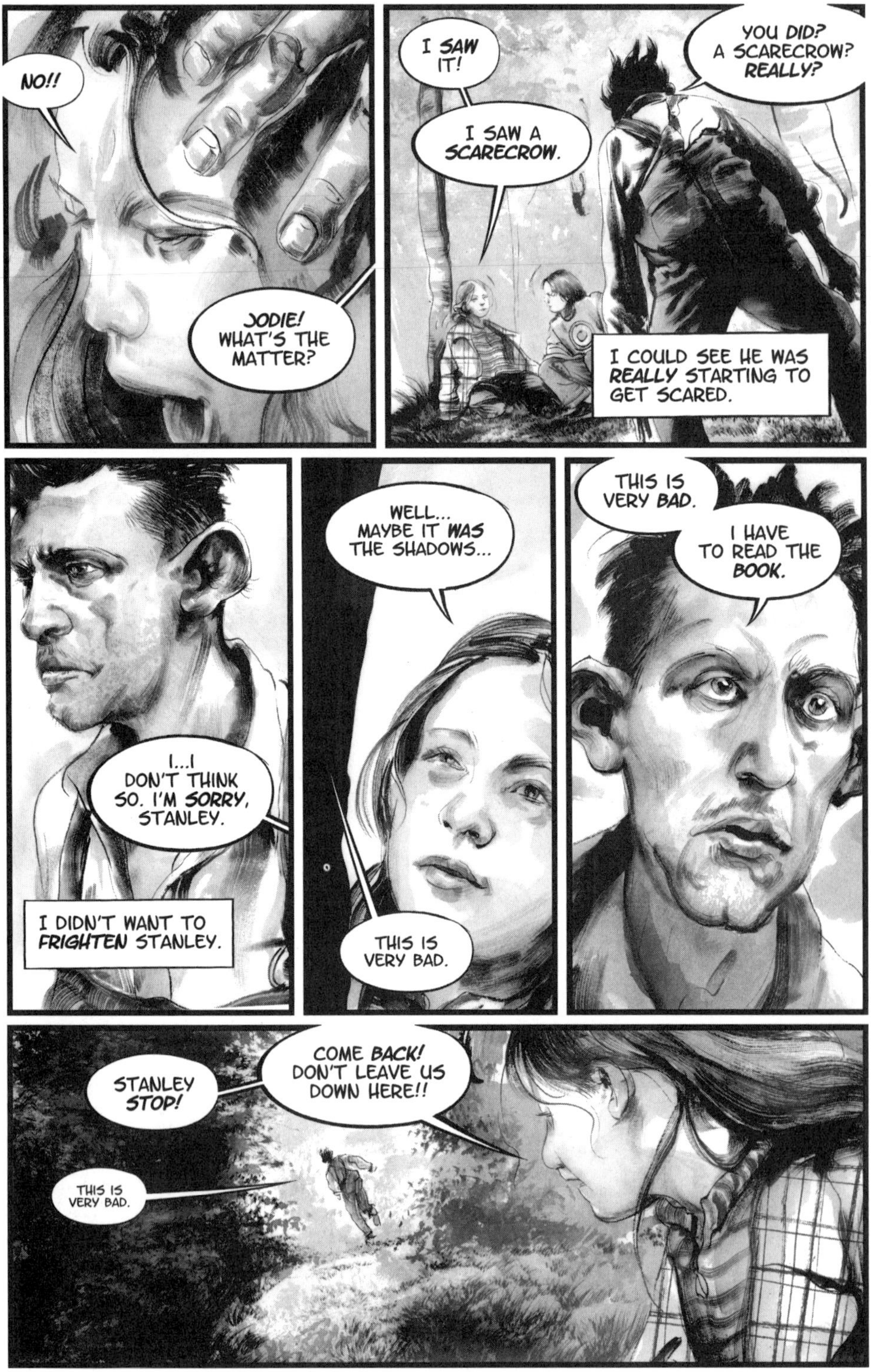
NO!!
JODIE! WHAT'S THE MATTER?
I SAW IT!
I SAW A SCARECROW.
YOU DID? A SCARECROW? REALLY?
I COULD SEE HE WAS REALLY STARTING TO GET SCARED.
I...I DON'T THINK SO. I'M SORRY, STANLEY.
I DIDN'T WANT TO FRIGHTEN STANLEY.
WELL... MAYBE IT WAS THE SHADOWS...
THIS IS VERY BAD.
THIS IS VERY BAD.
I HAVE TO READ THE BOOK.
STANLEY STOP!
COME BACK! DON'T LEAVE US DOWN HERE!!
THIS IS VERY BAD.

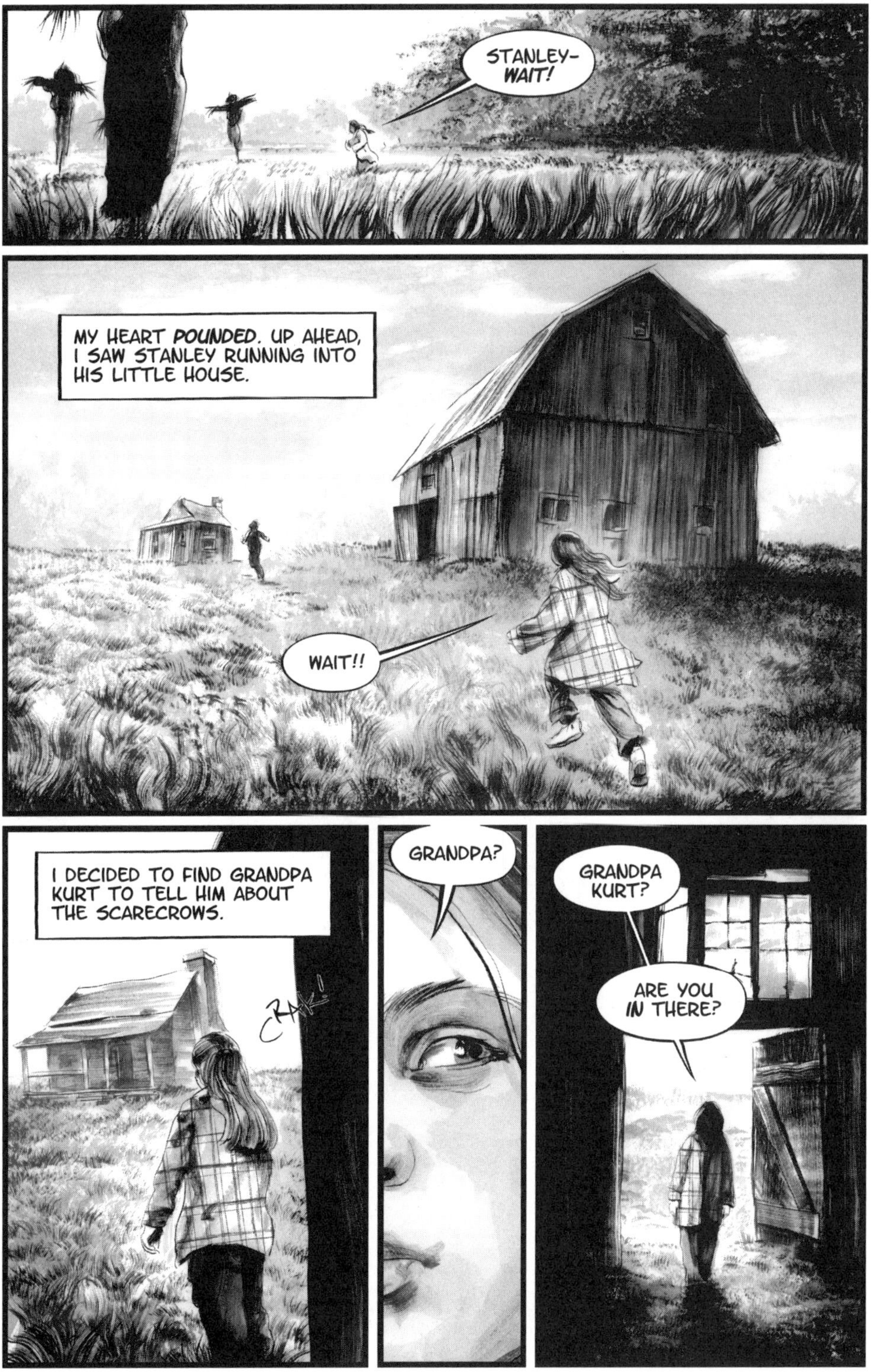
STANLEY-
WAIT!
MY HEART POUNDED. UP AHEAD, I SAW STANLEY RUNNING INTO HIS LITTLE HOUSE.
WAIT!!
I DECIDED TO FIND GRANDPA KURT TO TELL HIM ABOUT THE SCARECROWS.
CRAK!
GRANDPA?
GRANDPA KURT?
ARE YOU IN THERE?

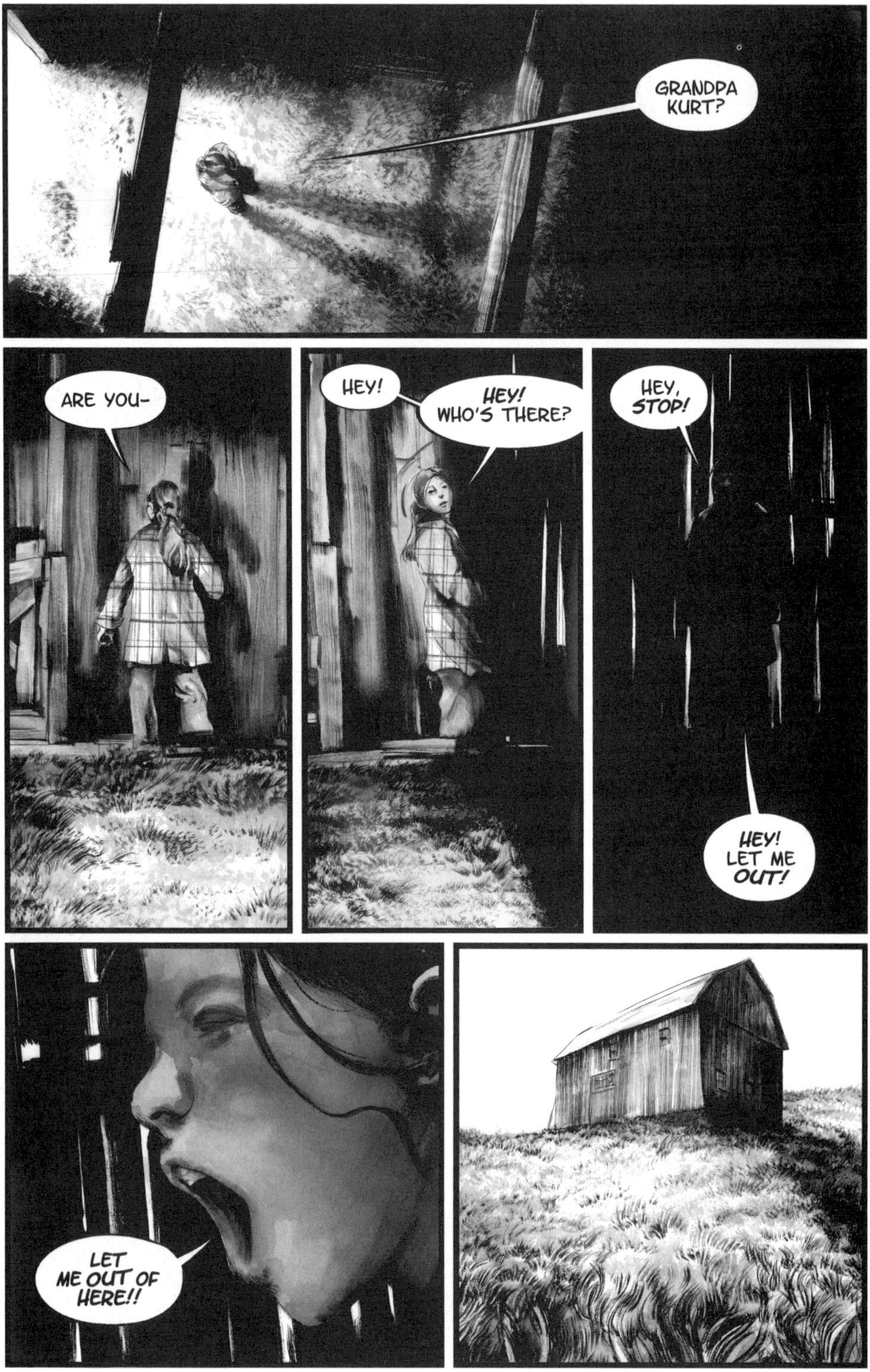
GRANDPA KURT?
ARE YOU-
HEY!
HEY! WHO'S THERE?
HEY, STOP!
HEY! LET ME OUT!
LET ME OUT OF HERE!!

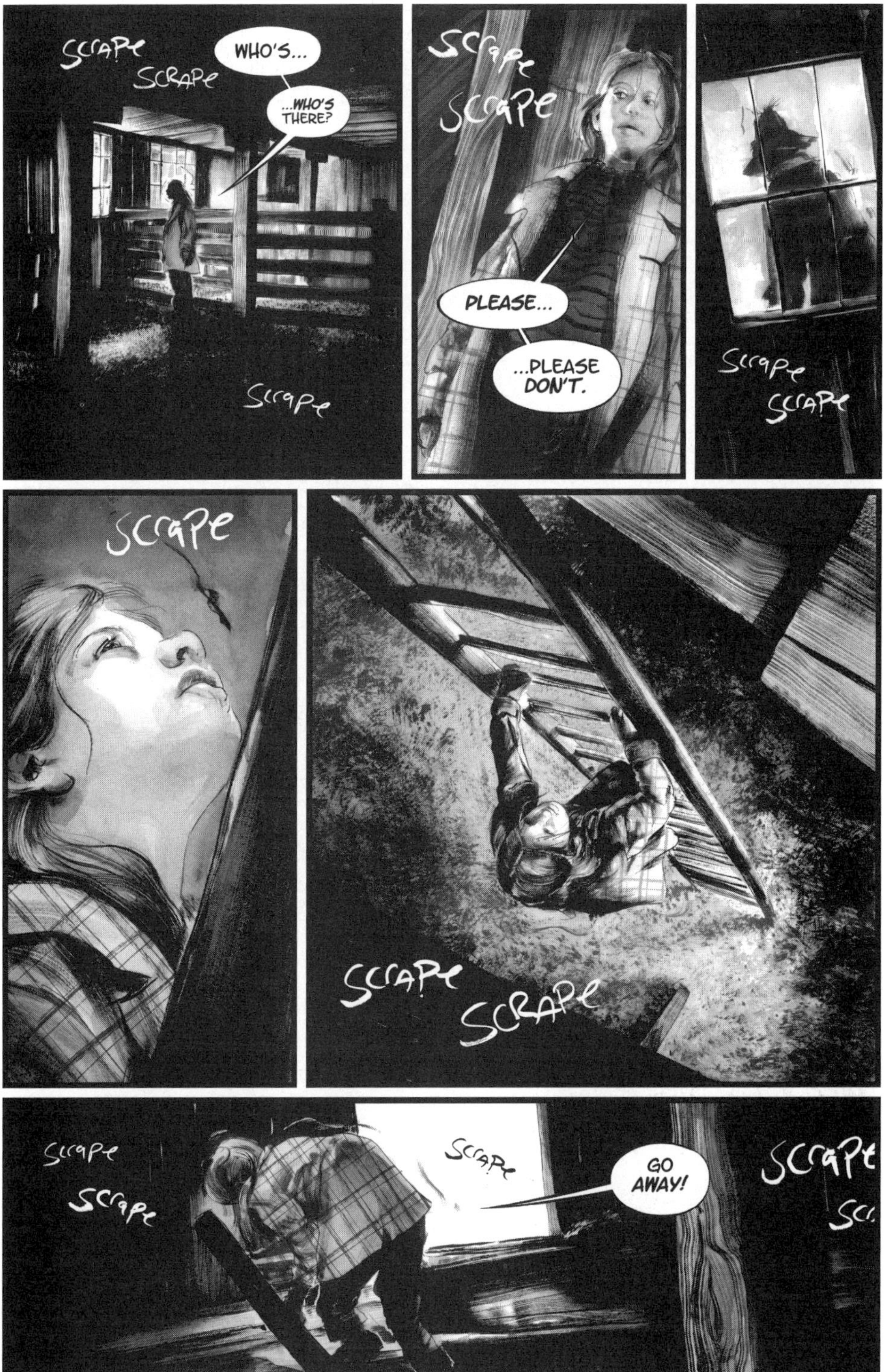
SCRAPE
SCRAPE
WHO'S...
...WHO'S THERE?
SCRAPE
SCRAPE
SCRAPE
PLEASE...
...PLEASE DON'T.
SCRAPE
SCRAPE
SCRAPE
SCRAPE
SCRAPE
SCRAPE
SCRAPE
SCRAPE
GO AWAY!
SCRAPE

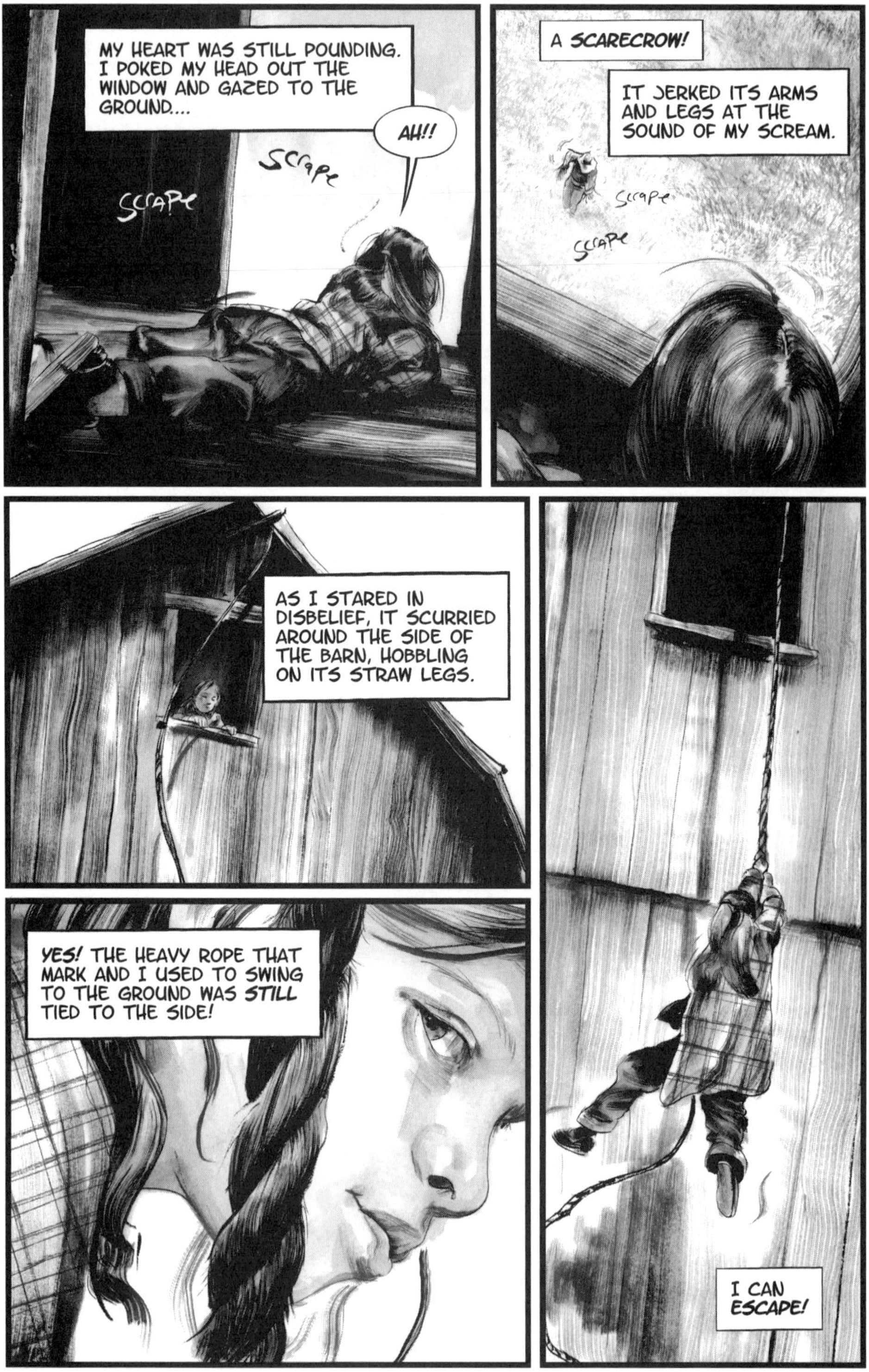
MY HEART WAS STILL POUNDING. I POKED MY HEAD OUT THE WINDOW AND GAZED TO THE GROUND....
AH!!
SCRAPE
SCRAPE
A SCARECROW!
IT JERKED ITS ARMS AND LEGS AT THE SOUND OF MY SCREAM.
SCRAPE
SCRAPE
AS I STARED IN DISBELIEF, IT SCURRIED AROUND THE SIDE OF THE BARN, HOBBLING ON ITS STRAW LEGS.
YES! THE HEAVY ROPE THAT MARK AND I USED TO SWING TO THE GROUND WAS STILL TIED TO THE SIDE!
I CAN ESCAPE!

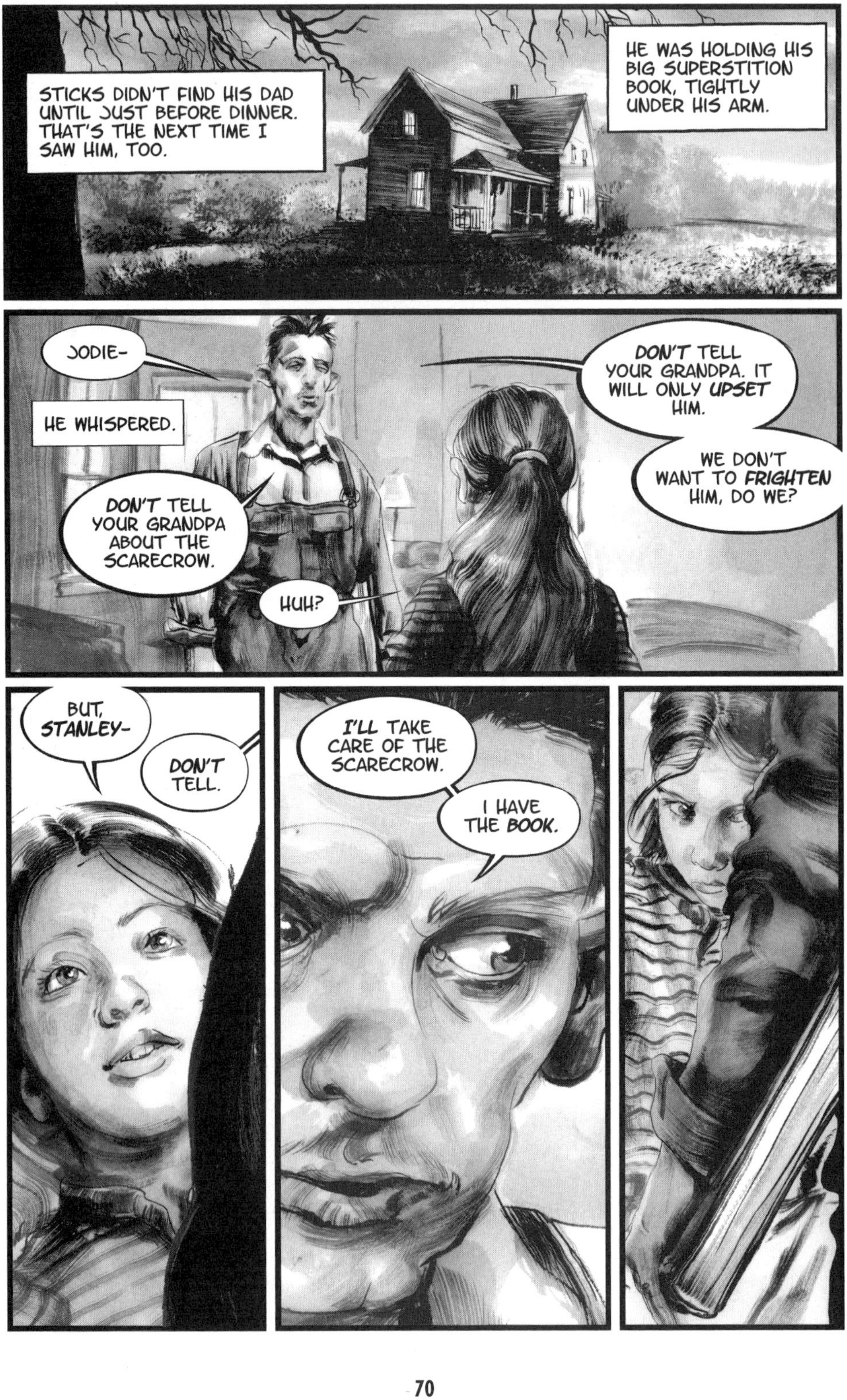
STICKS DIDN'T FIND HIS DAD UNTIL JUST BEFORE DINNER. THAT'S THE NEXT TIME I SAW HIM, TOO.
HE WAS HOLDING HIS BIG SUPERSTITION BOOK, TIGHTLY UNDER HIS ARM.
JODIE-
HE WHISPERED.
DON'T TELL YOUR GRANDPA ABOUT THE SCARECROW.
HUH?
DON'T TELL YOUR GRANDPA. IT WILL ONLY UPSET HIM.
WE DON'T WANT TO FRIGHTEN HIM, DO WE?
BUT, STANLEY-
DON'T TELL.
I'LL TAKE CARE OF THE SCARECROW.
I HAVE THE BOOK.

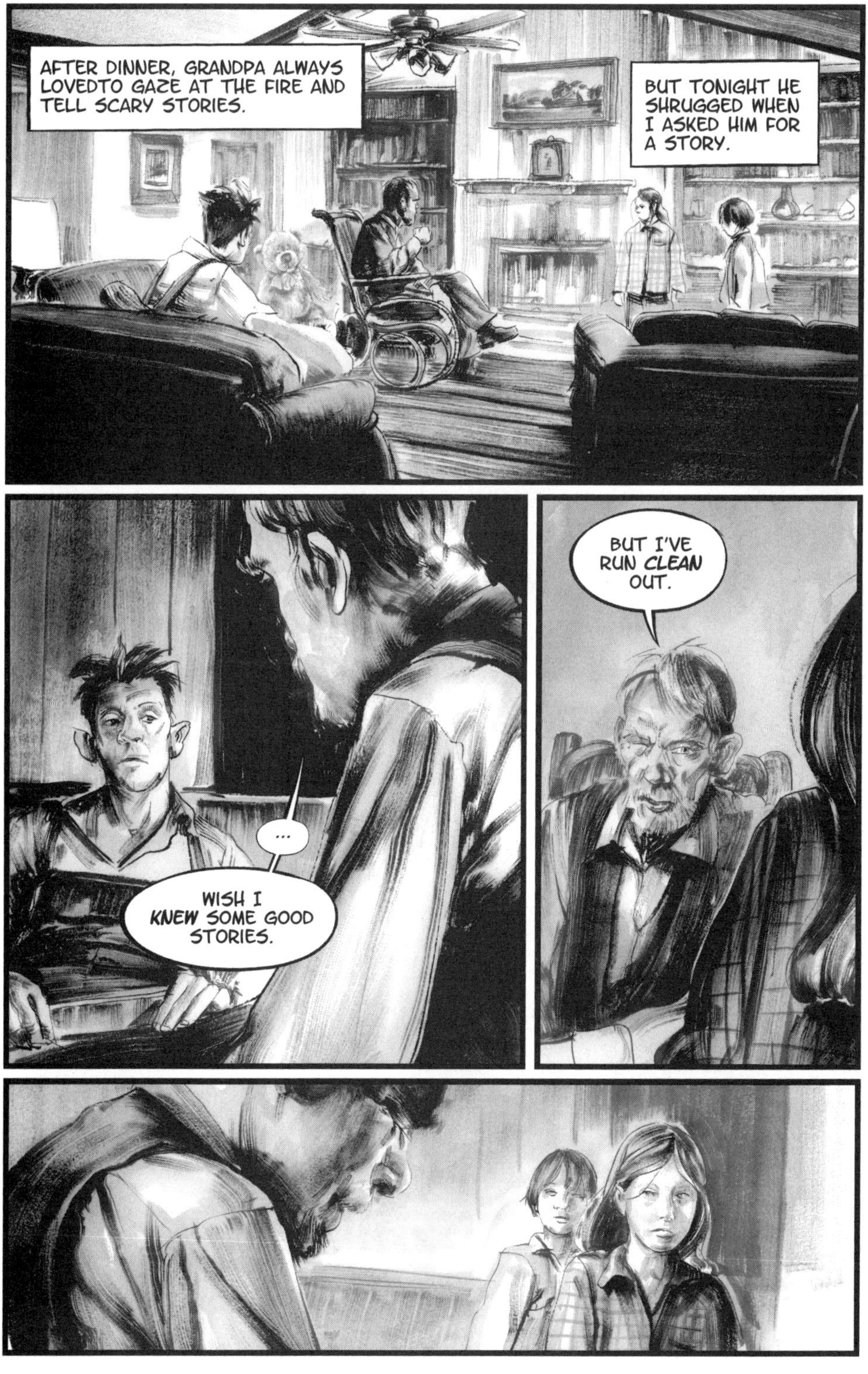
AFTER DINNER, GRANDPA ALWAYS LOVEDTO GAZE AT THE FIRE AND TELL SCARY STORIES.
BUT TONIGHT HE SHRUGGED WHEN I ASKED HIM FOR A STORY.
...
WISH I KNEW SOME GOOD STORIES.
BUT I'VE RUN CLEAN OUT.

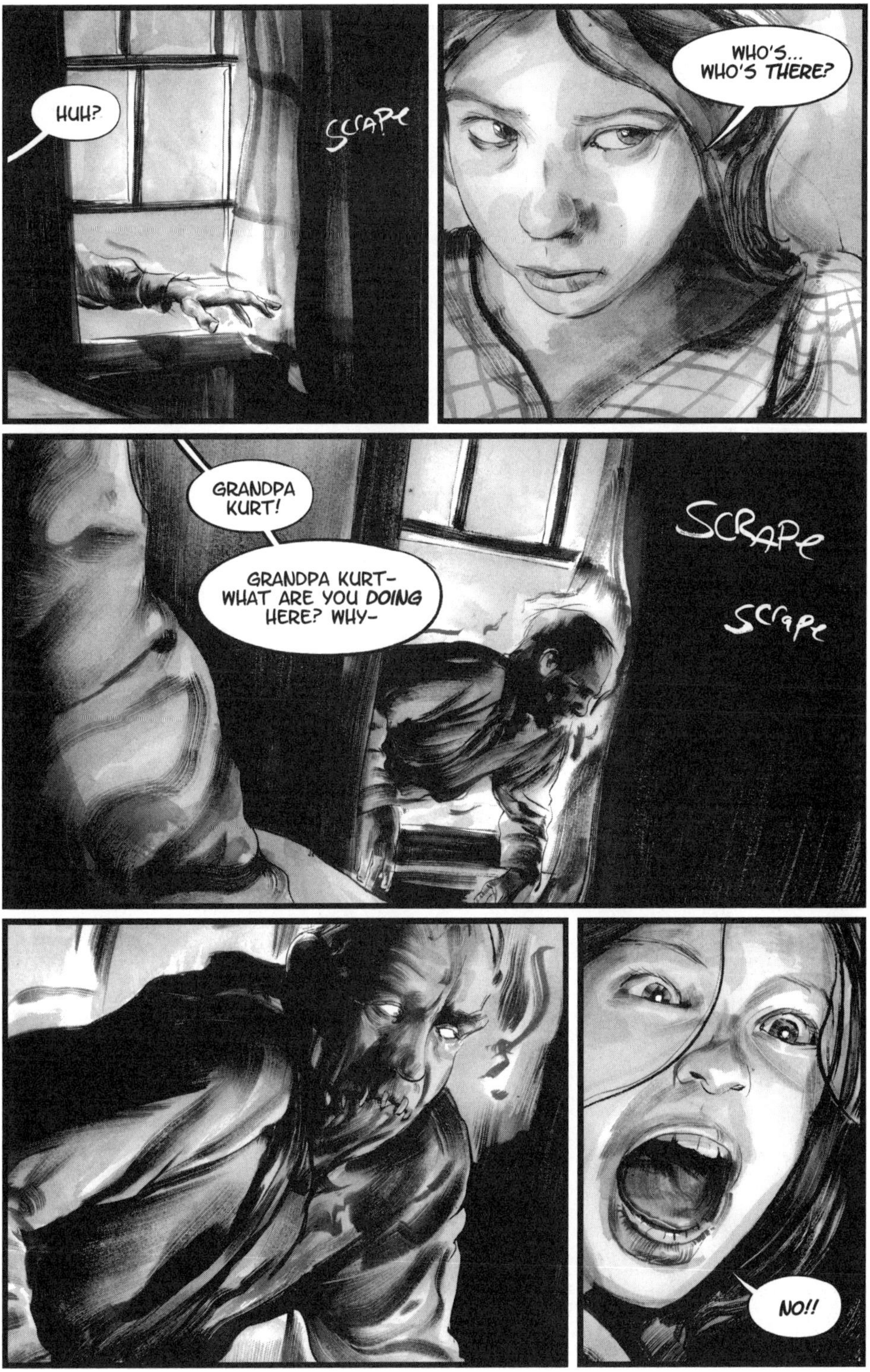
HUH?
SCRAPE
WHO'S... WHO'S THERE?
GRANDPA KURT!
GRANDPA KURT- WHAT ARE YOU DOING HERE? WHY-
SCRAPE
SCRAPE
NO!!

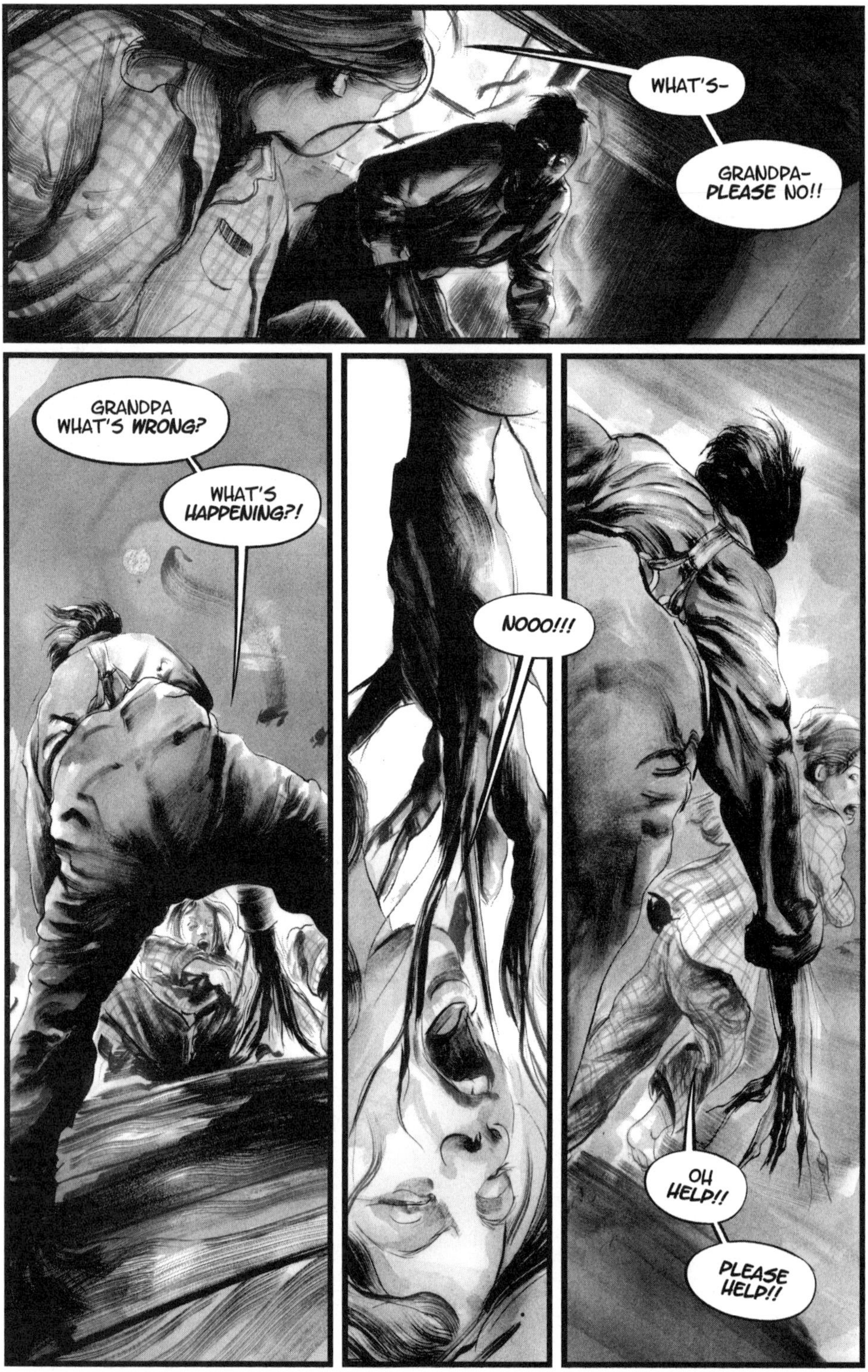
WHAT'S-
GRANDPA-
PLEASE NO!!
GRANDPA
WHAT'S WRONG?
WHAT'S
HAPPENING?!
NOOO!!!
OH
HELP!!
PLEASE
HELP!!

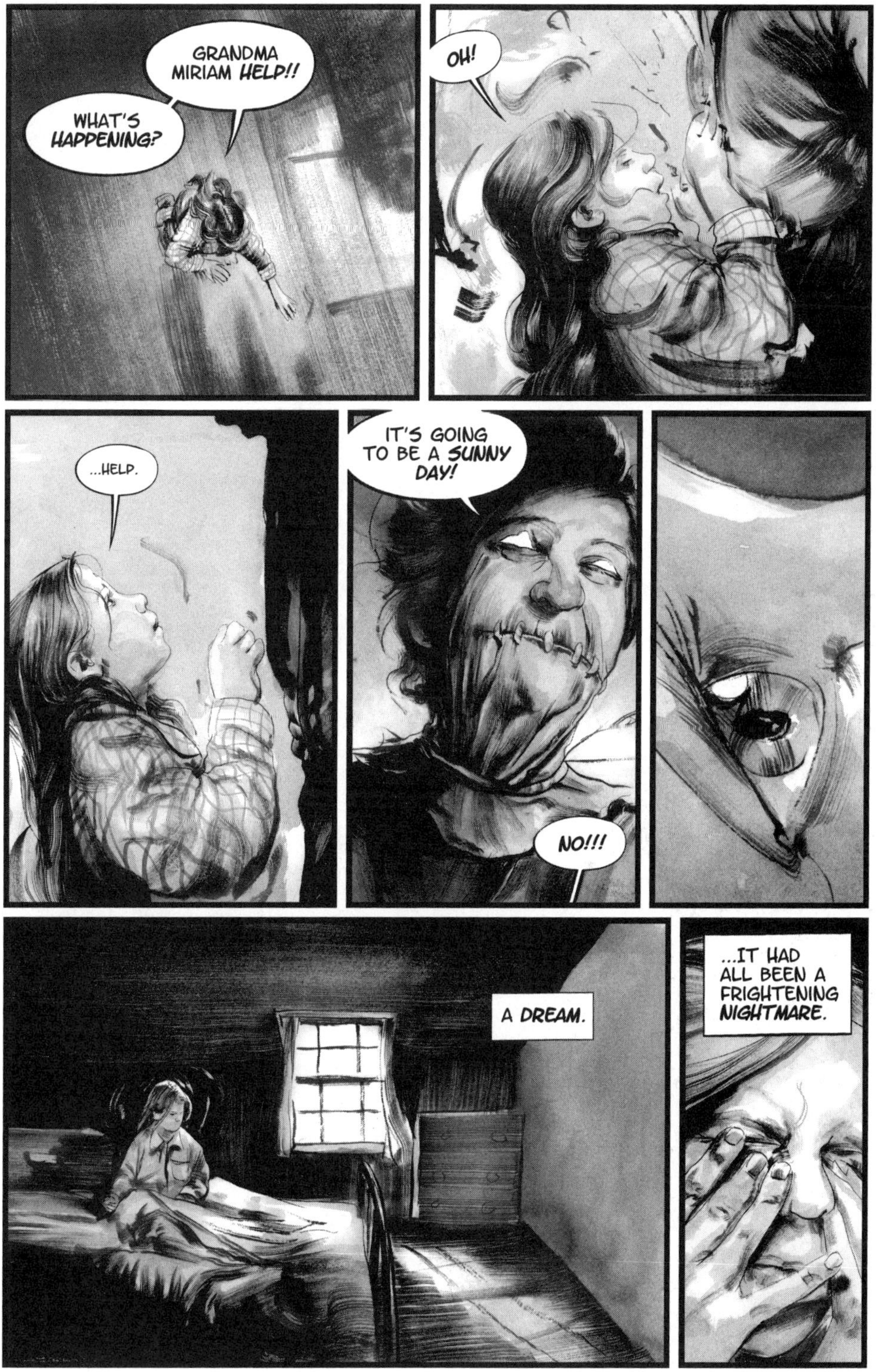
WHAT'S HAPPENING?
GRANDMA MIRIAM HELP!!
OH!
...HELP.
IT'S GOING TO BE A SUNNY DAY!
NO!!!
A DREAM.
...IT HAD ALL BEEN A FRIGHTENING NIGHTMARE.

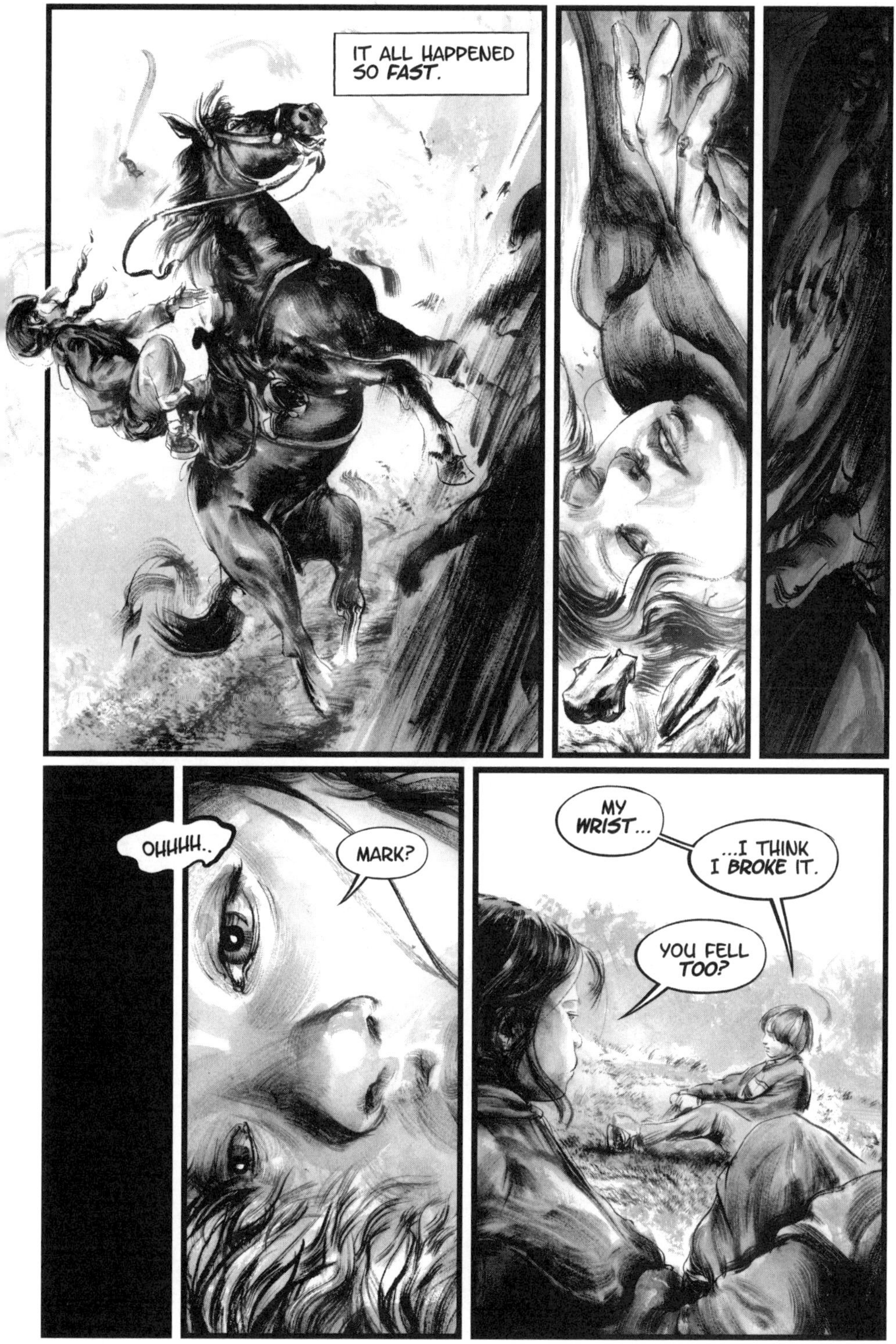
IT ALL HAPPENED SO FAST.
OHHHH..
MARK?
MY WRIST...
...I THINK I BROKE IT.
YOU FELL TOO?

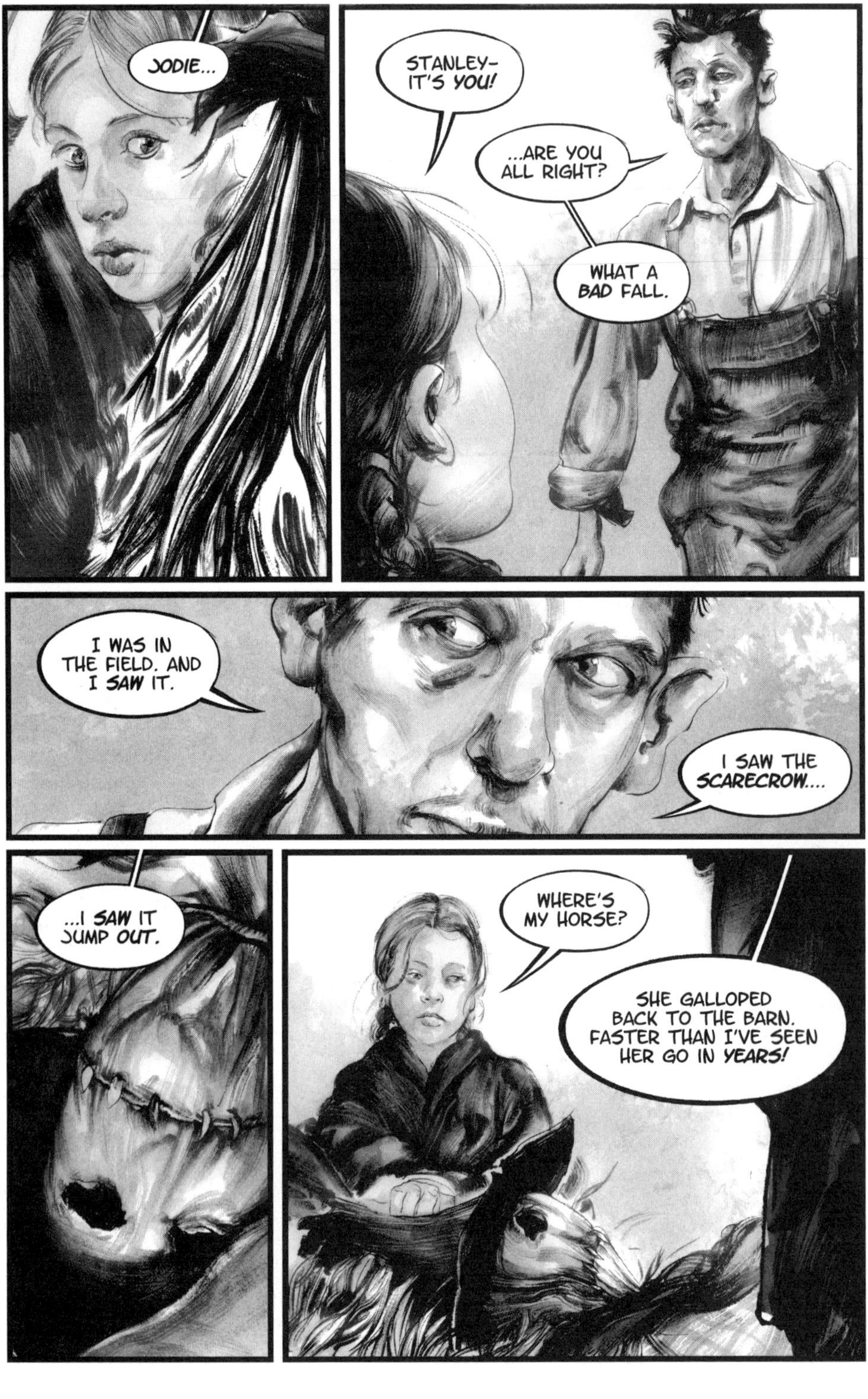
JODIE...
STANLEY- IT'S YOU!
...ARE YOU ALL RIGHT?
WHAT A BAD FALL.
I WAS IN THE FIELD. AND I SAW IT.
I SAW THE SCARECROW....
...I SAW IT JUMP OUT.
WHERE'S MY HORSE?
SHE GALLOPED BACK TO THE BARN. FASTER THAN I'VE SEEN HER GO IN YEARS!

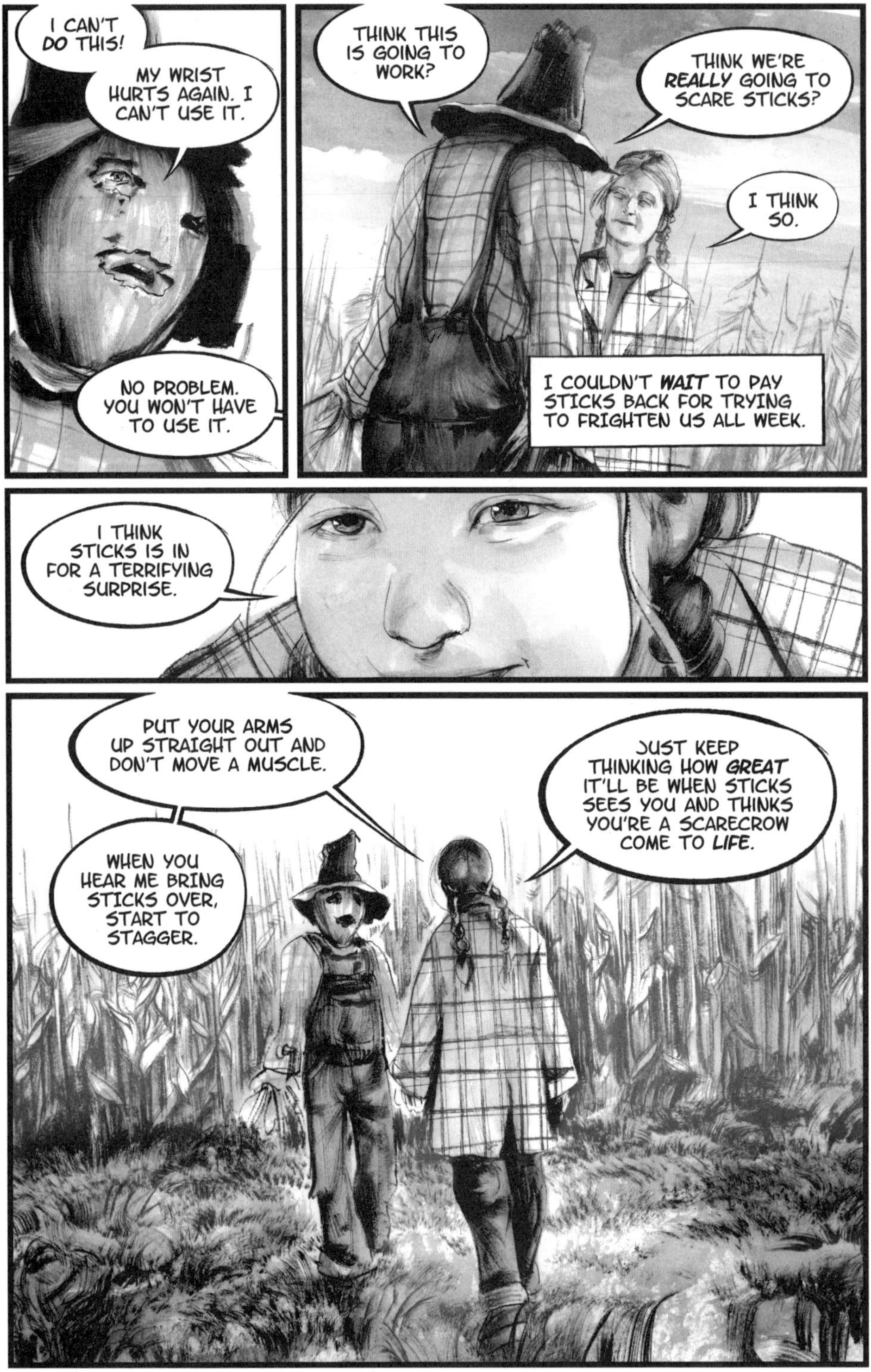
I CAN'T DO THIS!
MY WRIST HURTS AGAIN. I CAN'T USE IT.
NO PROBLEM. YOU WON'T HAVE TO USE IT.
THINK THIS IS GOING TO WORK?
THINK WE'RE *REALLY* GOING TO SCARE STICKS?
I THINK SO.
I COULDN'T *WAIT* TO PAY STICKS BACK FOR TRYING TO FRIGHTEN US ALL WEEK.
I THINK STICKS IS IN FOR A TERRIFYING SURPRISE.
PUT YOUR ARMS UP STRAIGHT OUT AND DON'T MOVE A MUSCLE.
WHEN YOU HEAR ME BRING STICKS OVER, START TO STAGGER.
JUST KEEP THINKING HOW *GREAT* IT'LL BE WHEN STICKS SEES YOU AND THINKS YOU'RE A SCARECROW COME TO *LIFE*.

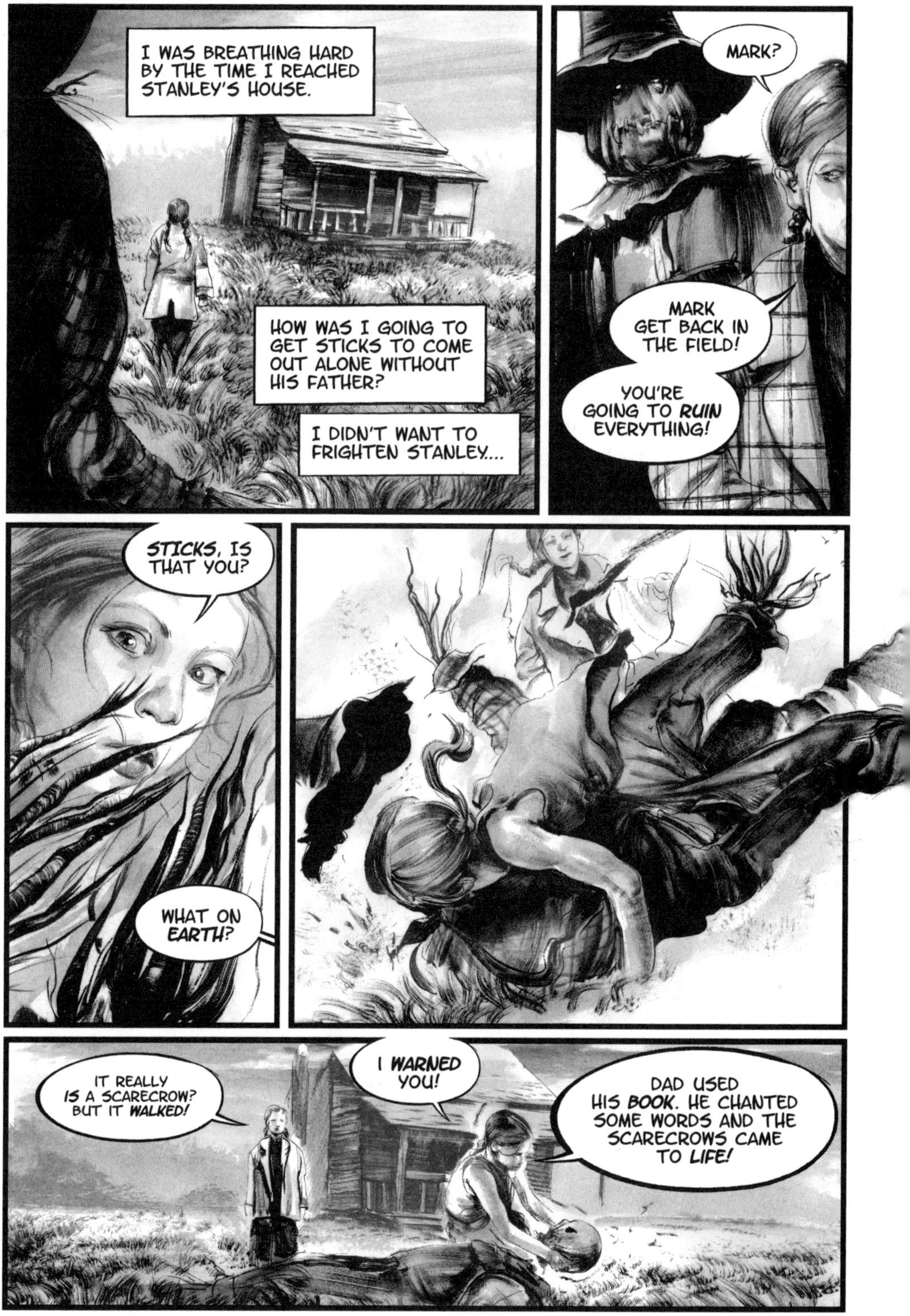
I WAS BREATHING HARD BY THE TIME I REACHED STANLEY'S HOUSE.
HOW WAS I GOING TO GET STICKS TO COME OUT ALONE WITHOUT HIS FATHER?
I DIDN'T WANT TO FRIGHTEN STANLEY....
MARK?
MARK GET BACK IN THE FIELD!
YOU'RE GOING TO RUIN EVERYTHING!
STICKS, IS THAT YOU?
WHAT ON EARTH?
IT REALLY IS A SCARECROW? BUT IT WALKED!
I WARNED YOU!
DAD USED HIS BOOK. HE CHANTED SOME WORDS AND THE SCARECROWS CAME TO LIFE!

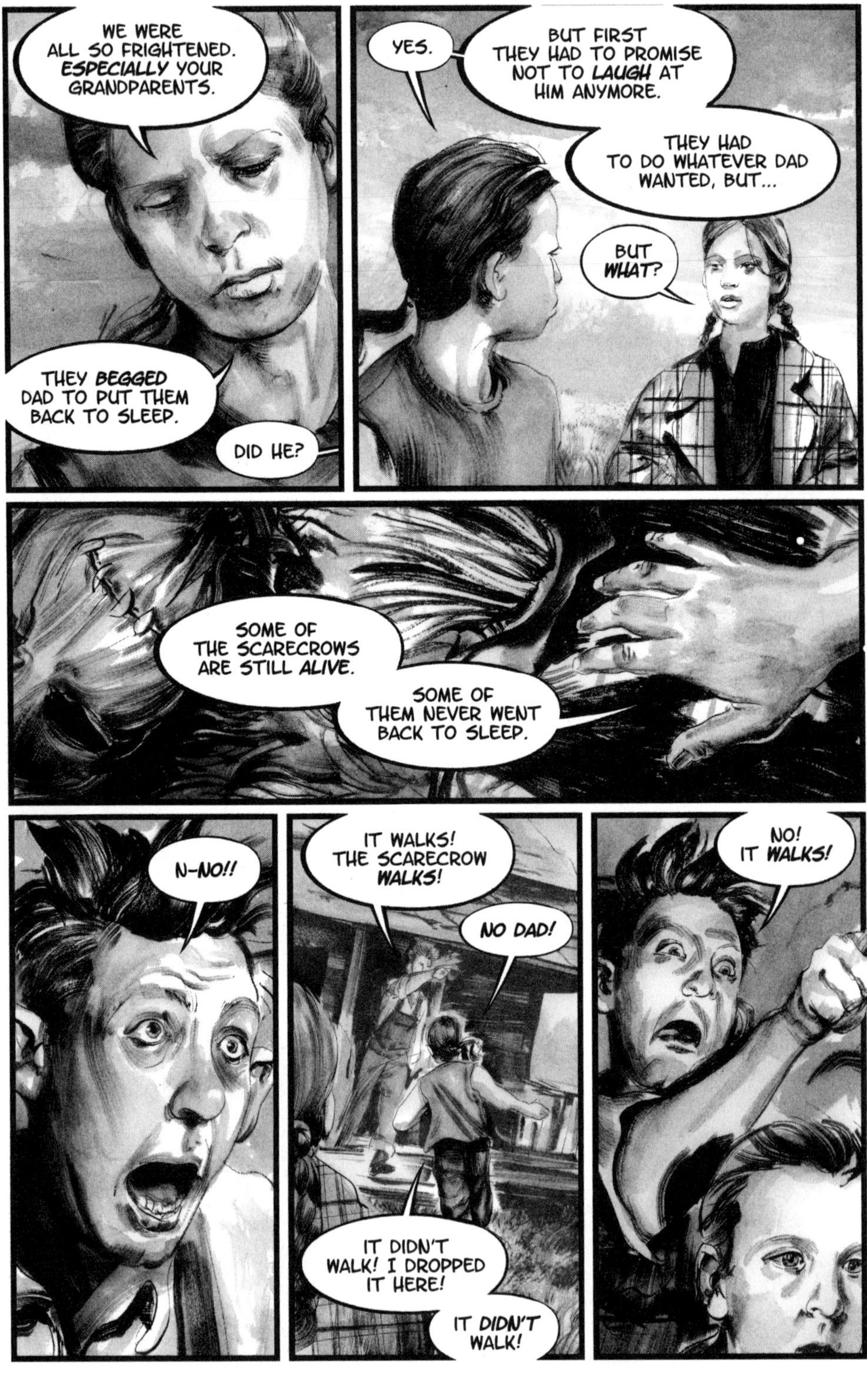
WE WERE ALL SO FRIGHTENED. *ESPECIALLY* YOUR GRANDPARENTS.
THEY *BEGGED* DAD TO PUT THEM BACK TO SLEEP.
DID HE?
YES.
BUT FIRST THEY HAD TO PROMISE NOT TO *LAUGH* AT HIM ANYMORE.
THEY HAD TO DO WHATEVER DAD WANTED, BUT...
BUT *WHAT?*
SOME OF THE SCARECROWS ARE STILL *ALIVE*.
SOME OF THEM NEVER WENT BACK TO SLEEP.
N-*NO!!*
IT WALKS! THE SCARECROW *WALKS!*
NO DAD!
IT DIDN'T WALK! I DROPPED IT HERE!
IT *DIDN'T* WALK!
NO! IT *WALKS!*

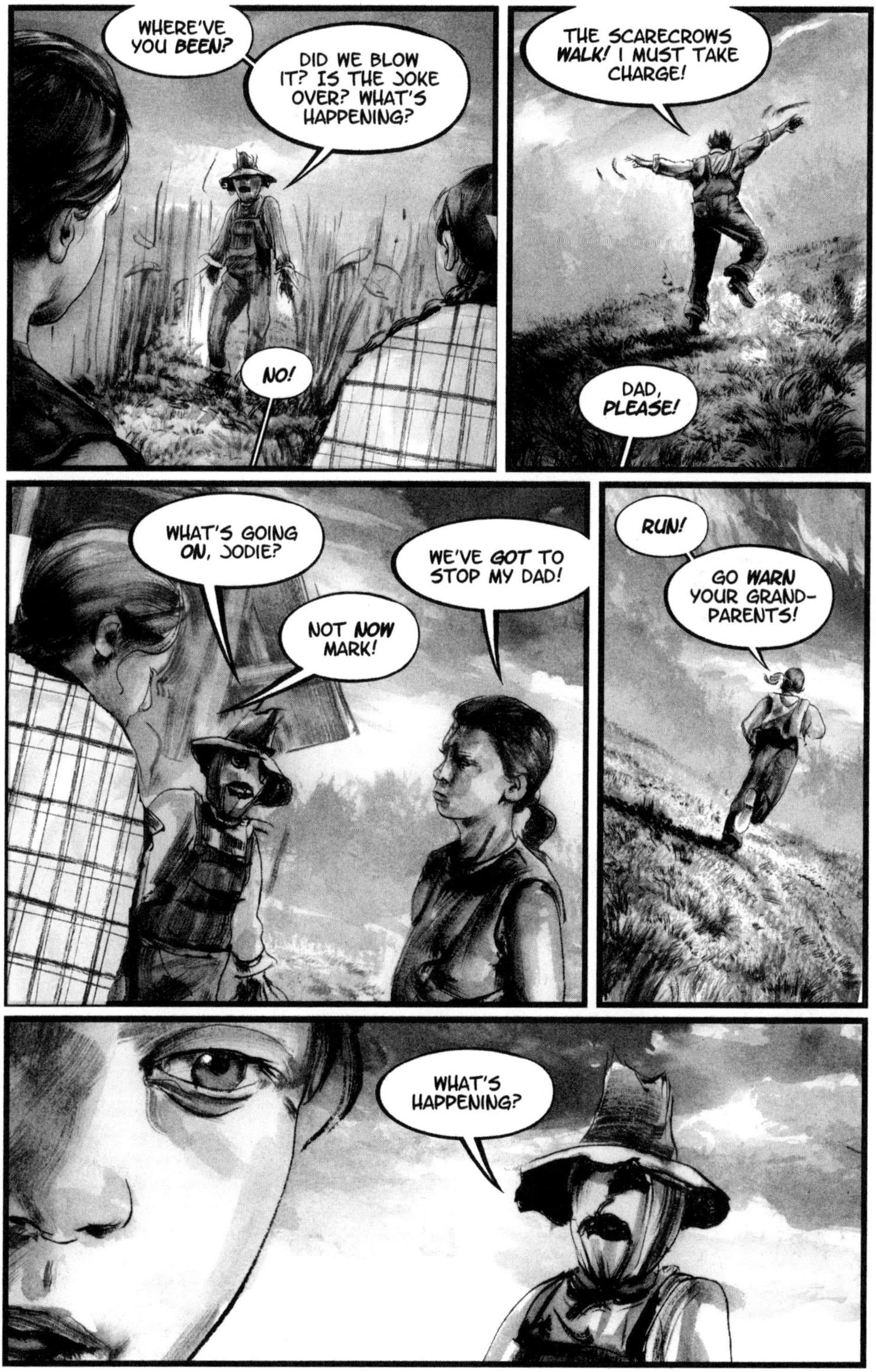
WHERE'VE YOU BEEN?
DID WE BLOW IT? IS THE JOKE OVER? WHAT'S HAPPENING?
NO!
THE SCARECROWS WALK! I MUST TAKE CHARGE!
DAD, PLEASE!
WHAT'S GOING ON, JODIE?
NOT NOW MARK!
WE'VE GOT TO STOP MY DAD!
RUN!
GO WARN YOUR GRAND-PARENTS!
WHAT'S HAPPENING?

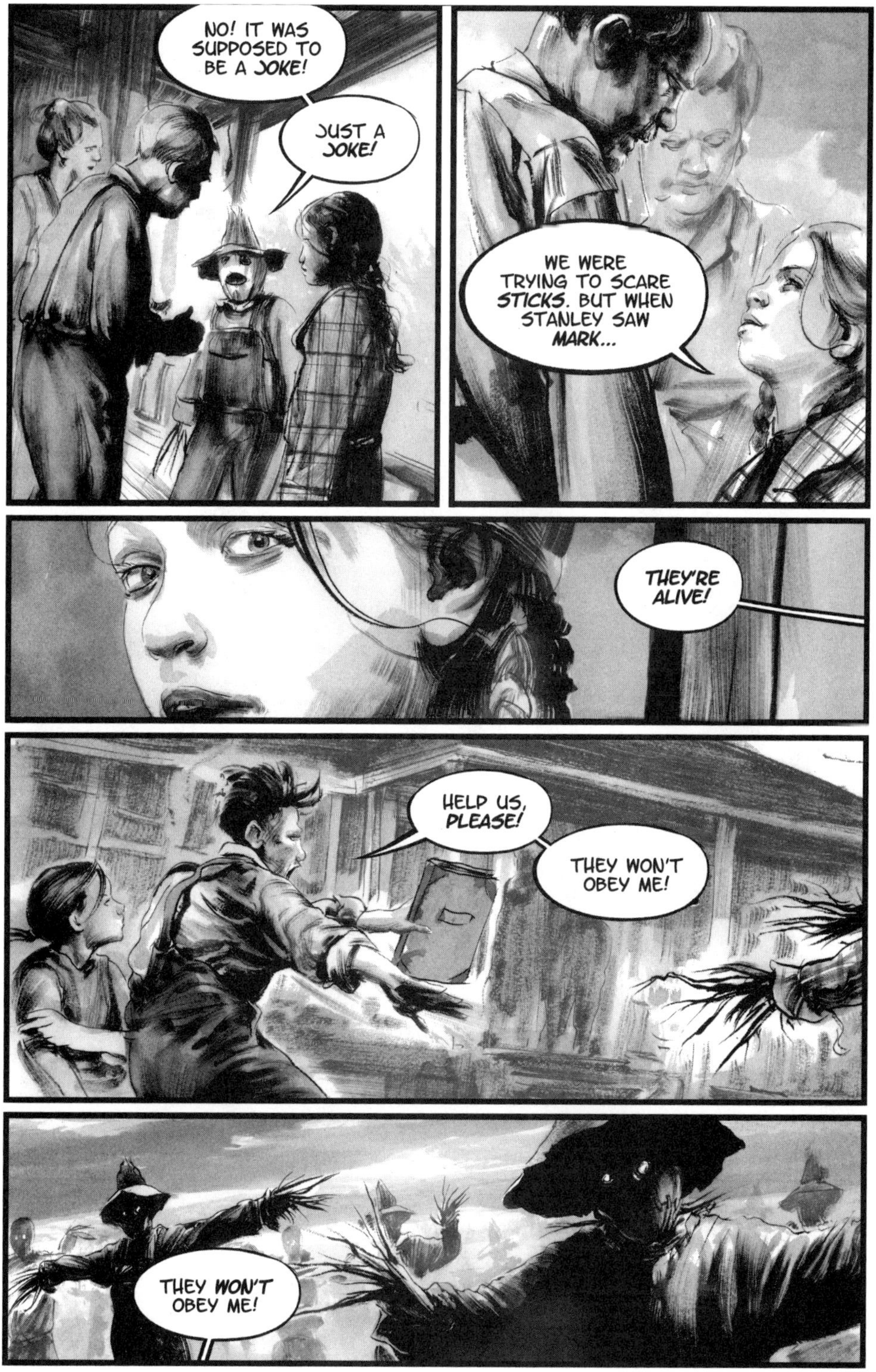
NO! IT WAS SUPPOSED TO BE A JOKE!
JUST A JOKE!
WE WERE TRYING TO SCARE STICKS. BUT WHEN STANLEY SAW MARK...
THEY'RE ALIVE!
HELP US, PLEASE!
THEY WON'T OBEY ME!
THEY WON'T OBEY ME!

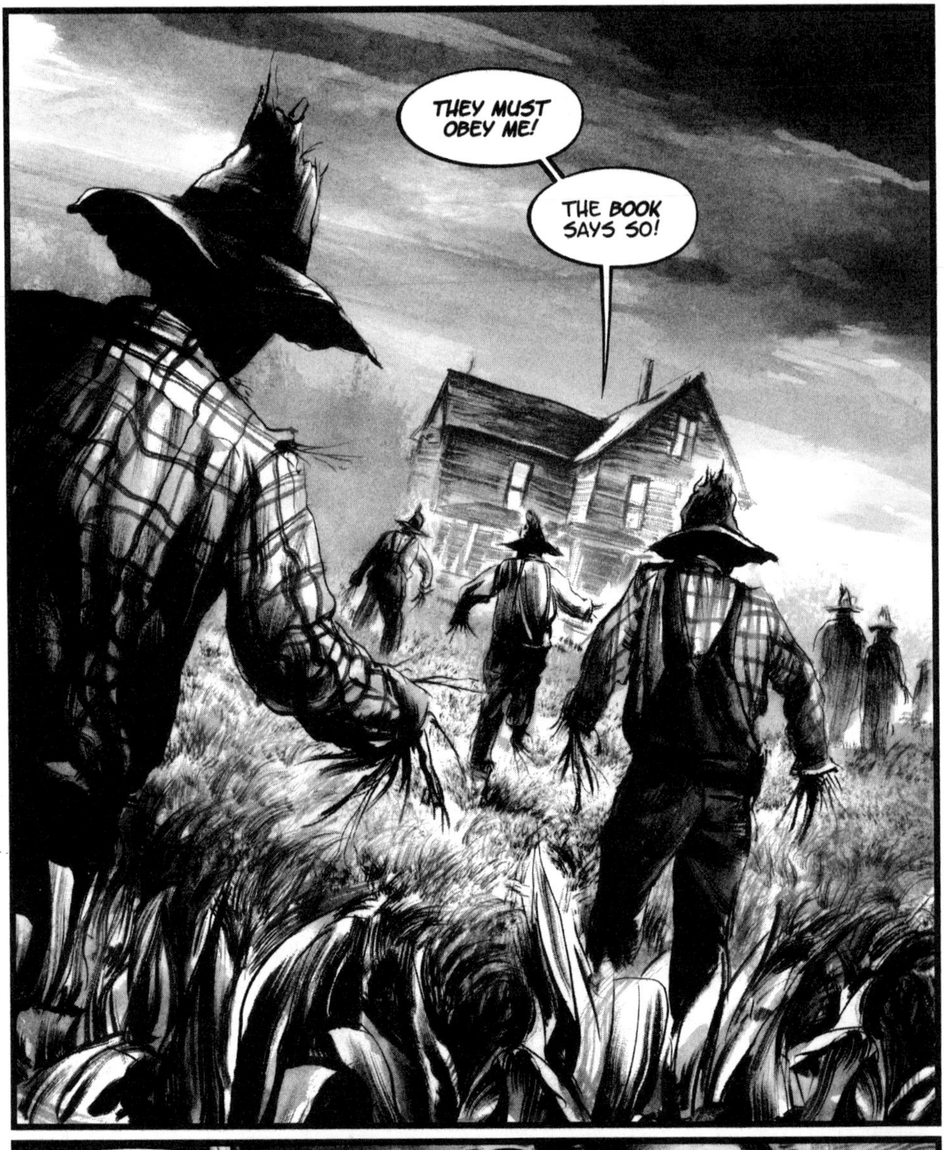
THEY MUST OBEY ME!
THE BOOK SAYS SO!

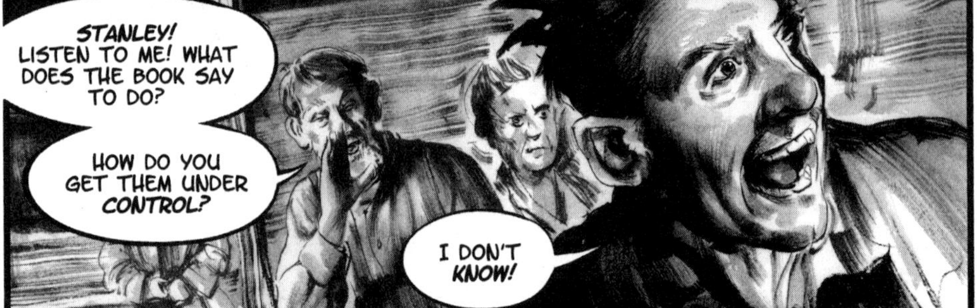
STANLEY! LISTEN TO ME! WHAT DOES THE BOOK SAY TO DO?
HOW DO YOU GET THEM UNDER CONTROL?
I DON'T KNOW!

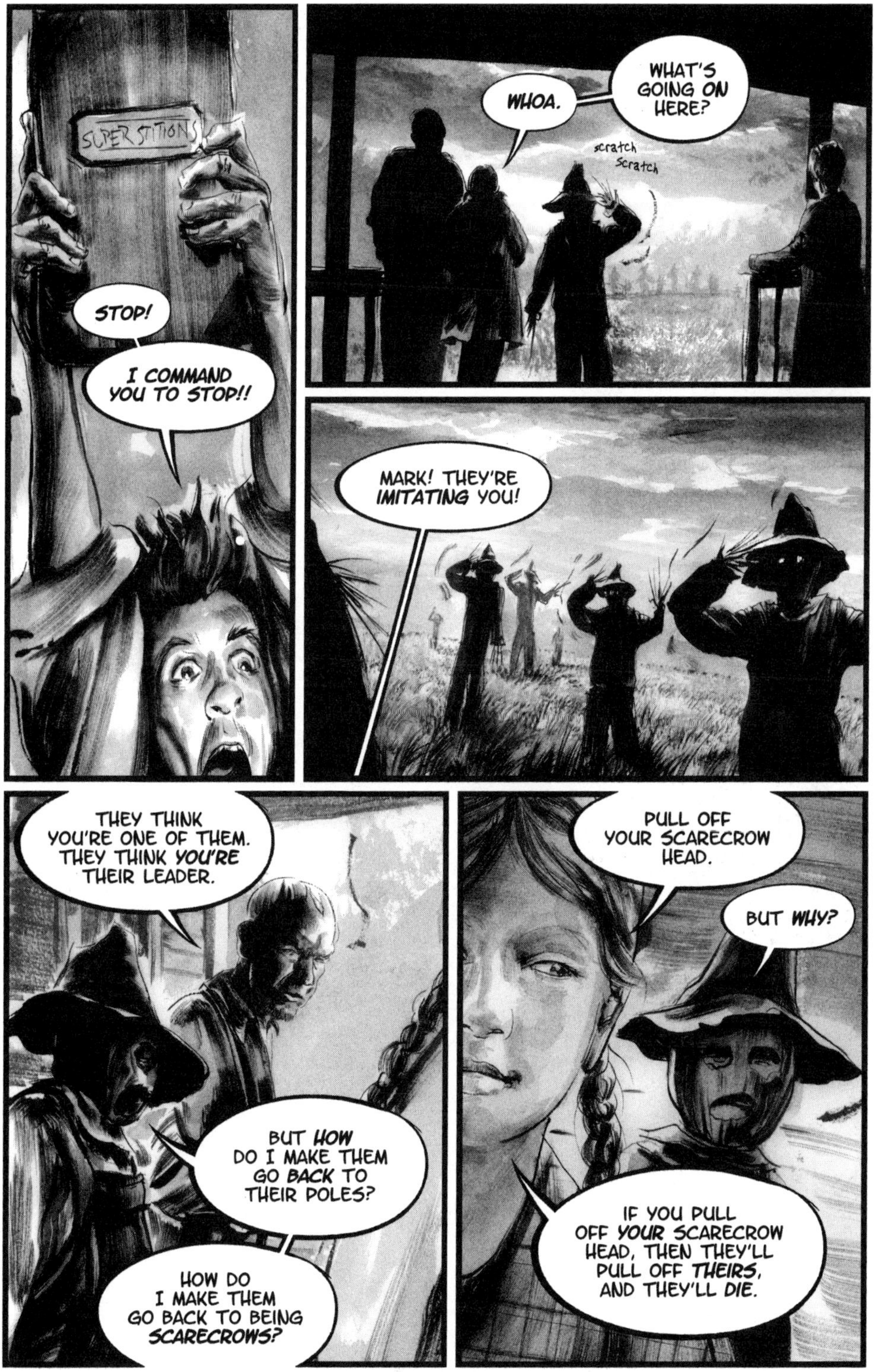
SUPERSTITIONS
STOP!
I COMMAND YOU TO STOP!!
WHOA.
WHAT'S GOING ON HERE?
scratch
scratch
MARK! THEY'RE IMITATING YOU!
THEY THINK YOU'RE ONE OF THEM. THEY THINK YOU'RE THEIR LEADER.
BUT HOW DO I MAKE THEM GO BACK TO THEIR POLES?
HOW DO I MAKE THEM GO BACK TO BEING SCARECROWS?
PULL OFF YOUR SCARECROW HEAD.
BUT WHY?
IF YOU PULL OFF YOUR SCARECROW HEAD, THEN THEY'LL PULL OFF THEIRS, AND THEY'LL DIE.

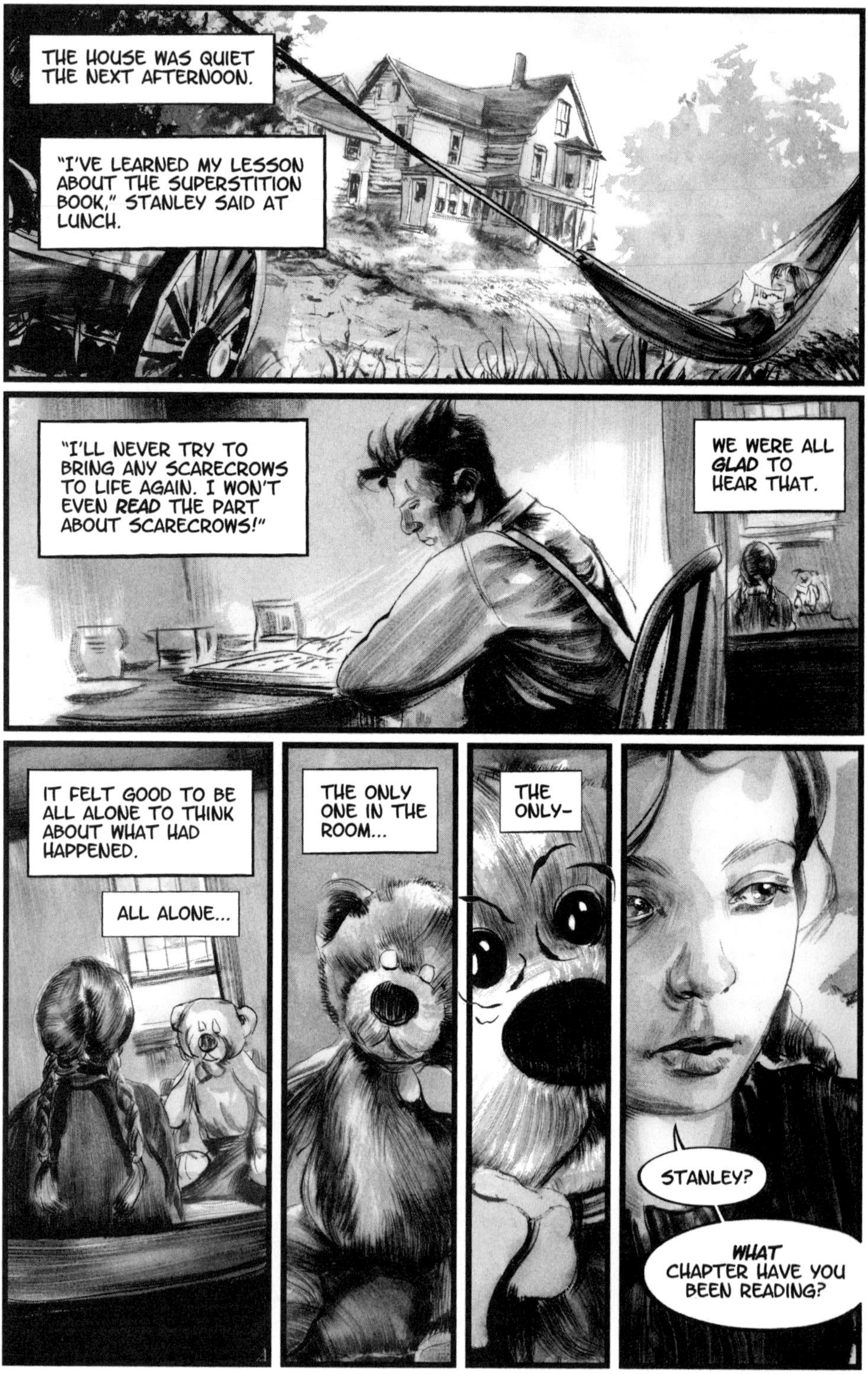
THE HOUSE WAS QUIET THE NEXT AFTERNOON.
"I'VE LEARNED MY LESSON ABOUT THE SUPERSTITION BOOK," STANLEY SAID AT LUNCH.
"I'LL NEVER TRY TO BRING ANY SCARECROWS TO LIFE AGAIN. I WON'T EVEN *READ* THE PART ABOUT SCARECROWS!"
WE WERE ALL *GLAD* TO HEAR THAT.
IT FELT GOOD TO BE ALL ALONE TO THINK ABOUT WHAT HAD HAPPENED.
ALL ALONE...
THE ONLY ONE IN THE ROOM...
THE ONLY-
STANLEY?
WHAT CHAPTER HAVE YOU BEEN READING?

THE
ABOMINABLE
SNOWMAN
OF PASADENA

ADAPTED AND ILLUSTRATED BY

Scott Morse

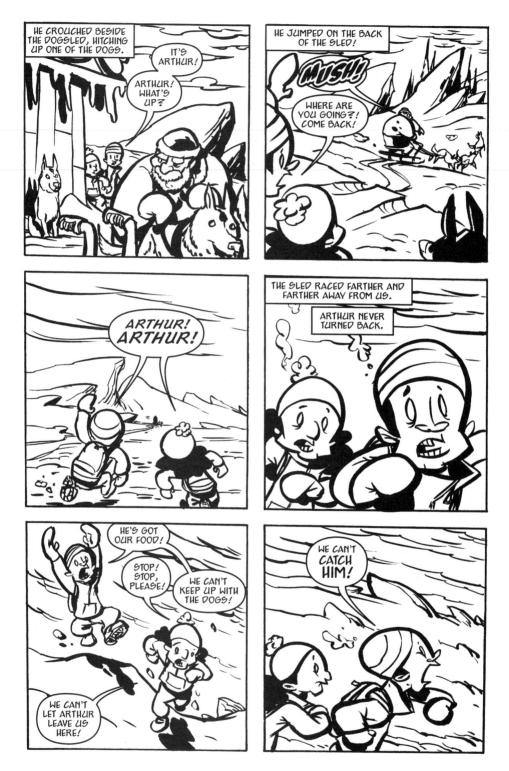

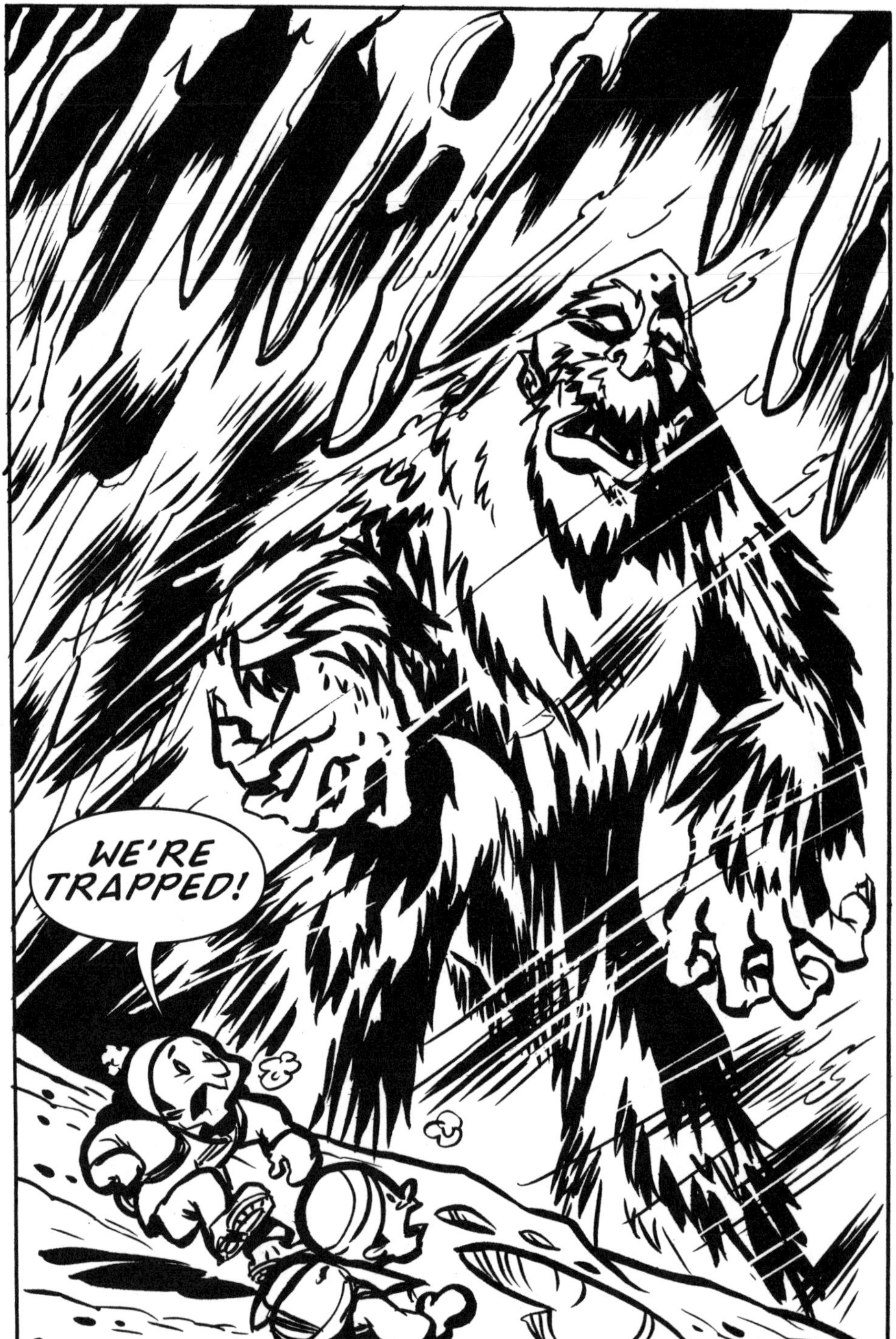
WE'RE TRAPPED!

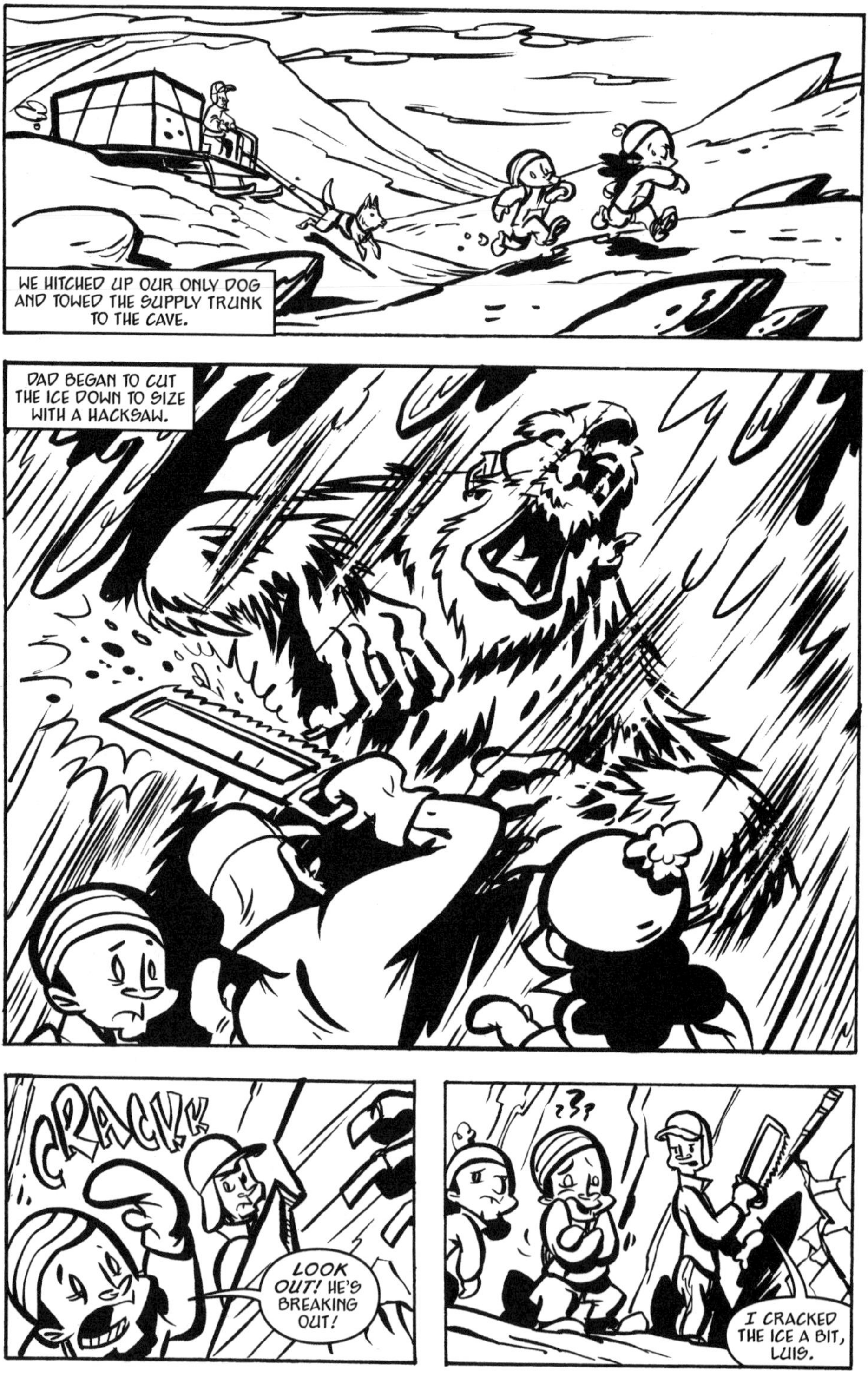
WE HITCHED UP OUR ONLY DOG AND TOWED THE SUPPLY TRUNK TO THE CAVE.
DAD BEGAN TO CUT THE ICE DOWN TO SIZE WITH A HACKSAW.
CRACKK
LOOK OUT! HE'S BREAKING OUT!
I CRACKED THE ICE A BIT, LUIS.

127

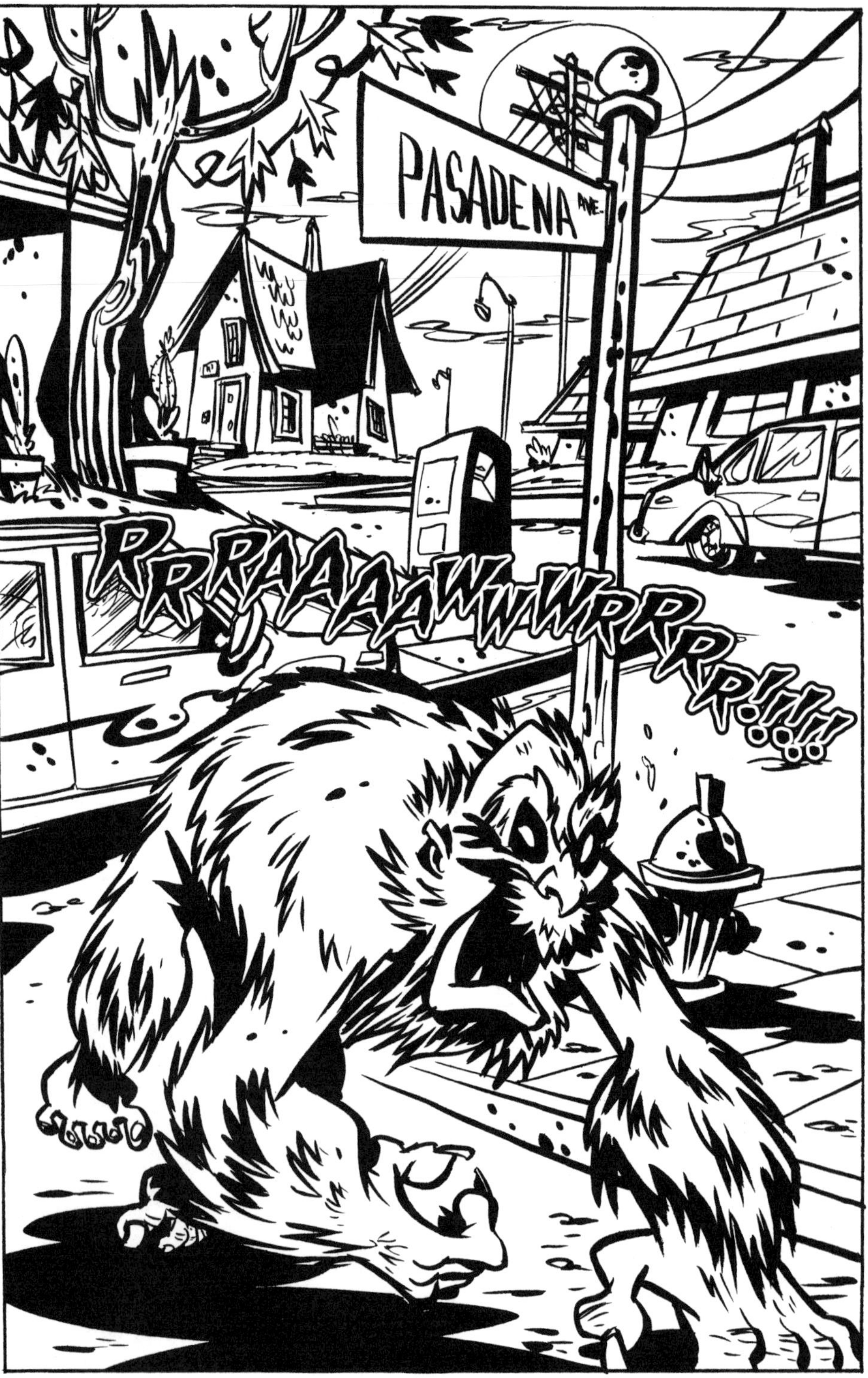
PASADENA AVE.
RRRAAAAAWWWRRRRR!!!!!

MEET THE ARTIST
Gabriel Hernandez

Gabriel Hernandez studied fine arts in Granada, Spain, where he now lives with his wife, Violeta, and his daughters, Clara and Lucia. He has illustrated several childrens' books and exhibited his paintings. Gabriel has created comic art for IDW comics; *CVO: Artifact;* and *CVO: Human Touch*, among others. He also is the artist for Clive Barker's The Thief of Always graphic novel series.

Gabriel sketched and summarized the text for *The Werewolf of Fever Swamp*. Then he created a rough storyboard without text (**A**), followed by one with text. Then he did a definitive storyboard. (**B**) He drew sketches of key characters, including expressions, movements, as well as some scenery. (**C**) Finally, Gabriel drew all the page sketches, inked over his sketches, filled in the details, added watercolors, and did all the speech bubbles and lettering by hand so it became part of the artwork.

137

Greg Ruth

Born in Texas, Greg Ruth began working in comics in 1993 with *Sudden Gravity* and has produced work for The Factoid Books, The Duplex Planet, The Matrix Comics, *Freaks of the Heartland*, and *Conan*. He has also done illustrations for *The New York Times*, worked on murals for Grand Central Terminal, and contributed to two music videos for Prince and Rob Thomas. Greg recently illustrated a new Scholastic series, *Sherlock Holmes and The Baker Street Irregulars*, and is currently at work on his own original graphic novel for Graphix, a spooky, suspenseful story of a child who disappeared, the tape of clues he left behind, and the boy who sets off into an unearthly forest world to solve the mystery.

Greg doesn't do sketches. He boldly jumps in and draws the art all at once.

Greg read through the original book of *The Scarecrow Walks at Midnight*, scribbled notes, and crossed out blocks of text or whole chapters with page counts. He then created a group of drawings to go with the scenes he had left, basically figuring out what each page contained and how it would break out into panels. Greg drew by hand, first doing the big parts of the page, its "beats," and then filling in the rest. He electronically scanned the artwork into his computer so he could assemble the pages and create the speech balloons and lettering. Finally, he went to bed each night, just as the sun was coming up, for a few hours of nightmares and then woke up — to repeat the process again and again and again!

MEET THE ARTIST

Scott Morse

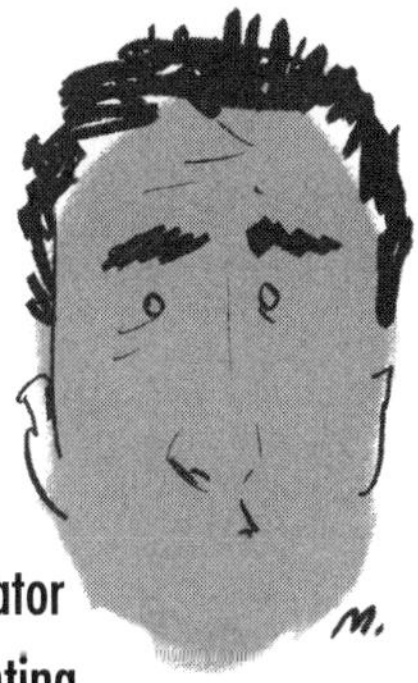

Scott Morse is the award-winning author of more than ten graphic novels, including *Soulwind; The Barefoot Serpent;* and *Southpaw.* He is also the creator of the *Magic Pickle*, a hilarious story about a dilly of a superhero who's fighting against evil vegetables trying to take over the world. Scott is working on two illustrated *Magic Pickle* chapter books and a graphic novel for Scholastic. He lives with his family in Oakland, California, where he works as a storyteller in both animation and comics.

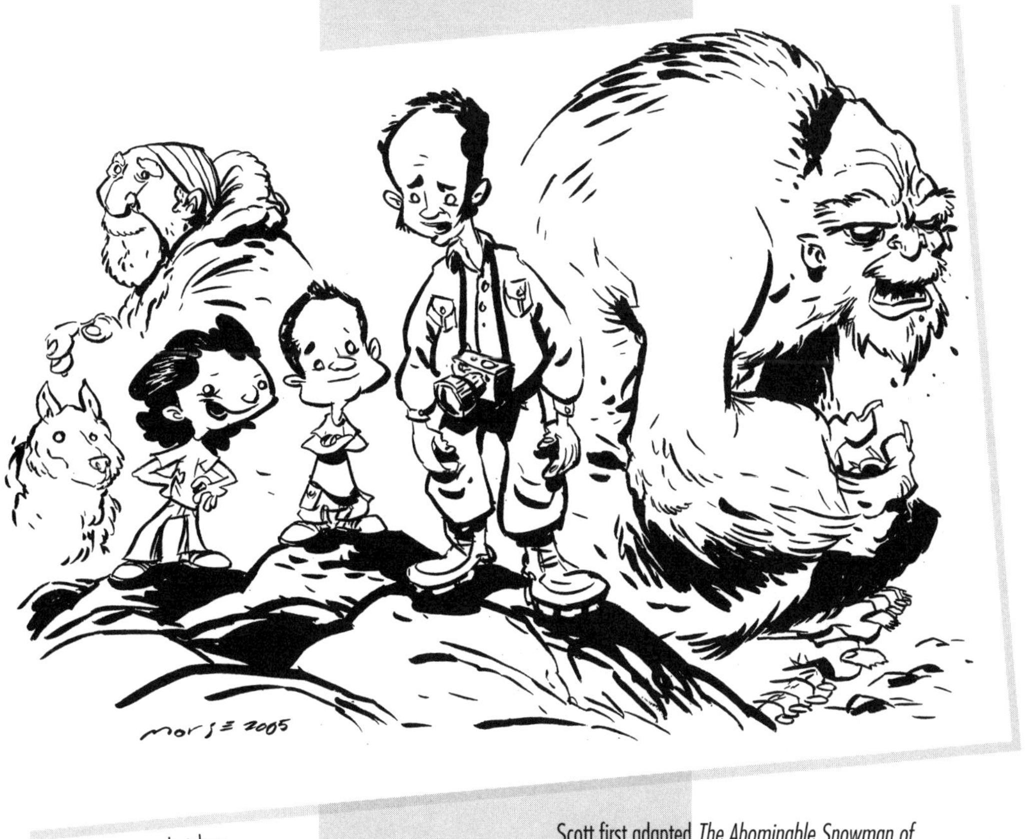
MORSE 2005

Scott's character sketches

Scott first adapted *The Abominable Snowman of Pasadena* into a script that broke down the story into pages and panels. He drew sketches, based on this script, and then penciled and inked the final art. This original art was scanned and sent as an electronic file to a professional letterer who added the speech bubbles, dialogue, and captions to the pages by computer.

GOOSEBUMPS

MORE GHOULISH graphix

TERROR TRIPS

Come along for the ride . . . though it could be one-way!!!

Jamie Tolagson, artist on *The Crow; The Dreaming;* and The Books of Magic series turns up the juice in *A Shocker on Shock Street*, the story of a brother and sister who land a dream job: testing the rides in a movie-studio theme park, where the special effects are REALLY special!

Or how about spending *One Day at Horrorland*? Award-winning artist **Jill Thompson**, creator of the Scary Godmother series, brings her quirky humor and madcap illustrations to this story about a family lost in an amusement park. Funny: there's no crowds, no lines, nobody around . . . to tell them the next ride might be their last!

The splashy, spooky fun of **Amy Kim Ganter**'s art is perfect for this story about two kids who find themselves in *Deep Trouble* while snorkeling. There's something dark, scaly, and *very* fishy swimming along with them! Amy is the creator of Tokyopop's Sorcerers & Secretaries series.

AVAILABLE IN MARCH 2007

TALES TO COME!

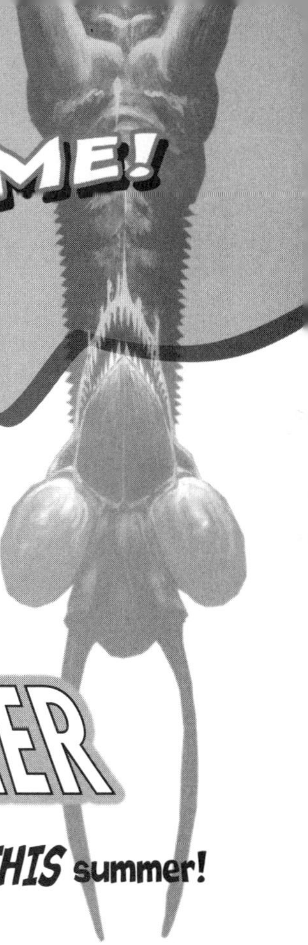

SCARY SUMMER

Wish that summer would never end? Not *THIS* summer!

Someone's creeping through the garden, whispering nasty things, smashing melons and squashing tomatoes, but those funky lawn ornaments can't move . . . *right?* **Dean Haspiel**, a veteran of Batman and Justice League comics and the acclaimed artist on *The Quitter*, knows just how to portray the ***Revenge of The Lawn Gnomes***.

In his award-winning comic series like The Bakers and Plastic Man, **Kyle Baker** proves he's one funny artist. The perfect guy to draw a story about a summer camp where it's all fun and games and everybody's happy. Too happy . . . That's why one young girl is out to uncover ***The Horror at Camp Jellyjam***.

Sandy beaches, tidal pools, shoreline caves . . . *ghosts!* A brother and sister's seaside vacation turns spooky at ***Ghost Beach*** by **Ted Naifeh**, Gothic master and creator of the creepy Courtney Crumrin series; the upcoming Polly and the Pirates series; and Unearthly, a sci-fi comedy manga series.

AVAILABLE IN JULY 2007

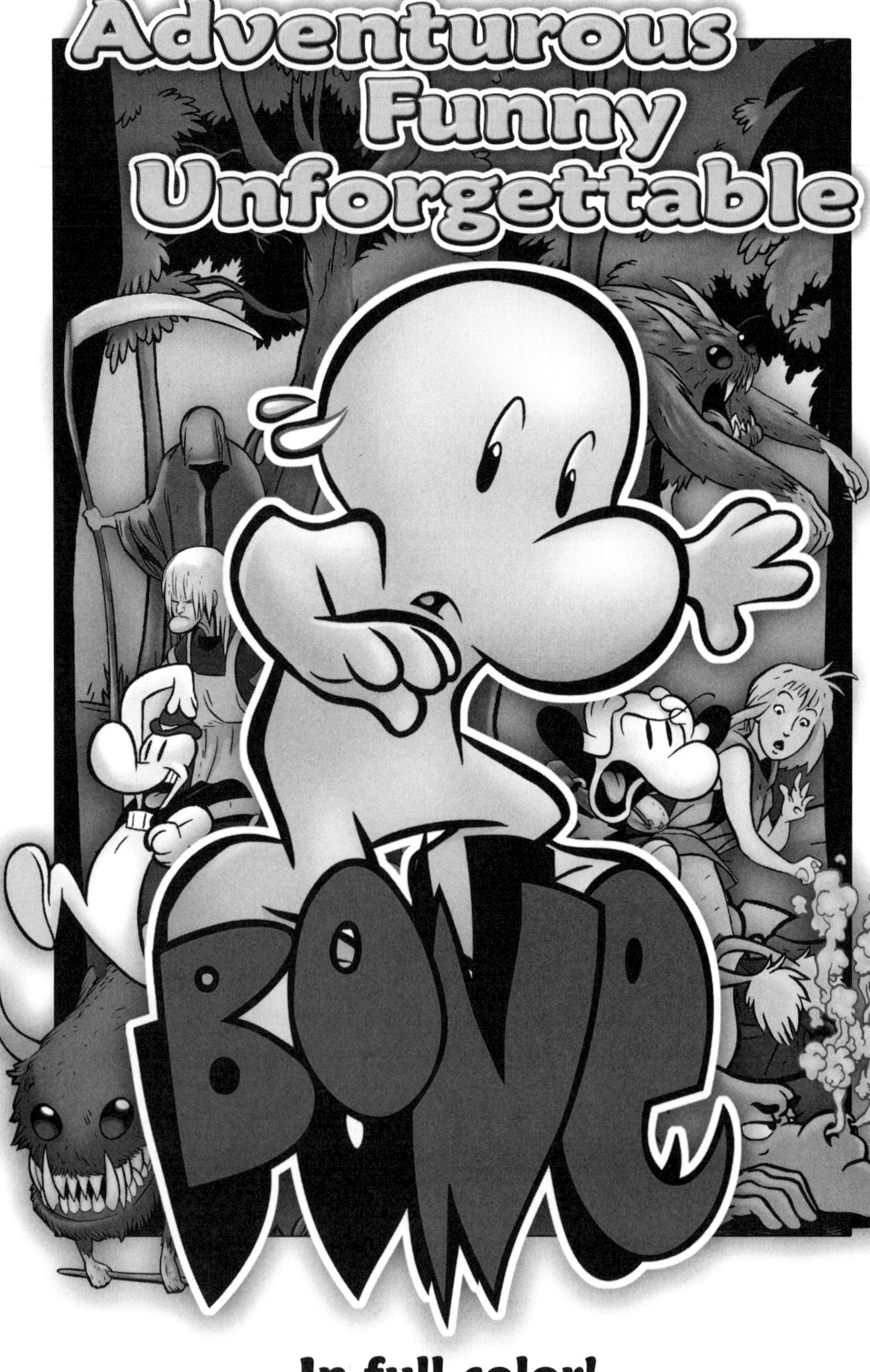
Adventurous
Funny
Unforgettable
BONE

In full color!

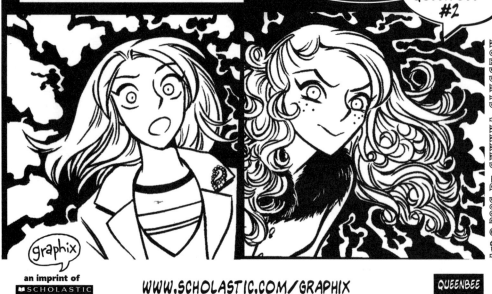